CW01202985

The Fox Spirit

by

Ash Warren

A Penelope Middleton
Japanese Murder Mystery

For Linda and Geoffrey

Chapter 1

The Coldest Snow

November 1992…

Outside in the gathering dusk, a light snow was beginning to dust the treetops with a quiet white blanket, which seemed to make the branches almost sparkle in the late afternoon light.

At the old inn, there was a soft knocking on the door of their room which she didn't hear at first.

Penelope Middleton, lying on the sofa of their comfortable room half asleep, lifted her head groggily and rose to see who it was, the novel she had been trying to read slipping from her lap onto the floor as she did so.

She opened the door to find their friend Hayashi-san, a pleasant man who ran his family's old inn on the *Nakasendo* road, at the far end of the village of Tsumago, deep in the mountains of the Kiso Valley in Nagano prefecture, and where they had often stayed before.

He smiled at her, but she could tell he was concerned about something.

"Didn't Hiro-san say he would be back by now?" he asked, stroking the stubble on his chin with his long white fingers.

Penelope cast a glance at her watch.

"Yes, you're right. I've been expecting him for the last few hours. He's late... as usual," she said.

Hayashi-san shrugged and leaned on the doorframe.

"Oh well... he knows what he's doing. I was just wondering, you know, because the forecast says we're going to get a lot of snow tonight. I wouldn't like to think of him caught out in that...."

Penelope looked him in the eye and got the feeling that the Kiso Valley native was probably more worried than he cared to admit.

"Well... you know Hiro-san. He forgets the time. He was probably ages taking photos at that temple. Maybe they let him into the museum too... that would have been the end of things..." she smiled, and turned to look out the window of their room, where, true to the innkeeper's prediction, the snow was indeed falling more heavily.

"Well... probably nothing to worry about. I just thought I would check... we are about to start putting together that *inoshishi nabe* I mentioned for dinner. You know, I told you we got some fresh boar's meat from one of the hunters the other day. That's still all right with you?" he asked.

"Oh, yes!" Penelope smiled. "That would be lovely, thank you. Hiro will probably turn up starving any minute."

The innkeeper nodded and headed downstairs to the kitchen to talk to his wife. There were only one other couple of hikers staying at the inn that night, which was a rambling old wooden building that had served the travelers on the *Nakasendo* road for over four hundred years now, and Hiro and Penelope often headed here when they wanted a break from their jobs at the university in Kamakura where they both worked.

The *Nakasendo* road had once been one of the two major 'highways' that stretched between the ancient capital of Kyoto and what had been Edo, now Tokyo, and the section of the old road through the village of Tsumago was extremely popular with tourists and hikers as it passed through a series of untouched villages just like this one, where the old wooden houses on either side of its single cobbled road were hundreds of years old and seemed to have been forgotten entirely by the modern age, thus making the area a favorite of artists and travelers from all over the country.

The *Nakasendo*, or "Mountain Way', was shorter than its sister road, the *Tokaido*, which ran along the sea to the south, but much more challenging to walk due to the many mountain passes that had to be traversed along the way. Nevertheless, it was also a lot more scenic, and for Penelope's boyfriend, Hiro Yamana, who taught painting and fine arts at the university where Penelope was a young Associate Professor in the department of Japanese Literature, was a keen amateur photographer, so it was the perfect place to spend a few days away now and again and where they could explore the many sights of the ancient road and make short hikes to visit the nearby temples and shrines.

Today, Hiro had set out to visit a small temple in the hills above Tsumago. This place also had a tiny museum dedicated to the eighteenth-century mountain ascetic and sculptor Enku, who had spent his life in this region and whose practice had involved making simple yet highly idiosyncratic Buddhist sculptures. This devotional work was said to have been done to honor his late mother, who had died when he was a child. Hiro had been especially excited to visit this temple, which had no less than three of the rare statues on display and was not too far from where they were staying, perhaps only a few hour's walk along the lovely old mountain routes which also had the benefit of being very well-marked trails.

That afternoon though, Penelope had opted for the comforts of their cozy old inn and a good book, and left him to his more energetic pursuits while she waited for him in their room. Hiro had been more than happy with this arrangement, as he preferred to be alone when he went on his hikes, and relished the chance to get away from people and be by himself in the natural world, which was something he missed, plunged as he was into a job which necessitated being surrounded by young students seven days a week. Penelope, who appreciated the solitary life even more than him, also enjoyed the time alone, moments when she could read whatever she liked for a change and perhaps write, yet also anticipate the moment when the man she was growing to love would return to her, full of good spirits and a revived enthusiasm for life, his skin smelling of the pines and the good mountain air.

An hour later, she awoke again and realized she had fallen asleep reading her book, and once again, she heard Hayashi-san tapping on her door.

"Just came to let you know dinner will be at seven," he said as he looked around their room over her shoulder.

"He's still not here?" the innkeeper asked.

Penelope shook her head.

"Actually, I've been asleep. What time is it?"

Hayashi-san stuck out his wrist so she could see his watch.

"Almost six-thirty. It's been dark for over an hour now. That seems a bit strange… I would have thought he'd be back by now, for sure. The snow is really getting heavy…" he said with a concerned look.

Penelope went over to the window and stared out into the darkness, where she could see the snow falling like a solid white curtain in front of the light from the window of the house across the road.

"Hmmm… That's odd, you're right," she said.

"Do you want me to go and have a look for him? Maybe he's in one of the cafes or shops up the street…" offered the older man.

Penelope looked at him and stared out the window again.

"No… don't worry. I'll go and have a look. I know where the trail he took branches off from the main road, too… I'll just walk up there a bit and see if I can see him. He'll probably be here very soon, I imagine…"

Hayashi-san nodded.

"OK. Dress warm. And if you don't see him, come straight back, OK? It's not like him to be this late usually. It's probably nothing. He might be just having a chat with someone in one of the cafes or bars or something. I can't imagine he wants to be trudging around in all this…Watch yourself on the cobbles too, OK? It's pretty slippery," he gestured out the window to the snow, then turned and went downstairs again.

Penelope stared out her window along the dark cobbled road that snaked between the old wooden houses, and suddenly had a strange sense of foreboding that she had rarely felt before.

"Where have you got to, Hiro…" she whispered to herself as she pulled on her heavy coat.

=====================

A few kilometers from the inn, and fighting to see his way in the increasingly heavy snow, Hiro was tapping his walking pole in front of him as he made his way down the old stone staircase that emptied onto the forest road that led to Tsumago, and pointed his little flashlight somewhat ineffectually up the dark and empty dirt road.

He had been forced to take his time on the return trip, at times inching his way down the stone staircase and the slippery upper parts of the trail that descended from the temple, as the snow was now falling quite hard and the icy stone steps in front of him had all but disappeared as the world quickly changed to white. On either side of the path, the branches of the pine trees were lowering themselves towards him with their increasing load of the new snow. Whenever he accidentally brushed against one of them, he was hit with another ample dusting of the stuff.

Hiro was not particularly concerned though, as he was a very experienced hiker and had been out in weather like this many times before. Nevertheless, he was relieved when he finally found himself at the bottom of the slippery stairs and once more on the firmer ground of the old forestry road, which now unwound itself before him towards Tsumago, an unblemished white carpet where clearly not a living soul had been since the snow had begun to fall a few hours before.

He checked his watch, saw that it was nearly five o'clock, and cursed himself for not leaving the old temple and its talkative priest earlier. The old man had been more than happy to show a rare guest around his treasures, and had plied him with tea and cakes and also a lot of interesting tales about the sculptor Enku and the local area, a place that was full of ancient legends and superstitions stretching back to the Heian period of a thousand years before.

The priest, a tiny little man with a wisp of white beard dangling from his chin that made him look like an ancient Chinese sage, was also a fund of information about the *yamabushi*, the mountain ascetics that practiced the esoteric rituals of *shugendo* in these hills, and also about the local history of the beautiful Kiso Valley, which he had only read about before in books like the famous one by Shimazaki Toson. Still, when he thought about his young girlfriend waiting for him back in their cozy room, he wondered, and not for the first time, what on earth had possessed him to have ventured out in the middle of nowhere just to see a few old Buddhist sculptures when he could have been with her instead.

Seeing the forestry road before him now and knowing he was close to home again, he trudged along more quickly though, his walking pole measuring his strides and feeling refreshed to be on level ground again and with just a few kilometers to the where the road met the *Nakasendo* and the village of Tsumago began.

But then, something unexpected happened.

"Hello," said a soft voice just behind him. "What are you doing here?"

Hiro almost jumped out of his skin, and wheeled around.

He was astonished to find the voice belonged to a beautiful young girl, standing by the side of the road in a long white cape with the hood pulled over her head. Startled, Hiro realized he must have walked right past her in the snow and never noticed, probably because of how perfectly camouflaged she had been in her long white robe.

"Wow…. you scared me there for a moment!" he said with a smile after he had recovered from his shock. "I thought I was the only person crazy enough to be out here in the dark. Are you OK?"

The girl nodded and smiled, and Hiro thought immediately how outstandingly pretty she was.

She was, perhaps, in her mid-twenties, with beautiful eyes and a long black ponytail trailing over her shoulder and down almost to her waist.

"Yes, I'm fine, thanks. What brings you out here?" she said.

Hiro leaned on his walking pole and shifted the weight of the heavy rucksack on his shoulders.

"I've been up to the old temple. To look at the Enku statues…" he said, gesturing towards the old stone staircase he had just descended. "How about you? I missed you completely standing there in that white dress…"

The girl laughed, a pretty, trilling laugh that seemed more animal than human.

"Oh! Enku… that old scallywag," she said, almost as if she had known the long-dead Buddhist ascetic. "And did you talk to that priest? What an old windbag he is. Never shuts up…" She smiled, and her dark eyes sparkled.

Hiro nodded. "Yes, well… he is very… hospitable, I suppose. I guess that's why I'm so late. I suppose you live around here?"

The girl nodded and stretched out her long, white-robed arms as if to embrace something rather than to point anywhere.

"Oh yes… I've been here… ages. Ages and ages. It's so nice here. You know, especially when it snows. And I meet people sometimes. Like you…"

She took a step towards him, and as she did, he felt something move inside him and almost take him off balance. There was something so fresh and young about her, but at the same time, powerful beyond anything he had expected. It was a kind of aethereal loveliness he had rarely encountered before, and being here so close to her felt like taking a draught of strong red wine and feeling a sudden drunken warmth rush to his head.

"Right… I see…" he slurred. "That's nice… do you live in Tsugamo?" he asked, unable to draw his eyes away from hers.

She nodded. "Tsugamo... well... I've been there. I prefer the forest, though. Less people... you know."

Hiro nodded helplessly and stood there staring into her eyes as she stepped closer to him and put her soft white hand on his arm. She leaned upwards to him, and for a moment, he wondered if she was going to kiss him.

But then she put her hand up to his face and whispered in his ear.

"Would you like to meet my boyfriend?" she said quietly.

Hiro heard a heavy footstep behind them, turned his head slowly away from her to look over his shoulder, and found himself looking directly into the face of a giant bird.

Frozen with shock, he stared into the animal's glittering dark eyes, its beak just a few centimeters from his face and so close he could feel the warmth of its breath on his skin.

Hiro tried to scream, but no sound came out of his mouth at all, and as he fell on his back in the snow, the camera gear in his rucksack dug painfully into his spine.

Unable to process what he was seeing, he saw that the 'bird' was dressed in a long, dark grey robe like a monk, its huge beak protruding from under a dark cowl, and from the arms of his robes hung long bone-colored talons where his hands should have been, that glistened like sharp knives.

Hiro watched in absolute terror as the girl went and stood next to the animal and looked adoringly into its menacing face.

Then she smiled down at Hiro, who was now trying to crawl backwards away from them.

"This is my boyfriend," she said happily. "He's been sooooo looking forward to meeting you… Hiro Yamana…"

=====================

Warmly dressed in her hiking boots and a thick down jacket, Penelope left the inn and wandered up the street, all the time expecting to see her errant boyfriend walking towards her, tired after his long trek in the freezing mountains.

After checking in at the various bars and cafes that lined the single street of the little village and being told in a few of the places they usually frequented that no one had seen Hiro all day, Penelope found herself standing finally at the far end of the village, where the little forestry road that branched to the right led off into the trees and where Hiro would eventually have to emerge to make his way back to their inn.

The spot she chose for her vigil that night was a lonely, dark place lit by a single dim lamppost. It was also unnaturally quiet, or at least it felt like that to someone like her who was not used to living in the countryside. The snow was swirling, and a mist was beginning to rise, yet she stood there in the cold night air for almost an hour. However, there was no sign either of him nor of anyone that evening abroad on the little snow-covered road.

There was just silence, broken only by the occasional soft tumbling of snow from the heavily laden branches of the dark pines.

She thought several times rather angrily about leaving, but each time she did, something made her wait, until in the end she could no longer fight the thought that, after all, she was probably just wasting her time and that, in all likelihood, Hiro was now back at their inn, soaking in the bath and wondering where she was after taking some alternate route home she didn't know about.

She decided to call it quits and go back.

Just as she turned her back though, she heard what sounded like a dog barking in the distance. She looked up the road, but all was quiet again. The road remained as it had been, empty and dark, with nothing moving at all in the stillness except the gently falling snow.

She turned away again and took a few steps, and then once more, she heard it. A high-pitched yelping, far away, and just for a moment, some instinct told her it was not a dog, but a person pretending to be a dog.

It was a weird feeling, a strange thought, like when you hear something untrue, but you cannot quite put your finger on what it was that made you doubt.

She decided to walk down the road a little bit, just out of curiosity, and stepped carefully along the icy little road toward the great forest, her footsteps leaving a lonely trail across the pristine snow. She walked as far as the first bend in the road, and peered out into the blackness and the thickening mists.

There was nothing to see, just the shadowy trees floating in the darkness and the empty dirt road winding away between them. The snow was falling much more heavily now, and from where she stood, her visibility was down to perhaps no more than thirty meters or so.

She waited for several minutes, feeling more and more alone and cold, and then just as she was about to turn around again, she saw a shadow move in the distance.

At first, she thought it was just the mist, but then she began to make out a shape slowly moving towards her, and then as it got closer, she realized there was not one shape, but two. Two people, moving towards her.

But it was not Hiro.

As the strangers drew nearer, it looked like a man and a woman with walking staves in their hands coming towards her, both oddly dressed in long robes that made them look like ancient monks. The man's robe was a dark grey, almost black, but the woman's was a dazzling white, just like the snow, which perhaps accounted for why she had not seen her at first. Both of them were looking down, and their hoods were drawn about their heads, making their faces almost impossible to see.

Penelope shouted 'hello!" in a loud voice, but they did not acknowledge her in any way.

As they drew level with her, she caught the faintest glimpse of the side of the man's face, which looked strange and somehow angular, almost like that of a bird's, but it was only the merest glimpse, and obscured by the falling snow and mist. She also saw that the woman seemed to be trailing something white from the bottom of her robe, almost resembling a fox's tail.

"Say… did you see anyone else on the road? A man with a backpack?" she asked them as they walked past, but neither made the slightest effort to reply, nor even turned their heads towards her. Perhaps the man shook his head under his cowl, but it was hard to tell.

The couple proceeded wordlessly past her on the other side of the road, and she watched them as they went off down the road that led to the next village.

Penelope turned her footsteps to the inn, her feeling of foreboding now worse than ever.

Chapter 2

Last Witness

Present day….

Several days after what came to be known the 'the Hachimangu murder' by the salivating Japanese press, Chief Inspector Eiji Yamashita of the Kamakura police heard a soft knock on his office door, which in an effort at workplace transparency he left open at all times, and saw his brawny sidekick, Detective Sergeant Yokota, standing there with a look of odd expectancy on his face.

"What is it?" asked his boss as he continued to type on his laptop, quietly fearing it would be yet another departmental blunder he was going to have to clear up.

"Well, sir, you aren't going to believe this one, I promise you," he said in his usual drawl, handing him one of the dark blue files so standard in the police department.

Yamashita, a well-dressed man in his late fifties with a long, aquiline face and greying hair around the temples, looked up from his screen and raised an eyebrow at his DS, whom he knew was not a man prone to any form of exaggeration.

He shut his laptop and opened the file, to find that the top page was a summary of the 'Hachimangu' forensic findings and the results of the autopsy.

Yokota waited patiently until his boss read down to the second half of the report when, as expected, he sat bolt upright and started reading a passage aloud from the document.

"... fur consistent with the species *vulpes vulpes japonica* or a subspecies of said animal..." he read, and looked up at Yokota, both eyebrows raised.

"Fox, sir. The common Japanese red fox, and there's more..." Yokota said, gesturing at the file.

Yamashita nodded, pointed his DS to the chair in front of his desk, and spent the next few minutes silently and carefully reading the rest of the report.

"Ah... there it is... the crow feather..." he said softly, again halfway through the document.

Closing the file, he stared meditatively out the window of his office.

"Well... that rings a bell, doesn't it?" he said quietly.

"It did with me too, sir," said Yokota, leaning forward with his big hands clasped together. "*Il Monstro*? I never thought he would darken our doorstep. But... here we are...".

Yamashita nodded.

"Yes... here we are, indeed. One of this country's oldest, and, more to the point, most uncaught serial killers. I must admit, you know, when I saw the body... it made me think. But the feather... well, well, well...." he said, rubbing his hands together.

Yokota nodded. "Yeah. That caught my eye too. But many of the previous *Il Monstro* killings… they were… kind of way before my time, you know. But I've been familiar with the case since I was in high school…"

Yamashita smiled. "So, you read Sal Nakamura and Ran Maeda's book?"

Yokota nodded. He and his boss were old friends of the investigative journalist Sal Nakamura, who had written several books on political scandals and crime over the years, and Yokota, who had grown up in a police family, had been a voracious reader of anything connected to crime since he was a child.

"There's no need to remind me of my age, you know…" said his boss wearily.

"Oh… that wasn't my intent, sir," smiled Yokota.

"I'm sure… But you're right. This guy has been leaving bodies behind for quite a while. Mainly in western Japan and Tokyo, however. I think this will be the fifth if it turns out to be him. I'm sure their task force will be all over it once they see this."

Yokota stood up and reclaimed the file from his boss's desk.

"You want to go and have another look at the crime scene, sir?"

Yamashita leaned back in his chair.

"Yes. Why not. Let's go and see if inspiration strikes… After all, our turf, our case. Let's see if we can't at least be helpful, though."

That afternoon the two detectives parked their car around the corner from Kamakura's huge Tsurugaoka

Hachimangu shrine, which was, without question, the most important shrine in the ancient city and one of its largest tourist attractions.

The men walked a short distance along the long, straight road that led up to the main shrine, bowed deeply as they passed under the great red *torii* gate, and entered the sacred grounds of the shrine proper. They then made their way around the *maiden,* a large, ornate stage that was used for ceremonial dance and other performances, and began to walk up the huge stone staircase that led to the main hall at the top, where the body of *Il Monstro's* latest victim had been found earlier in the week.

Halfway up the steps, Yamashita stopped and pointed to the stump of a giant ginkgo tree off to one side that seemed to be sprouting some new leaves.

"That's our famous tree there. It looks like it might be coming back to life," he said as they proceeded up the stairs.

Both men, natives of Kamakura, were well aware of the story of the thousand-year-old tree, behind which the assassin Kugyo, the nephew of the *shogun* Minamoto no Sanetomo had reputedly hidden before carrying out the murder of the famous leader one snowy February day in the year 1219. The tree had ever since been nicknamed the *kakure-ichō,* or the 'hiding ginkgo,' before being knocked down by a great storm in 2010. However, recently the tree had been sprouting new leaves, much to the relief of the shrine and its throngs of visitors.

Compared to the ancient *shogun,* however, the victim of the shrine's latest murder had been found in a much more important ceremonial place than outside in the grounds. It had been found inside the main shrine itself by some shrine attendants early in the morning, a sacrilege that had not gone unnoticed by anyone.

The crime was also somewhat unique in its gruesome nature.

The victim had been decapitated after death, and the torso laid out face up in front of the main altar with the hands folded peacefully across the chest, almost like an English effigy that you found in old churches in Europe. Perhaps most curiously of all, it had been dressed in the formal ten-layer black robes of a Heian period courtier. The victim's head also appeared in this strange tableau, placed on a large silver salver on the floor in front of it, somewhat like it was being served for dinner.

Even considering the way the victim had been dressed, in the court robes of ancient Japan, Yamashita had immediately thought that the whole picture had a rather Renaissance nuance to it. His first thought had been of the famous Caravaggio painting of Salome with the head of John the Baptist that he had seen once, and he had even wondered in the back of his mind if this was not some kind of arcane reference to it.

For the time being though, he kept these thoughts to himself.

Finally arriving at the top of the stone staircase, the two policemen received a brisk salute from the officer left on duty to watch over the crime scene, lifted the familiar yellow tape, and stepped into the main hall.

The body had long since been removed for autopsy, and the shrine now looked as if nothing whatsoever had ever happened there, especially in comparison to the last time they had visited and found the dark scene created there by the murderer.

"OK," said Yamashita briskly, looking around at the ornate main altar and the mass of gold and silver shrine decorations. "Run me through what we know."

"Yes, sir," replied Yokota, opening his briefcase and pulling out a large file of case notes.

He rifled through the pages for a moment, and then loudly cleared his throat.

"The body was found on a table before the main altar. Said table had been stored behind the platform with several other tables and positioned by the killer. The deceased was dressed in antique black courtiers' robes reflective of the Heian period. We are still looking into these and exactly what period they came from to see if that tells us anything. These robes were most likely antiques, but copies of stuff like them can be found at a lot of places, like wedding rental shops and the like, *noh* and *kabuki* theatres, costume rentals, etc., and we are trying to trace if anything has been reported stolen, but so far, no joy."

"Dressed before or after death?"

"Best guess - after. The body had been drained of blood after death, so - no mess. There was no blood on the robes, and no DNA traces from our killer. Cause of death, lethal injection, we are still waiting on the results of the full chemical analysis. Of course, it wasn't done here, so we are going through a mountain of local CCTV trying to find the vehicle that transported the body here. Also - no joy so far."

"What about cameras here?"

"Yes, this really sucks. Full security system, very expensive, and all disabled a few days before the murder, about a week ago. No one noticed."

"No one noticed?"

"No, sir. No one ever looks at it. The camera feed is in a little room in the back of the shrine offices over there," he pointed with his pen at a small wooden building behind the shrine.

"Figures…. The head?"

"Fine-toothed electric power saw. Pretty quick with that. Again, not done here."

"And he took the tongue this time?"

"Yes, sir. This time it's the tongue."

"Dead men tell no tales…. What about the dish it's sitting on?"

"One of the shrine's sir. They are very pissed about that. Used in some religious services. They have a pile of them in a locker behind the altar."

Yamashita folded his arms and leaned against the table that had been set up by the forensic department in the center of the room.

"And we still have no idea who he is?"

Yokota shook his head. "None at all, sir. Still combing through missing persons."

Yamashita sighed. "Time of death?"

"The evening of the third of March. We can't be very specific about time, however. It appears the body may have been kept on ice or in a freezer or something, at least according to the autopsy."

"A week ago, then."

"Yes, sir. Most likely."

"OK. Now tell me about the fox fur," he said, gesturing towards the forensic file in Yokota's hand.

"Found on the front of the robes. Doesn't look like transfer. It looks like it was put there."

"The usual calling card, then."

"Very likely, sir. I can't think of any reason why someone would have fox fur on their clothes. It looks like the killer was trying to tell us something."

Yamashita nodded. "Yep. He absolutely was. He was waving at us. 'Hello, remember me?' No question about it."

The two men were quiet for a while.

"Why here?" wondered Yamashita out loud.

Yokota shrugged and gestured back the way they had come.

"Well, this guy is pretty theatrical sir, as you know. Do you think the victim is supposed to represent Kugyo?"

Yamashita looked at his younger sidekick with some admiration.

"That's not a bad thought, Yokota. Kugyo was beheaded a few hours after he assassinated the *shogun*... Yes. That could be it exactly. A kind of re-enactment of what happened at the shrine's most famous event.... Interesting. What about the feather?"

"As before, sir, in the victim's right hand. And the same as in the previous killings all those years ago, a black crow's feather."

This final piece of evidence had only been divulged to a select group of people investigating the case and never to the press. That being said, Yamashita knew that Sal and his co-author were aware of it, but they had left it out of their best-selling book at the urging of the task force. The presence of the fox fur was supposed to be a closely guarded secret, however.

"OK. Access?"

"Looks like he had keys, sir. There is no sign of a break-in."

Yamashita shrugged and walked around the room a little in obvious frustration.

"Keys… *shimmatta*…. This guy is thorough…" he muttered.

Yokota nodded. "And a risk taker. That's what really blows my mind if you want my opinion, sir. This place is *extremely* public. There is nearly always someone around, twenty-four-seven. It's got cameras, even if no one looks at them. There are even cameras outside in the grounds. The shrine has both police *and* private security too. There's a *koban* with more than eight officers on duty just down the street. No one saw anything."

"And yet he was able to carry a body in here with no one noticing…. that takes balls."

"Yes, I would say so… that and also a shitload of planning," said Yokota, scratching his close-shaven skull.

Yamashita nodded in agreement and walked around the room with his hands in his pockets. "Yes. Balls and an off-the-scale level of planning and long experience. Three decades of it. Go figure *that* out. What we *do* know is that in the case of this place particularly," he stood and waved his hands at the ceiling, "he must have spent a long time planning it. Access and egress. Timing. Coming here. Leaving here. Finding out where the keys were. Maybe copying them? If that's how he accessed the place. All the little details. He had to have spent days or weeks casing the place. And all for what? He could have killed this guy a lot easier and left him in the forest somewhere like some of his other victims. But no, that's no fun. Because he

25

enjoys the theatre of it all. He enjoys the shock. And he thinks he is just cleverer than all of us…."

Yokota smiled. "He might be on the money with that."

Yamashita nodded. "Indeed, he might. I mean, he's been getting away with this stuff for nigh on thirty years, after all."

Yokota sighed and looked down at his file.

"So, in summary, sir. We don't know how or why he picks his victims. We don't know where he kills half of them. We don't know why he kills them. We don't know how he arranged this little *tableau vivant* …We have no murder weapon, and no witnesses to either this crime or any of his previous… displays…"

Yamashita looked at him and smiled. "*Tableau vivant?* What nice phrases you're picking up these days, Yokota."

The big man blushed. "The wife is a French major, sir."

Yamashita laughed. "I see. No witnesses, you say? Well, maybe not to this one… but there was one witness…"

"Wow, sir…" said Yokota. "That was a long time ago. You want to go over it with her again?"

Yamashita nodded. "Well, why not? Seeing that he's chosen to honor Kamakura with his latest abomination, she might be due a visit. Plus, I know her quite well, as you know, *and* she has a pretty good memory… And we have a couple of other folks here in this town who are experts on this case…"

"Sal? And Maeda?"

"Yes. That's what I'm thinking. Ran Maeda and Sal wrote a bestseller on this case several years ago, the one you mentioned before that you read. I think we should pull them both in. Let's tell them what we can and see if it rings any bells with them. It can't hurt."

Yokota nodded. "'Yep. I agree, sir. The more, the merrier."

The two men stepped out of the main hall into the sunshine.

"You really think we can crack *Il Monstro*, sir? After thirty years? A national case?" asked Yokota as they descended the stone staircase.

Yamashita looked at him seriously and put his hand on his shoulder.

"Every criminal makes a mistake, Yokota. *Every* criminal. No exceptions. We just need to find it. And then… he's ours."

=====================

Penelope Middleton, who was now a recently retired full professor of Japanese literature from Kamakura's Hassei University, had actually first met Chief Inspector Yamashita, now one of her closest friends, when as a young detective he had been sent to interview her about the killing of her boyfriend, Hiro, nearly thirty years previously.

At that time, the young officer had been on secondment from Kamakura to the Tokyo Metropolitan police and placed on the *'Il Monstro'* case task force, as the Japanese press had later dubbed it. His bosses wanted someone to go over the witness testimony that the Nagano prefectural police had provided, and he had been the man chosen for the job.

Over the years that followed, and as he had rapidly risen to his current rank, he had worked on several cases that Penelope had been involved with in one way or another, and the chief inspector had come to see her as an indispensable aid and sounding board when it came to the most difficult ones. These were the hard ones, the ones that had baffled the police, and cases that, if not for her unique gifts, would have gone unsolved. She had, he always said, a genius for looking at the facts in a different way and for coming up with solutions of such astounding originality and precision that had convinced him over the years that she was severely wasted in spending her life lecturing and writing papers on Edo period poetry.

And he knew that, more than any of them, she had a personal reason to want to catch this particular murderer.

This morning, as they sat together once again in her sunny living room with its view out over her large vegetable garden, he felt a wave of sadness at having to open, once again, an ancient wound that he thought she and nearly anybody else in a similar situation would have rather put behind them.

In this, though, he could not have been more mistaken.

The truth was that Penelope had never once ceased to think about the man she had lost that day, nor had she ever given up on the idea that one day she would watch as his killer was finally brought to justice.

Her best friend, Dr. Fei Chen, who lived in the house next door with her elderly aunt, and who was also Yamashita's confident as well as being a Kamakura police coroner, was a person far more direct about the opening of wounds, ancient or otherwise.

As Penelope put a mug of coffee in front of Yamashita, the slender Chinese lady bustled in from the garden and threw herself in her usual old wicker chair in the sunshine.

"Oh, I know why you're here, Eiji. Start talking," she commanded, throwing the old straw hat she used for gardening on the floor and running her hands threw her short dark hair. "I told her a few days ago you would be wanting a chat. And here you are…"

Yamashita put both hands together and made a mock bow towards her sagacity.

"Let the man have his coffee first, Fei. The poor devil just walked in the door," said Penelope with a reproving look.

Fei smiled. "OK. Make one for me too, then. But I want to hear all the gossip… Is it true we have an *Il Monstro* case in Kamakura? Because from the autopsy report and forensics I read, it sure looks like that to me…."

"I suppose you, too, have read Sal and Maeda's book?"

"Twice," said Fei with a grin.

Yamashita took a sip of his coffee. "God, you always seem to know more than me, Fei. But in answer to your question, yes. That's what we've got. Almost definitely."

He cast a glance into the kitchen where Penelope was busying herself with the coffee, and Fei shook her head and looked at the floor.

"Excellent...Wow..." she said. "I thought that bastard just operated in Tokyo these days...."

"Hmmm... that's actually not true. Only the last one was in Tokyo. He moved around before that. Nagano, Kyoto, Nara...then Tokyo. That's just the press hype," he said.

Long ago, the Japanese press had grasped the similarities between the famous 'Monster of Florence' cases in Italy and the similar cases in Japan, the last of which had taken place in the Japanese capital, and dubbed the killer the '*Il Monstro di Tokyo*' or "The Tokyo *Il Monstro*.' This was partly because of the similarities in the killings in the sense of their seemingly random and theatrical nature, but Yamashita suspected it was mainly because it gave them a chance to use the word 'monster' in big letters and because it sold more newspapers.

Both the Italian and the Japanese cases had similarities, the staging and mutilation of bodies, the random nature of the slayings, the sheer brutality inflicted on the victims, and mainly the fact that they had both remained unsolved, even though it was suspected that the Italian '*Il Monstro di Firenze*' was probably dead, presuming the police and the journalist who had pursued him for so many decades indeed had the right man.

To Yamashita's trained mind, the Japanese *Il Monstro* case was an utterly different animal.

The biggest difference lay in the choice of location for the slayings and in the victimology. In Italy, *Il Monstro* had focused exclusively on killing couples in lonely lovers' lanes in the countryside, usually shooting them and mutilating the females. In Tokyo, however, the victims had always been single men, and he had never once used a gun.

"Anyway, I'm glad there's at last something to divert you from your duties down in the cellar, Fei. I see you didn't do the autopsy?" he asked.

Fei accepted a mug of coffee from her friend and placed it on the floor next to her, where one of Penelope's four cats suddenly appeared and sniffed at it like it was something to eat.

Fei shook her head.

"Nah. They wouldn't let us touch it. Once they heard it might be *Il Monstro* they rushed some specialist they've been using down from Tokyo. I still read the report though, and I heard about it from one of the assistant coroners who they asked to help out. Very weird indeed. What's all this stuff with robes?"

"You tell me," said Yamashita with a shrug. "It's a mystery. That's why I'm here. To throw myself on Penny-*sensei's* mercy…"

"You seem to do that quite often…" quipped Fei with a smile.

Penelope came and sat down between them at the dining table.

"Don't be rude. How can I help you, Eiji?"

"Well… I was wondering if I couldn't invite you to dinner. You too, of course, Fei. There's someone I'd like you to meet, and he has kindly offered to cook at his place, which is a way better deal than if you came to mine. He's the guy who wrote the book on *Il Monstro,* with Sal..."

Sal Nakamura was another old friend who had been Penelope's student many years ago at Hassei. At the mention of his name, Penny looked up at Yamashita and cocked her blonde head to one side.

"Would that be Ran Maeda?"

Yamashita nodded. "The same. I think he and Sal mentioned you in their book, without using your name, of course."

Penelope nodded. "Yes, I asked them to keep my name out of it. And I haven't actually met Maeda-san. Sal interviewed me about it, that was all. But is it true, I'm still the only living witness? Not that 'witness' is the right word. I didn't see anything useful at all that day, I think..."

Yamashita shook his head and leaned forward towards her. "That's not true at all. You saw something... two people. That was very significant, and it's been a factor in the investigation for decades. And you're right, no one else has ever seen a thing. Even though we've had five killings now. So... what you saw was very important. Even if you don't know exactly what it was."

Penelope looked down at the floor.

"You know... I've always felt guilty in a way... I wondered if what I said just sent everyone off on some wild goose chase and that maybe I did more harm than good. I mean, telling the story about the two figures I saw in the snowstorm that day. I know what I saw was extremely strange, but what if they had nothing to do with what happened to Hiro?"

Yamashita nodded, but looked at her thoughtfully.

"But what if they did?" he asked quietly.

Chapter 3

Don't Believe Your Eyes

The Kamakurayama area of the city of Kamakura was a quiet, heavily-wooded, hilly area with many older houses in its leafy streets and was also dotted with several tiny shrines and temples that reflected the more rural atmosphere that the area was famous for. The town itself had long been a retreat for artists and writers, especially after the war finished, and now, due to its many charms and proximity to the capital, older areas like this had become much sought after.

As their taxi negotiated the tiny streets searching for the old Maeda home, a feat which seemed to defeat the little GPS on the dashboard, Yamashita filled Penelope and Fei in on a few details about their host they had been unaware of.

"We were at school together actually, Maeda and I," said Yamashita, smiling a little at what was obviously a nice memory for him. "He was always someone with a real interest in crime from a psychological point of view, so I wasn't really very surprised when Sal said he had asked him to help write their book on *Il Monstro*. He was pretty much the perfect choice, I thought, and he had previously written another successful book on the Italian *Il Monstro di Firenze*, so he knew that case well too," he said as he gazed out the window at the old wooden houses they were passing, with their high walls enclosing traditional gardens that were full of maples and cherry trees.

"Maeda is a polymath, I mean, a seriously clever guy. He's written more than forty books on a dozen different subjects, and he has an interest in criminal psychology and things like that for which he is pretty well known internationally. But he's also written books, I dunno, on art, philosophy, music… even cooking. He has a bunch of degrees from some of the top universities in the world, and speaks I don't know how many languages. His family… well, that's another interesting story. They are the direct line of the old Maeda family, who were the old feudal lords of Kanazawa, you may have heard of them. They were the richest of all the feudal families. Maeda's great-grandfather was a count or something like that, but then the family lost everything after the war. Titles, lands, the works. It's really hard to imagine for normal folk, but for the old aristocracy like his family, everything just changed in the blink of an eye. One moment they ruled like princes, the next, they were like everyone else."

"Yes, I've heard this story before. A lot of the old aristocratic families like his had to change," said Penelope. "Kind of reminds me of that book by Dazai … what was that? Oh yes… *The Setting Sun*…some of those people never really managed to adjust to the modern world."

Yamashita nodded. "Yeah, that book could well have been written about his family, especially the grandparents. But Maeda's father was a bit of a rebel, and the family nearly disowned him when he married someone they thought was 'beneath him,' or however it went. He was an artist and a poet, quite a well-known one too, and his mother was also an artist or something like that. I met them a few times when I was a student, they were very nice people. They still had a bit of money, and I think they managed to keep the house we're going to tonight, but not much else. They died a long time ago, in a boating accident, when we were at school. Tragic… I remember going to the funeral. There were several members of the royal family there too… Ah, here we are…."

The taxi had headed up a narrow, winding road with nothing but woodland and a cliff on one side, and stopped in front of a large, old two-story house surrounded by a long white concrete wall topped with ceramic tiles and a traditional wooden-roofed entrance gate. Penelope noted that the wood on the gate looked like it was rotten in some parts, and the garden they could glimpse inside also looked like it could do with some attention as well.

Yamashita pressed the buzzer, and their host appeared at the gate a minute later to welcome them inside.

"Eiji… it's been a long time…" he said with a polite bow to Yamashita. He greeted Penelope and Fei, and both were pleasantly surprised by this quietly graceful man, who seemed to evince an air of natural dignity and calm.

Ran Maeda was tall and slender with slightly longish grey hair that reached the collar of his shirt, and which he wore in a ponytail. He was wearing black slacks and a long-sleeved light-blue shirt with the sleeves casually rolled up and looked somehow a tad more glamorous than many men his age had a right to.

But what immediately caught their attention was his eyes.

They were blue.

This was the first time in her life that Penelope had ever met a Japanese with blue eyes, even if Maeda's were a very, very dark shade of indigo. She had heard of this rare phenomenon before, even if she had never encountered it, and knew that it stemmed from some long distant ancestor, usually from the far north of Japan, sometimes from the indigenous Ainu people, who had intermingled with people from the ancient Slavic tribes that had become Russia, and which very occasionally manifested itself far down the genetic chain in the modern day.

She and Fei were far too polite to comment on it, though, and followed Maeda into his charming old wooden house through a very attractive, slightly run-down, western-style garden with sweeping lawns and flower beds full of colorful plants.

In the kitchen-dining room, they found Maeda's co-writer and their old friend Sal Nakamura sitting on a stool next to a large marble-topped kitchen island drinking beer from a bottle and smoking his usual hand-rolled cigarettes. He rose and greeted them all, and Maeda told them to have a seat while he busied himself pouring drinks.

Sal and Maeda actually looked a little similar. Sal was younger and taller, but he also wore his hair in a long ponytail, which had never changed since the first time Penelope had met him when he was one of her Japanese Literature students at Hassei some decades before. It was also why he always called Penelope '*sensei*' whenever he spoke to her, perhaps to remind them of their old bond.

"Did you know Ran and Eiji were at school together?" he asked Penelope.

"Yes, he was just telling us. Is that true?"

Ran laughed and handed her a long champagne flute of sparkling wine.

"Yes, it's true. We were even in the same class. At the bottom somewhere, I expect."

Yamashita shook his head. "If I remember correctly, I was at the bottom, and you were always at the top. We all thought the teachers wanted to adopt you."

Maeda waved away the compliment.

"It's true," said Sal with a mischievous smile. "He had an odd nickname in his schooldays, didn't he, Eiji?" he said, looking at Yamashita to supply it.

Maeda rolled his eyes and made a face, and Penelope marveled again at their beautiful deep color.

"Leo," said Yamashita. "After Leonardo Da Vinci. Because he was so good at everything."

"Ladies," said Maeda giving Sal and Yamashita a rueful look, "don't listen to this nonsense. It's purely apocryphal..."

Penelope and Fei laughed, and Maeda passed one of the champagne flutes to Fei, and then stopped and looked at her carefully.

"*Ni lai zi zhonguo ma?* ("Are you from China?") he asked her, in beautifully accented and rapid Mandarin.

"*Wo de jia ren lai zi Shanghai.*" (My family is from Shanghai) Fei replied, looking rather shocked at the unexpected change in language.

Maeda nodded. *"Yi ge fei chang hao di. Wo yijing tai jiu mei guguo nalile…"* (A very nice place. It's been too long since I've been there…") he said with a smile.

Fei smiled back and looked at Penelope.

"His pronunciation is perfect," she complimented.

"Very rusty, but I can still get around. It's such a relief to get away from Japanese now and again," he said as he began taking plates from one of the cabinets.

"Yes… I know the feeling…" said Penelope, who rarely had the chance to speak English these days as nearly everyone she knew was either Japanese or just monolingual.

Yamashita offered to help, and together the two of them began to serve the meal.

"Is this a chicken *ragout*?" Penelope asked a few minutes into the meal. "It's sensational…" she smiled.

"It's actually really simple," said Maeda with a smile as he brushed away a long strand of hair from his face. "I was taught it in Sicily by a chef once. In Palermo. Someone told me that he used to be the go-to chef for some big mafia kingpin. Anyway, like in most of Italy, food is the second most important religion."

"What's the first?" asked Penelope.

Ran smiled. "Football. Then food, and then Catholicism is a poor third. I'll give you the recipe if you like…"

"Yes, please. And do teach Eiji to cook sometime. I've failed in that respect over the years, I think…" she joked.

"Now, now… I bring the wine… I know my place," said Yamashita, filling her glass as he spoke.

"So," said Maeda leaning forward and placing the tips of his fingers together. "I must say this is very exciting, Eiji. A visit from you, *and* a visit from our old friend *Il Monstro* to our little town," he shot a glance at Sal, who nodded happily. "And finally, at last, I get to meet the only person who has ever seen him," he said, giving Penelope an admiring look.

He raised his glass to her, and Penelope made a non-committal gesture.

"I think the word 'see,' as I was explaining to Eiji the other day, is a bit of an exaggeration…" she said.

Maeda nodded. "Still, a very rare thing. Where was it, in Nagano, right? Maybe thirty years ago or so… *a yamatengu*… a mountain *tengu*… and you saw his accomplice, the fox spirit too… I read the report… it was like something from an old fairy story…"

Fei looked up, surprised.

"The fox spirit? Sorry, we haven't really discussed this much…" she looked at her old friend, as if to ask if it was all right if they ventured down this path, and Penelope nodded briefly. Even though they had known each other for decades, Fei knew this was one topic that Penelope would usually rather they left alone.

Maeda had no such qualms though, and seemed to warm to his theme.

"Sure. The *kitsune*, the fox spirit. A shape-shifter from the ancient times. It's said that if a fox lives to be over a hundred years old it can take human form, and usually they appear as a beautiful young girl who waylays travelers on lonely roads. There are even *kyubi-no-kitsune*, or nine-tailed foxes, who have the ability to see and hear anything happening anywhere in the world. And her friend,

40

the *tengu*, the great bird god of the mountains. According to legend, they sometimes traveled together. In fact, Dr. Chen, you might know that the fox spirit was originally Chinese. The *huli-jing*, it was called. Like many good things, such as yourself, they were imported here…"

Fei laughed. "I think you'll find I'm a more recent import."

"Of that, my dear doctor, I have no doubt. Both the *tengu* and the fox could be good - and they could be bad. The *inari* foxes you see at some shrines are messengers of the gods, so they are the good foxes. The *tengu* could also be beneficent, or they were the other kind that ripped you apart. It kind of depended on where you lived. But people in the countryside still believe very strongly in both, I assure you."

"Yeah, he's right about that," chimed Sal. "I have relatives in western Japan. They think fox spirits are as real as yesterday's baseball scores."

Fei laughed. "Sal's redneck relatives… like the Beverley hillbillies…" referring to the old television show she had seen as a child.

"And also… there's the feather," Ran said, looking at Yamashita with a smile, who looked back at him surprised.

"You're not supposed to, er… talk about that, Ran," he said with a sigh. "But I guess it doesn't matter here…"

Maeda stood up and walked behind him to top up his glass.

"I know… but don't worry, you're secret is safe with us. Sal and I have known about the feather and the fox fur for years, haven't we?"

Sal looked apologetically at Yamashita.

"That's true. But we never wrote about it, or the fur, as you know. We knew you wanted that kept, er… private, for now."

Yamashita rolled his eyes and swore softly.

"Well, damn you both. If you know, who else knows?"

Maeda put his hand on his shoulder consolingly.

"Probably a lot of people, I guess. That's the press for you. And you know the police department leaks like the proverbial sieve as well…"

"Wasn't there some fox connection to the *Il Monstro* case in Italy?" asked Penelope. "Do they have fox spirits there too?"

Sal shook his head. "Yeah, well… kinda. We wondered if our guy used that idea to link himself to the Italian crimes at one point. But yes… the chief suspect was this Sicilian peasant guy; I forget the name now. And yes, he kept various animals in his family home in Naples. But it's not a really solid link."

"If it was indeed *him* at all. The jury is still out on that," said Maeda, resuming his seat at the head of the table after fetching another bottle of wine. Penelope thought he had a kind of quiet academic authority about him, like a professor briefing a less informed student.

"Yes… I read there was some doubt about it," said Yamashita.

"Well, Eiji. We don't live in a perfect world, do we? Even good policemen like you don't always get their man, and I think the *polizia de Firenze* made quite a pig's breakfast of it," said Maeda. "But let's face it, there's no connection with the Italian crimes other than the Japanese media grabbing the name *Il Monstro*, probably because they think anything foreign sounds cool. It's why half the professional football clubs in this country have Italian names, something I've always considered rather bizarre… But this latest one here in Kamakura… that's *very* strange. I believe the victim was dressed up? Would you care to elaborate?"

Yamashita nodded, reached into his briefcase, and passed Maeda a thick file.

"Sorry to spoil your dinner, folks…" he apologized.

"Don't worry about me," said Fei. "I'm used to it…"

"So… what do we have here?" Maeda took out a set of photographs that were held together with a bulldog clip. He started going through them one by one and passing them around the table to the others. The pictures showed the victim's body as it was found at the shrine, including various closeups of the garments he had been wearing.

"Astonishing. Everything about this case is … astonishing…" he said quietly.

"Wow… These look, what… Heian period stuff?" said Sal, pointing to the robes the victim was dressed in.

"Probably Kamakura or Muromachi period," said Maeda fetching a large magnifying glass from his study and scrutinizing one of the close-up photographs. "The material and the stitching look more recent than Heian. But very good. Yeah…these aren't made today, no one does that kind of stitching in replica couture… Do you see this type of very ornate cross-stitching here on the sleeve? That was common with the early seamstresses around the

43

eleventh century and later. I would be looking at museums if I were you, Eiji, see if they've had anything filched lately…"

"Seriously? They're antique?" said Yamashita, impressed as always by the depth of his friend's knowledge of obscure subjects. "We never thought about that. I'll ask my DS and the forensic people to look into it. But I guess my question is… why? What's the point of all this? Is he trying to give us some message?"

"Yes, why dress him up like that? That's my question, too," said Penelope. "I mean, why go to all the trouble? Why take the risk?"

Maeda nodded. "Why indeed?" he said, sitting back and folding his arms. "Well, I think he's an entertainer at heart, our boy. He thinks he's some kind of artist. A little like the Italian *Il Monstro*, who used to lay out his victims like in the Botticelli painting *Il Primavera*. I'll give you that they had that much in common, at least. I think our lad is even the same type of creature. An extrovert, who probably pretends to be the exact opposite. He has a sense of *le théâtre du macabre*. The theatre of horror, if you like. He likes creating these little… artistic scenes. It may be no more than that. Not really much to go on, despite all the pantomime."

"That's what my DS said too. I think you're right, actually."

"Well, as such it might also indicate either or both of two personality traits, if you don't mind me putting on my psychiatrist's hat for a moment. One is that he thinks he is superior to everyone else, thus he's not scared of taking even the most absurd risks. Or…" Maeda looked around the table for dramatic effect and then at Yamashita.

"…he wants you to catch him. Because he wants to stop. Both are very common traits in serial killers. Although the level of attention-seeking in our current friend is interesting…" said Maeda, taking a small sip of his wine. Watching him closely, Penelope noted that he ate and drank extremely little, but took the time to savor everything he put into his mouth.

Penny put her knife and fork together on her plate.

"The question is: how do we use it to catch him? And by the way, that was the best *ragout* I have ever eaten, Maeda-san."

Maeda smiled and gave a little bow.

"Please call me Ran. It's the character for 'indigo,' after these…" he waved the end of his fork to indicate his eyes. "I thought it might be apropos since we were talking about things related to Italy."

Penelope smiled. "It was."

"But in answer to your question, Eiji… I wouldn't be going down that path. I mean, trying to figure out all the quirks and the meaning of these displays he makes. I think that's exactly where he wants you to go," said Maeda.

"I agree," said Penelope. "All this scene setting, all these different ways he kills… Do you want to know what I think?"

Yamashita nodded. "Always."

Penelope took a sip of wine.

"I think that's all a red herring. I think it's done for two reasons. One is because it pleases *him*, and the other is because it confuses *you*…"

There was a dead silence in the room for a moment, and then Maeda began to clap.

45

"That's *exactly* what I think, too, Penelope-san. I couldn't have put it better. Wherever did you find this lady, Eiji?"

Penelope blushed, and Yamashita sighed and looked at Sal.

"It's terrible when clever people ambush you," he joked.

"Never happened to me," quipped Sal.

"Well, I dunno…." said Fei. "You can't just ignore all the theatrics. It must point to *something*, especially if, as Ran says, he wants to get caught… and anyway, what else do you have to go on?"

Maeda looked at them all.

"The doctor is right, we don't have much else. So, we have to use what we have. And what we have are five killings. The first four were all committed in quiet places outdoors in both Nagano and then in wooded areas in Kyoto, Nara, and Tokyo… and then this one. This one is the first time he has gone in for some historical motif. But it probably won't be the last. I think he's obsessed with the past, by the way."

"Why do you say that?" asked Sal.

Maeda put his forefingers together under his chin, which made him, if anything, look even more professorial.

"Well, that's what these crimes have in common. The first four – killed by an ancient mountain legend, the bodies torn apart and the various parts left hanging from trees, and now this last one, where he seems to have gone to a lot more trouble than usual, reflective of the twelfth-century and the death of the *shogun* Minamoto… our boy loves the past. He's got a real thing for it," he said.

Penelope leaned back in her chair and folded her arms.

"One thing I've wondered over the years is why people said I saw a *tengu*? I mean, those things are supposed to have large red noses, aren't they?"

Sal and Maeda shook their heads.

"Not always," said Sal. "There are different types of *tengu*, you know… they're one of the most ancient spirits in Japan, older even than the *kitsune*… almost certainly from the shamanistic time that predated the ideas that eventually formed into the indigenous Shinto religion thousands of years ago. Some look like birds, like the *crow tengu*. He's from Nagano too, where your friend was killed. The *crow tengu* looks like a human, except he has the head of a crow. Which may even be indicative in a way of how our boy sees himself… Anyway, that's why the locals in Nagano thought it might be that. For them, these creatures are very much a part of life, a part of their history. And, of course, there was the way your friend was killed too…"

Penelope looked down at her plate and gave a small sigh.

Though no one wanted to talk about the details of Hiro's death, they were all, including Fei, well aware of what had happened that night.

That night, so long ago now, after giving up her lonely wait on the snowy road and returning to the inn, Penelope found, to her concern, that Hiro had failed to return and waited up the whole night for him with the innkeeper and his wife. Then, at first light, a search team had headed up the little forest path, and in less than a kilometer, they had come upon a scene that none of them would ever forget, and that was still spoken about to this day.

One of the men at the front of the party had spotted a small trail of blood heading into the trees by the side of the road, and after advancing into the forest, they had come upon a giant pine. There, suspended from ropes like decorations on a Christmas tree, they were shocked to see the various parts of Hiro's body hanging from its branches suspended in the cold winter air. A foot here, a hand somewhere else, the internal organs... the head with the eyes eaten by the birds... it looked like he had been ripped apart.

The superstitious locals had all thought the same thing, and some of the searchers, older men from the village, had taken one look at it and whispered the same word: *tengu*... a reference to an old story of the *crow tengu*, who used to kill his victims and hang the pieces of their bodies from the branches of a tree to keep them fresh so it could come back and eat them later.

"Well, that was a long time ago," said Penelope sadly.

Sal nodded and patted her on the shoulder. "Yes, it was... but this time, things have changed, and he's up against modern science now. I think this time we have a chance..."

Maeda nodded.

"Yes, I agree. I think it's now only a matter of time. I take it you've read our little book on the subject?"

Penelope nodded. "Yes, a few times, actually. It was very interesting. And I've also read your book on the Italian *Il Monstro* case, which was quite thrilling. Is it true you think that the monster of Florence is dead?"

Maeda poured them all some more wine.

"Yes. I think they missed him. In fact, I'm convinced of it. I think they jailed the wrong man… and yes, I think he's dead. He would never have stopped killing, and I believe he was certainly free to do so. I even know who it was… I made a point of visiting his grave, too. Just to make sure…" he said, swirling the dark red Nerello Mascalese wine he had served them that he had explained was made from a native Sicilian grape variety mostly cultivated around Mount Etna.

He took the merest sip from his glass and closed his eyes, silently savoring the strong, rustic taste.

Then he looked up and gave them all a grim smile.

"Unfortunately, though, our friend here in Japan… seems to be showing no signs of slowing down…"

Chapter 4.

Prius Dementat

A few days after their sumptuous dinner at Maeda's house, which they had all enjoyed greatly, Chief Inspector Yamashita made good on an offer to take them all to the crime scene at the great shrine in Kamakura to get their views on the case,

Penelope was a little surprised at her friend's request for them to join him, as from past experience she knew he was usually more than a little reluctant to have non-police involved in a homicide case, and she knew that his bosses would have been furious if they had found out. But she sensed there was something about the odd nature of this murder that had driven him to look for help from people like herself and Maeda, who had an ability to think a little outside the box.

Whatever the reason though, she had to admit that she was intrigued, not only because there was a connection to the death of her old boyfriend, but also by the sheer weirdness of it all. A victim dressed in Heian period robes was not your typical murder in twenty-first-century Japan. Somehow, she felt, this murderer was trying to communicate something in a kind of code that she could not understand, but if she could figure out what that was, she might be able to help finally stop him. For Hiro's sake, if not her own, she was determined to try.

She arrived quite early at the main gate of the shrine where they had all agreed to meet, and thought she would be the first there, however, as she turned the corner, she saw Sal and Ran were already standing there under the huge red *torii* gate deep in discussion about something. It wasn't until she walked up behind Ran and tapped him on the elbow that they even noticed her.

Both men smiled and bowed to her, and she noticed Maeda was well-dressed that day in a sharp black suit with an open-necked white shirt, which, coupled with his longish swept-back grey hair, reminded her of a certain good-looking concert violinist that she had been involved with several years before. If she had been honest with herself, or with Fei, who had asked her directly what she thought of Ran after the dinner, she would have admitted that he was, in many ways, the type of man who she would normally find quite attractive, and that if she had a 'type,' it might just well be him.

However, it had been a long time now since her last relationship, and it was difficult for her to kindle anything in that direction anymore, or to overcome the strong sense of inertia that her romantic interests seemed to lay hidden under. Still... she thought, as she looked at him that morning, you never knew...

"Sorry, Penny-*sensei*," said Sal. "We were just discussing our old book on *Il Monstro*. Ran here is talking sequels..." he said, gesturing to Maeda, who rolled his eyes and smiled mischievously.

"Well... and why not? There's been a lot of developments, including the recent one here, since we last published. It seems our villain has awoken from his slumbers, wouldn't you say? And that usually spells a publisher wanting to cash in. Ours called me yesterday to ask if we were interested in ah... revisiting the crime, so to speak... you should at least think about it, right?"

Sal sighed and shuffled his feet. He was always somewhat reluctant to start new projects until he had finished what he was currently engaged in, and he had enough self-knowledge by this time to know that once he started something like this with Ran again, it would most likely be all-consuming until it was finished, like the last one had been. That was just how Ran was, and Sal knew it.

Penelope, who was also a writer, laughed at his discomfort. "Well... I kind of agree. Strike while the iron is hot and the publisher is feeling generous... and speaking of crime..." she nodded towards the road where she had just spotted the chief inspector climbing out of an unmarked car that was being driven by DS Yokota, whom they had met several times before.

Yamashita strode quickly up to them and gave them all a quick bow before gesturing that they should make their way into the shrine proper.

"Yokota's just going to park the car, and then he'll join us. Thanks so much for coming, by the way, it's good of you all to spare the time," he said as they walked across the grounds toward the main hall.

"I guess you've been spending a bit of time here recently?" asked Ran.

Yamashita nodded.

"Too much. We were here the other day too, going over things. There's a couple of points about this we are still not sure of. And don't forget, this is confidential, right everyone?"

He shot a glance at Sal, who was the only professional media person in the group.

"Mum's the word. Don't worry…" said Sal with an understanding look.

"Just thought I'd mention it…" said Yamashita with a smile.

Penelope looked up at the big shrine buildings they were approaching.

"You know, even though I've lived in Kamakura for thirty years, I can't even remember the last time I was inside the main hall. Must be donkey's years ago. Mainly I just cut across the grounds here to save time going somewhere else," she said as she looked around as if trying to orient herself.

"Anyway, my first question is this. Why do you think he chose *this* place for his latest er… display?"

Yamashita fell into step beside her as they walked up the long stone staircase past the stump of the ancient ginkgo tree.

"That's very much my question, too," he said. "I mean, like you said before, it just makes zero sense, unless the fear of getting caught is less than the hope of showing off somehow. Take a look around! This is one of the most used public spaces in the city. It's never closed, twenty-four-seven. Why take the risk? Unless it's all theatrics, as Ran was saying. Though I doubt I would wager my freedom on getting a round of applause…"

He turned at the top of the stairs, and they stared out over the huge complex that was the Tsurugaoka Hachimangu shrine, which contained several sub-shrines and museums and which had constant access from the busy Komachi shopping street just outside as well as other entrances.

"Hmmm…." said Ran. "Yes, I give you it's hard to understand. Maybe he likes the challenge. But that at least tells us something about him…"

The four friends turned and entered the main hall, where Yokota had suddenly appeared in front of them to hold up the yellow crime scene tape for them all to go under.

"Well, Detective Sergeant. Long time no see…" said Sal to the younger policeman, who smiled and bowed.

"Yes, it's been a while. Good to see you again, Nakamura-san. Let's see… it's not long since I rescued you from that guy's woodshed, I believe…" said Yokota, referencing the last case they had all been involved in.

"Yes. You know, I think I still owe you dinner for that…" said Sal with a grin.

"I think so, too." said the detective.

They now stood in the main hall where the body had been found, and which they all recognized from the photographs the chief inspector had shared a few nights previously.

"So… this is it, eh?" said Maeda, looking around the large high-ceilinged room with a grave air. "Have there been any developments since we last spoke?"

Yamashita nodded.

"Yep… there have indeed. I wanted to fill you all in on it now that we're all here and get your perspectives. You and Sal know this killer as well as the police do, I think. And Penny-*sensei*… well, you *are* connected to this in a way."

He looked up at Yokota who opened his briefcase and passed his boss a large ring-bound folder, which Yamashita placed on a side table near the entrance and began to flip over some pages before he found what he was looking for.

"So… first, the main news," he said, looking up at them all. "We now know who the victim is, or rather was."

"Go on," said Maeda, coming to look over his shoulder at the open folder.

"OK. He was one Keito Imada, sixty-two years old, from Tokyo. There was a missing person's report filed on him about a week ago, and the body was identified by a family member yesterday evening. So, it's definitely him."

"So, who was he?" asked Sal.

"Exactly. He was, apparently, a wealthy art gallery owner from an old and prominent Tokyo family, and he owned a sort of second home here in Kamakura, not too far from where you live, Ran. He spent a lot of time down here lately, so his brother tells us."

"Married? Family?" asked Penelope.

"Divorced. No kids. The brother and his family are his only relatives. The brother also lives down here, in Zushi."

They all knew the little town on the coast that the chief inspector mentioned, a wealthy enclave with a marina that also claimed an estate owned by the imperial family.

"You said he was from a prominent family? How so?" asked Penelope.

Yamashita nodded and turned a page in his file.

"He was the grandson of Keisuke Imada, the wartime politician and later Speaker of the House of Representatives," he said, without looking up.

Sal gave a low whistle. "If memory serves, didn't his grandad spend some time in jail after the war? For war crimes?" he asked, folding his arms and looking up at the painted ceiling above them.

"That he did, not unlike the late and unlamented prime minister Abe's grandfather and a lot of other ruling party grandpas. Apparently going to jail for war crimes does no harm at all to your political career," said Yamashita

"So it would seem," sighed Penelope.

Sal drummed his fingers on the altar table and Penelope could tell he was dying to go outside and smoke. But then the journalist turned round to them all with an inquiring look on his face.

"There's another reason we know this guy's name, isn't there… it's in the back of my head…"

Maeda nodded. "Kaede Suimura?" he offered.

Sal slapped his thigh, and Yamashita and Yokota both nodded.

"That's it. I knew I'd heard his name before…" said Sal, frowning.

Penelope looked up at them all.

"Sorry, who?" she asked pleadingly.

Maeda turned to her. "Suimura Kaede was a beautiful and quite famous actress. You've probably seen some of her films. She committed suicide about fifteen years ago," he said sadly.

"That's right," said Yokota, who had been standing quietly behind his boss. "With her husband. I was a young copper in uniform at the time. One of my first cases after joining the force."

"She lived in Kamakura?" asked Penelope.

"She did. They left behind a young daughter who was in college at the time," Yokota looked at the floor, and Penelope could tell the memory of it still affected him.

"Why, though?" she asked. "Why both of them?"

Yamashita sighed.

"Shame. Shame and guilt and because they loved each other. But the main reason was that she had an affair. With our victim. They tried to keep it quiet, but the media got hold of it somehow."

Penelope shook her head.

"Lots of people have affairs. They don't kill themselves over it," she said sadly.

Yokota shook his head. "Not in this case. The connection ran deeper than that. It was discovered that Imada was involved in some kind of art business with Suimura's husband. It went bankrupt, and the husband lost a lot of money. Nearly everything, it seems. And then Imada dumped her, after which she went back to her husband, and was so overcome with remorse at what she had done to him… and what Imada had done to them, that they made a pact to die together. I was one of the first officers on the scene, actually."

"Wow. I'm sorry to hear that, Yokota-san," said Maeda.

Yokota nodded and looked away, clearly uncomfortable at the memory of it.

"How did they die?" asked Penelope.

"Carbon monoxide poisoning. In their car, in the garage. They left the daughter a long letter explaining what they did. It had been planned weeks before, we learned later…"

"Jesus…" Penelope whispered.

There was silence in the room for some time.

Finally, Yamashita spoke.

"Kugyo…" he said, looking at Maeda, who nodded thoughtfully.

"Kugyo… the assassin? Of Minamoto no Sanetomo? The *shogun*?" asked Penelope.

Maeda looked at her.

"You know your history, professor. Yes. He dressed him up as Kugyo. Kugyo the Betrayer. The man who turned on his friend and stabbed him in the back, just like our victim betrayed the husband and his wife," he said, and looked outside and towards the long staircase to where the remains of the 'hidden ginkgo' lay, the tree behind which the assassin had concealed himself.

He turned to Yamashita.

"If I were you… I'd have a look at that. This may well have something to do with the Suimura case…" he said. "You remember what our old teacher used to say, don't you? *Quos Deus vult perdere, prius dementat.*"

Yamashita smiled and nodded.

"That indeed has crossed our minds," he replied, casting a long look toward his friend.

They were about to leave the hall when Yamashita noticed Penelope move to a corner of the room and stand staring at the security camera, which had been placed high up on the wall and was pointed directly at the main altar where the victim's body had been laid out.

The chief inspector went over and stood next to her.

"So… this was switched off?" she asked.

"Yes. It'd been turned off a few days before the murder. No one noticed…"

"Why not?"

The chief inspector shrugged. "I guess because they had no need to look at the recordings. Nothing ever happened in here besides worshippers coming in and out."

"Which would have included our killer."

"Precisely."

Penelope turned and looked at him.

"So, there was a blank screen on one of their monitors… and no one did anything about it? Seems odd…. How do you turn this camera off?"

"The security setup is located in the shrine's offices. The camera can be turned off from there. He seems to have had keys to the office and to the main hall. No sign of a break-in."

"So, the camera was just switched off, not disabled in any way?"

"No, it seems to have been just switched off."

"I see… no sign of a break in… Who has access to the security office here?"

"The head priest is the only one with the keys, and he said he rarely went into that office, so he never noticed the monitor was off."

"So… how do you know it was our killer who turned it off?"

Yamashita looked at her carefully.

"We… er… well, we assume it must have been him. No one else would want to turn off the camera, after all…"

Penelope raised an eyebrow.

"Which company is responsible for the security here? ProSec?" she asked, pointing to a sticker on the side of the security camera?

Yamashita nodded. "Yeah. Very big company. Quite reputable."

"And can ProSec operate the cameras here remotely? I mean, from their offices?"

Yamashita stared at her.

"Shit. We never thought of that."

Penelope smiled.

"Maybe you need to go and see who had access at ProSec. Or have another look at whoever had access to that office here. But it seems to me it would be a lot simpler to turn off the camera from *there,* particularly if you knew someone or had access yourself, than to risk entering the shrine's offices, right? If there were no signs of a break-in in either place, that means you would probably need keys. That means you would need the key to this room, *and* a key to get into the security office here. That's two keys. So unless you suspect the Chief Priest… which is rather unlikely, wouldn't it be easier to turn off the camera at the security company and find another way in here?"

Yamashita and Penelope walked over to the heavy main doors.

"So how are these locked?" asked Penelope. "With this?"

She pointed to a large piece of wood that was slid in behind the doors to secure them in the traditional manner.

"Yes. So after the priest finished securing the main door, they would exit by the back stairs," said the chief inspector.

Yamashita led her down the narrow staircase behind the main altar, and they opened the door at the bottom, where a padlock was hanging open on the lock.

Penelope looked carefully at it, and also at where the locking mechanism was attached to the wall.

"This padlock is new," she said, pointing to where the padlock hung open on the door lock. You know, all he had to do was cut off the old padlock and replace it, and he could have gained access... as long as he could switch off the alarms. I bet you find the priest's keys don't match it, and he just left this one here for show. Then all he needed to do was make sure the camera was off too..."

Yamashita cursed.

"Forensics must have missed this. That's why I asked you to come... Shit. He had help... Someone to turn off the alarms and shut off the camera feed... from outside."

"Well, that would make sense... Occam's Razor, Eiji. If he didn't have keys to *this* room and just cut his way in with some bolt cutters..."

"He probably didn't have keys to the security office either," said Yamashita with a groan.

He thanked her profusely, and they hurried back upstairs where he gestured to Yokota to get the car.

"Right... we need to get going, I'm afraid, folks," he said as he picked up his file.

The group went out of the main hall into the sunlight again.

Detective Sergeant Yokota took the chance to whisper in Penelope's ear while his boss had his back to them.

"Do you know what all that Latin meant? What Maeda said?" he asked.

"Oh, that?" she asked "It's from *Antigone*.... An old Greek play. "*Those whom the gods wish to destroy, they first make mad.*"

Yokota gave her a quizzical look.

"Thanks," he said, and headed off to get the car from the parking lot.

As they walked down the long staircase, Penelope felt someone touch her on the shoulder and found Maeda just beside her.

"Could I interest you in a bite of lunch at my place?" he asked in a low voice so that no one else could hear.

She looked up into his dark blue eyes.

"As long as the conversation is not completely in Latin," she smiled.

Chapter 5

The Heron Maiden

An hour later they were standing in Ran's kitchen, which in the daytime looked completely different to what it had a few evenings previously when they had all come for dinner.

Somehow less formal and more welcoming than before, with the sun streaming into the room from a bright blue sky, it was a warm, sunny room with large windows looking over the garden, and Penelope noticed for the first time that it was exceptionally (and expensively) well equipped for someone who obviously knew how to cook.

There was a large range of different Japanese knives, some hanging on the wall and others arranged in a couple of large wooden knife blocks on the counter, and he also had a full set of shiny French copper pans hanging from a ceiling rack that lowered at the press of a button, and a professional-level Italian oven she had only seen in restaurants and which, although she privately coveted such a thing, had always remained stubbornly beyond her budget.

Ran busied himself at once with arranging their lunch, pulling various things from his pantry and refrigerator while she watched and observed that he knew exactly what he was doing in a kitchen, unlike a lot of other men in her experience. There is a certain way an experienced chef does things that is readily apparent to any other chef, just as it is very clear from the hesitant way someone else uses a knife, for example, that they are not so used to cooking.

"I overheard what you were saying to Eiji about the security system at the shrine... that was a clever observation of yours," he said as he poured her a glass of wine.

"Thank you. I'm confused why he didn't think of it himself, however. It's not really like him to miss things like that..."

"I know what you mean. I imagine he's under a lot of pressure. The press has been going crazy over these killings, especially the last one... To be honest, I think most forensic crews would have paid no attention to that lock. It was lucky you were there."

He laid out some heavy and rather antique-looking silver cutlery on the adjoining kitchen table and Penelope picked up one of the spoons and turned it over admiringly.

"How old are these? They look... I don't know...French?"

Ran smiled.

"Yes. I picked them up in Provence in an antique store many years ago. They were an extortionate price, but I just had to have them.... How about a small salad and some *vichyssoise*? Would that be OK? You're not gluten intolerant or anything, are you?"

"Sounds perfect," she said as they clinked glasses.

"That's good to hear. We don't do vegan here, I'm afraid…" he said with a serious look, as if it was some kind of disease.

He opened up some plastic containers from his refrigerator, and as soon as he had carefully warmed the contents on his stovetop, they were sitting down to lunch.

"This is very nice," she said, complimenting him on the soup.

"Yes, I made it yesterday. It's long been said, and it's true, that soup is always better the next day. It gives the flavors time to settle. At least that's what I've heard."

"You seem to know your way around the kitchen. That's a pretty rare thing with you Japanese guys, I've discovered…" she joked.

"Well, we are not all hopeless. Anyway, I've always loved food. I think it's one of the few creative things I can do with my hands, apart from music. My father liked to cook too, so maybe I got it from him. He used to make his own pasta, I remember. Even had one of those old Marcato pasta rolling machines. You know those? On Sundays, he allowed me to be his sous-chef… we usually ended up covered in flour."

They ate in silence for a while, and Penelope was surprised at how natural it felt to be with him, which was something she did not usually feel with men.

"So, are you always so observant?" he asked. "I'm talking about the lock on the shrine door again…"

Penelope looked down at the glass of chardonnay he had given her.

"Well, maybe… usually. I don't know. I just tend to notice things… things most people don't. It's just the weird way my mind works. When I was a kid we used to play *'I Spy'* whenever we went for long drives. You know that game, I guess?"

Rand said he did.

"Anyway," she continued. "I could always tell my parents what we had seen and where. Car models, number plates, names on buildings, etc., that kind of thing."

Ran smiled. "I think I remember reading somewhere, was it *le Carré* maybe? That kind of thing is a part of basic espionage training. You know, the ability to walk into a room, sit down and then tell your trainer all about the people there without looking and which ones were the enemy or suspicious or whatever, all just from a quick glance."

"I read that too. I think it was *le Carré. Smiley's People*? Something like that…" she said, taking a final spoonful of soup.

"You probably would have been an excellent spy."

"Missed calling, I guess," she smiled. "Do you have any superpowers? Apart from being a world-class chef and God knows what else? Eiji seems quite in awe of you. I've never heard him talk that way about anyone the way he talks about you."

Ran smiled modestly and waved away the compliment, and as he did so, Penelope saw that he wore an old gold signet ring with a finely cut rectangle of ruby on the middle finger of his right hand.

"Eiji is just being nice. And exaggerating. He's got plenty of talents himself. Have you ever heard him play the cello?"

Penelope nodded "Oh yes, I have. Several times. Though it's hard to coax him into performing. He's really quite good, I've always thought."

"Absolutely he is," said Ran, leaning back comfortably in his chair and crossing his arms. "I've always said he could have been a professional musician. His brother, too, though he preferred the mysteries of Zen Buddhism, I gather."

Penelope knew she was referring to Dokan, Eiji's brother, the head monk at Engakuji temple in Kamakura, and one of her closest friends.

"Yes, Dokan and I are old buddies. I see him every week at Engakujii for tea after my meditation session. Did they play together? He and Eiji? I knew Dokan was a violist… but he's never spoken about it, at least not to me."

Ran went into the adjoining room and returned a moment later with a small black and white photograph in a simple wooden frame, which he passed with a flourish to Penelope.

It was an old photograph of a string quartet playing in a wood-paneled room that looked like the lobby of a hotel, and Penny immediately identified the members as a very young-looking Chief Inspector Yamashita in a black tuxedo playing the cello, flanked by Dokan (whom she had never seen with hair before) holding a viola. There was also a strikingly beautiful young woman with long black hair on the violin and a pianist who was none other than her host.

"This was us - doing our side hustle while we were at university. We used to play at wedding receptions and other functions. For money. It was quite a good gig. We were actually in some demand once upon a time. And we weren't even music students…."

Penelope stared with interest at the old photo.

"Wow," she interned quietly. "This is a side of him I've never seen before - and I've known him for years, you know… Who's the girl with the violin?"

For a moment, she thought she saw a slight shadow pass across Ran's face, an almost indetectable falter in his usually composed smile.

"She, observant one, was Yuriko Nakatome, from the famous Nakatome real-estate family. You've probably heard of them I'm sure, they own half of Tokyo. I married her, actually…"

Penelope remembered suddenly that Ran was a widower, and lowered her head.

"I'm sorry, she's…."

Ran nodded.

"Yes, sadly. Many years ago, now." He accepted the photograph from Penelope's hands, their fingers brushing together slightly for a moment.

"Still," said Ran brightening, "our boy Eiji was… is, quite a musician. He's still concert-level. That sort of talent tends to stay with people, I find."

"I hope so. I'm beginning to think that whatever talent I have enjoyed over the years may be somewhat… evaporating with age…"

Ran laughed and looked at her in a strangely penetrating yet not oppressive way, a little like a cat looks at you. Still, from somewhere deep inside herself, she had the feeling that he was looking at her like she was some kind of interesting laboratory animal and somehow seeing into her head and watching her thoughts pass by. She also had the urge to reach over and stroke his face, an urge which she resisted, but nevertheless recognized.

"You know…" he began, as he continued to gaze into her eyes. "People love to conceal themselves. I think… it's almost one of our earliest instincts. To shield our weaknesses from others…"

Penelope looked down, seeking refuge from his eyes, which seemed to be mapping her like a newly discovered country.

"I guess they do… I forgot you were a psychiatrist for a moment… Do you still practice?"

Ran stood up and carried their plates over to the kitchen island.

"A psychiatrist… yes. Though I don't really think of myself in those terms anymore. But yes, I still keep my hand in. I do some pro-bono consulting for a mental hospital in Zushi. Just a few times a month. They have a few interesting patients I've been seeing for a long time. Mostly though…" He pointed to the living room, which opened onto his book-lined study and the gardens outside. "I hang around in here. Writing. It's much more relaxing… except when my publisher calls me every morning asking how I am getting on with things…"

"Are you writing anything particular at the moment?"

He made a pained gesture and threw up his hands.

"I'm *always* writing something. I wish I could stop sometimes. I should ask you the same thing. Why don't we have coffee in the library? I even have a few of *your* books, I think…"

"Oh God… do you? In that case, I owe you a debt of sympathy…" she smiled, and rolled her eyes modestly.

"Have a seat, and I'll bring the coffee in a moment," he said, gesturing for her to go into the adjoining room, which served as both his study and his library and where she could see a large black leather sofa in the middle of the room on an expensive looking Afghan rug.

She did as he asked and was left alone in the big room for a while to wander among his possessions.

Her first impression on seeing his massive collection of books was that she was back in her uncle's old library in the Cotswolds, except that this one looked out on a kind of run-down garden rather than a having a view of the rolling green limestone hills she used to hike as a girl.

It was also strikingly tidy, to the point of obsessive. There was a large antique desk with hardly anything on it other than a closed laptop and some neatly clipped-together papers facing a big window that looked to the south. The room had floor-to-ceiling dark oak shelving on all of the walls, lined with books of all shapes and sizes, all without a speck of dust on any of them. She noted that there were almost no paperbacks at all (she disliked these as well) and that many of the books were old, leather-bound editions or else pristine hardbacks.

The room shrieked of a man with an obsessive need for order and a taste for the finer things.

She seized the chance to browse the shelves and, sure enough, after less than a minute, found several of her own books. She took one off the shelf, a book she had written years ago on the haiku poet Takaboku Ishikawa, and noted, as she flipped through it, that several of the pages had various things underlined with cryptic notes in a very clear and meticulous hand along the tops and bottoms of the page.

Well, well…A student of poetry….

She put the book back, and as she did so, Ran appeared with the coffee on a tray, which he placed on the highly polished coffee table in front of the sofa.

"Oh… I see you've found your little shelf there. Some most illuminating stuff you've done too… I would love to discuss it with you sometime."

Penelope smiled and continued to gaze in wonder at his collection. There seemed to be a little of everything here, and it was all laid out by subject. One side of the room seemed to be non-fiction, with books on law, medicine, languages, music, philosophy, and history all collected together on different shelves, whereas the other side of the room was literature, which seemed to be divided by country. Greek classics in one area, then Roman, Chinese, British, French, Russian… a lot of them in the original languages. The collection showed a deep and wide-ranging learning, and told her much about what kind of passions governed him.

"This is really something… did you put all this together yourself?"

Ran nodded and poured the coffee from a solid silver pot.

"Alas, yes. Cream and sugar?"

"Yes, both please. It must have taken years…" she said as she looked around.

Ran nodded and looked around his collection.

"Yes. All my life. I'm still going, of course. There's even more in the bedrooms…" he said with a sigh.

"I know the problem," said Penelope as she joined him on the sofa. "My place is nothing as grand or neat as yours, but it has books everywhere too. Most of which I cannot find when I want…"

"Yeah, I know that problem. That's why I have that…" he pointed to a large cabinet full of small drawers next to the fireplace.

Penelope stared at it.

"Oh, my God. Is that what I think it is?"

Ran nodded.

"Card index file. Dewey system."

Penelope shook her head.

"I haven't seen one of those…."

"I know… since you were an undergraduate. It works, however. All the cards are cross-indexed too. It saves me a lot of time when I'm researching…."

"You made that yourself too?"

"Yep."

"Wow… you must never watch television."

Ran laughed.

"Yes… I rather miss out there. You're right. I've yet to darken the door of Netflix," he grinned.

She sipped her coffee, which had a rich, nutty flavor she liked.

"Is this… from Indonesia?" she said, nodding towards her cup.

Ran sat back with an impressed look on his face.

"Wow… that's some palate you have. Yes. Borneo. You know your coffee. It's a bit of a fixation of mine, I'm afraid. One of many…"

Penelope nodded.

"I was sure I'd had it before. I was at a conference there once, and one of the other speakers was a coffee nut. Or is it 'coffee nazi'? I've heard some people called that.

Anyway, he insisted we go to some coffee plantation there and try it. This kinda brought back a memory of that… by the way… what are those?"

She gestured to one of the other shelves in front of them, which was the only one in the room with no books on it, but was instead full of beautifully laid out but seemingly disconnected little items.

Ran looked up and over at where she was gazing.

"Oh, that. Nothing. Just a place to keep stuff I don't really have a place for."

Penelope stood up and wandered over to inspect the items on display.

There was a little wooden Buddha statue carved out of a single piece of rough wood, a set of three small green marbles, a black bird's feather, a brush resting on a piece of old washi paper with something written on it, and several other disparate looking bits and pieces, including a little silver frame which looked like it held a leaf from a tree she couldn't identify.

However, it was to the small Buddha statue that she was drawn, and she could not help but pick it up and turn it over lovingly in her hands.

"Enku… 18th century. Have you heard of him?" he said, referencing the famous Buddhist priest who had spent his life wandering Japan and carving thousands of Buddhist statues to pray for the soul of his mother, who had died in a flood when he had been a child.

Penelope nodded.

"Oh yes… I know him. I've just never held one in my hands before. Most of these are in museums or temples now… I knew someone once who really loved Enku pieces…"

Ran came and stood beside her.

"I've had him a long time. It belonged to my father, actually…"

She put the statue back carefully on the shelf.

"Your father? I think Eiji mentioned he was an artist?"

Ran nodded. "'Yes, that's right. Not a very well-known one or anything. Would you like to see?"

"You have some of his work here?"

"Oh yes, but most of it is in storage these days. Lack of space, I'm afraid. He had thousands of drawings and paintings here before he died. I didn't have the heart to throw them out, so I just put them away. I kept a few here, though… "

He led her into the living room, and she immediately saw what he meant.

Above the fireplace was a large portrait of a woman in a long white dress that reminded her of the dresses brides wore at old-fashioned Shinto weddings. She was standing alone in a snowy landscape and looking away to one side. In her hands, she grasped a dark-colored Japanese umbrella, which contrasted strongly with the white of her dress and the winter landscape.

"Wow…" Penelope exclaimed. "That's amazing. It reminds me of something actually… a play?"

Ran put his hands behind his back and stood before the portrait.

"Very good, Penny-*sensei*. Yes. It's a scene from The Heron Maiden, a *kabuki* play…"

Penelope nodded.

"I wondered… it seemed familiar. The woman's face is really striking, though…"

Ran looked up at the painting.

"That's my mother. He painted her many times. He always said she was his muse…"

They were silent momentarily, and Penelope looked into the quiet sadness of the woman's eyes that the artist had so beautifully captured.

"He must have loved her very much…" she said softly.

Ran nodded. "He did. He always said they were soulmates. A couple that finds each other somehow, life after life… Do you believe in that, Penny-*sensei*?"

"Reincarnation? That's a very romantic idea… but no, I can't say I do."

Ran shrugged, "I do. I think it explains a lot of things. Why we feel the way we do about things, people. Why we feel we have connections with them we can't explain…"

He did not look at her to see her response, and when she made none, he escorted her back to the library, and they finished their coffee.

"So… what do you make of the latest killing then? What do your eyes tell you?" he asked, leaning forward and clasping his hands together in a manner that rather reminded Penelope of a doctor quizzing a student during their rounds.

"Make of it… well… I'm not sure. There is something about it, though… something I dislike… I don't think it's an honest killing."

"Honest? An honest murder? What do you mean?"

Penelope looked at him carefully.

"I mean, it was too obviously staged, too carefully prepared. There's no passion about it. No obvious reason. It feels like the person was killed just for the sake of killing someone. Like when you present a play. It doesn't feel like real life."

Ran nodded.

"You mean it's a distraction? A red herring, as you British call it?"

Penelope tilted her head and smiled.

"Maybe…. Whatever it is… the killer is not being honest with us. I mean, I think he wanted to kill that particular person, but the rest of it is all smoke, all about something else. I get the feeling we are being led up the garden path somehow."

She put her cup down on its saucer and turned to him.

"I have a question for you too…"

"And what is that?"

"Do you *really* not see any connection to the original Italian case?"

"*Il Monstro di Firenze?* No. Not really. I think that's all, I don't know, media fluff. The Monster of Florence killed kids making out in lovers' lanes. He killed in pairs, and then he mutilated the women in a sort of grotesque sexual way. That's not what's going on here. Here this is dismemberment, but it's not the same kind of corpse desecration."

"So, no connection…."

Ran looked at her and smiled. "Well… I didn't say that. There is one…"

"What?"

"A clue, left behind at each killing… In Italy the Monster left us his desecrations of the female body. That was the clue from him to the police. A hint. And the cartridge cases, always from the same gun. Another clue. He didn't have to leave those behind. All these killers, they all leave behind their little clues, their little signatures, whether they mean to or not."

"And this guy?"

Ran pointed to a painting on his wall that depicted a hunting scene, probably from the 19th century in Britain. A group of horsemen, all dressed in red coats, were gathering at the start of a traditional British fox hunt.

"Fox fur," he said softly. "Always the fox fur and the feather… I know we are talking about ancient Japanese legends… but I wonder if there is also another meaning. Something we are missing…

Chapter Six.

The Bamboo Garden

"No, I haven't seen him since he left. It must be about, I dunno, about two weeks now, I guess."

Chief Inspector Yamashita took a sip of his coffee and placed the cup and saucer back on the large glass desk of the man they had come to see as Yokota continued making notes in his little pocketbook as they spoke.

"So, tell me, how long has your company been responsible for the security at the Tsurugaoka Hachimangu shrine?" asked Yamashita.

The president of ProSec, one of Japan's biggest private home security companies, relaxed into his oversized leather chair and looked out the window at the skyscraper next door. The office was located in the central business district near Shinjuku station in a huge building situated among dozens of other huge buildings not far from the west exit of the world's busiest station, and the company used most of the twenty or so floors for themselves.

The head of the company was a short, balding man in his early sixties by the name of Shunsuke Ishihara. He had cleared his schedule to see the two detectives that afternoon, and it was clear that he was more than a little concerned at the effect this scandal was going to have on his business.

"According to our records, we've done their security for over a decade. As you probably know, we look after many important cultural assets all over the country. Even the Imperial Palace. I don't know who got us the job with Kamakura and this shrine, but Murakami-san was responsible for that account. An excellent engineer, and he was with us for over twenty years. I recruited him myself, years ago, when my father ran the company, and I was looking after the Human Resources department. His family were our old friends; I think our grandfathers served in the war together… something like that anyway."

He tapped out his cigarette in the large crystal ashtray on his desk and directed his two guests over to the sofas in the middle of the office where they could talk more comfortably.

"But now this Murakami-san has left the company? Was that a sudden departure? Was he fired?" asked Yamashita.

The president shook his head and looked at the floor.

"Well, no… not at all. It's a bit embarrassing really, seeing he was a senior person with us… but he just… well, disappeared. It was a few weeks ago now. We've been trying to contact him for a while… but no luck. We've even sent people to his house and spoken to his family and the neighbors. After he disappeared, I got a full report from his manager about it, but no one has seen him lately. Even his relatives. I guess they've been over to his house too…I don't know the details, though."

Yamashita and Yokota exchanged glances.

"OK, well…" began the chief inspector. "Anyway, I take it you know why we're here… the murder at the shrine… where it seems all your cameras were turned off for some reason. Do you think your engineer, Murakami-san… had anything to do with that?"

Ishihara threw his hands in the air.

"I honestly couldn't tell you. Look, we've thoroughly investigated this, as per your request. He disappeared shortly before the murder at the shrine took place. Two days before, to be exact. But there are a number of people who could have turned off the cameras from here…. remotely, as you mentioned before. All you need is the right security clearance. And the thing is, many of our staff have this clearance, for reasons of access and convenience. You know, in case the alarms go off accidentally in people's properties and we have to turn them off. It all runs off a centralized server. The same systems control the cameras too."

"And is there some way of knowing precisely *who* turned them off?"

The president shook his head.

"No. We don't log that information. It could have been Murakami… it could have been someone else. We know *when* they were turned off, but not by whom exactly. It could have just been an error."

Yamashita leaned forward and rested his chin on his tented fingers.

"An error? I doubt that very much somehow," he said, arching an eyebrow. "So… did you know much about Murakami-san?"

Ishihara looked at the floor again a little nervously.

"Well… we didn't socialize if that's what you mean. However, I was told he had some rather strident… political opinions. Very right-wing. He once refused to work with one of our other engineers because the man was from Taiwan…."

Yokota tapped his pen on his notebook.

"Is that so… Did he have a family?"

"He was divorced, I think. Lived alone. He has a daughter… I think she lives in Osaka. Anyway, he kept to himself pretty much, apparently. His parents were from Hokkaido, I believe. That's where he grew up. They used to be pretty wealthy, but they lost their business in the war. At least, I think that's what my father told me once."

Yamashita tilted his head.

"What kind of business was that, do you know?"

The president looked at the ceiling as if trying to remember.

"They were fur traders. I think one of the ancestors was Russian and settled here. He started a fur trading business in the early 1900s. Very successful."

Yamashita and his detective sergeant exchanged another meaningful glance.

"Furs…" said Yokota. "That wouldn't happen to be fox furs, would it?"

=====================

The Human Resources department of ProSec having furnished them with the missing Murakami's address, the two policemen were soon standing outside an old house in the northern Adachi ward of Tokyo a few hours later, not far from the banks of the Arakawa River, one of the largest rivers in the region which formed the traditional border between the Tokyo Metropolis and the neighboring prefecture of Saitama. The name in front of them on the high wall of the house was inscribed on a weather-worn wooden shingle, but the family name 'MURAKAMI' could still be clearly distinguished.

On the way over to the house, Yamashita received a call from his friend Professor Morita, a historian at his old alma mater at Tokyo University, and he switched the call to video so he could see the caller's face as they talked.

"Thanks for your call, Hideo. Did you manage to find out anything?

Professor Morita's bearded face appeared on the screen, and Yamashita saw he was holding up a piece of paper.

"Yes, I did. By chance, one of my graduate students was researching the economy of the Taisho period last year and wrote something about the fur trade in Japan. I have the paper here actually..." he said, waving the document before him.

"So this story about the Murakami family being fur traders is true?"

Morita nodded.

"Yes. The great-grandfather was a Russian fur trader and trapper from an area near Vladivostok. He married a widow with a family from Hokkaido in the early years of the century, and they decided to set up a store in

Yokohama. He took her name of Murakami when they married, as there were no sons in the family, and then ended up inheriting her family's trading business as well. Her son by her first husband then took over in the 1930s. The fur industry was big business back then, and they got into making clothing and hats and that sort of thing. The son ran the business until the war, after which it went bankrupt, like many others. No demand for luxury fur in those days, and their supply line had been completely severed by the Russian government. So that was that. I don't have any more information as to what happened to the family after that. But the story you told me is true…

Yamashita nodded and smiled.

"You wouldn't be able to tell me what kind of furs they traded, would you?"

There was a pause on the line while the professor shuffled through his papers.

"Mink… that was big. Sable and martin, you can find those plentifully in the northern regions, including Hokkaido. Black bear, mainly used for hats and rugs and things….

"Fox?" asked Yamashita in a hopeful voice.

"Fox? Hmmm… yes. Fox fur was pretty plentiful. Yes. They traded in fox furs. Mainly used for women's stoles."

Yamashita shot a glance at Yokota, who nodded as he drove.

"Thank you, Hideo. You've made our day," he said cheerfully, and the professor smiled and waved as they hung up.

"Well… there you go, Yokota. Our first link to the fox fur," said Yamashita.

Yokota agreed. "Well, it's probably nothing, I suppose. But where there's smoke… you never know…"

Yamashita nodded. "I agree, it's not much to get excited about, but the way things are going, any clue is a good clue. Let's just see where it goes when we track down the elusive Murakami-san."

Standing in front of the house now, Yokota knocked hard on the gate and rang the buzzer repeatedly, only to hear it echoing inside the house each time it was pressed.

"Well… shall I?" asked Yokota after a few fruitless minutes had passed, gesturing towards the old wooden door set into the wall that led into the garden.

They had no warrant, and so no legal way to enter the premises without the owner's permission.

"Did you get through to the daughter?" asked the chief inspector.

Yokota nodded.

"Yeah. She just left me a message, saying it was fine by her if we went in and had a look. She didn't seem overly concerned about her old man to tell the truth…"

Yamashita nodded.

"I kind of get that, from what his boss said about him. He sounded rather unpleasant. Well, go ahead then… it's about as close to permission as we are going to get… Let's call it 'suspicion of a crime' or something if we get called out for this."

Yokota nodded and turned the latch on the gate, which opened with a sharp screech of rusty metal.

"Well, not locked anyway," he smiled.

"They never are around here," said his boss.

The two men proceeded into the small garden at the front of the old house, and walked up to the front door. After knocking and announcing themselves in loud voices, Yokota pushed hard on the door.

"Locked," he said, looking at his boss for permission.

Yamashita simply nodded at Yokota to proceed, and a few seconds later, his burly DS had managed to kick in the rather flimsy wooden door to reveal the empty entranceway to the house, where a single pair of black business shoes were placed neatly as if waiting for their owner to step into them.

Yokota shouted "POLICE" loudly, but the word simply echoed as before, and no sound greeted them in return.

They walked inside, and began to go from room to room, until they had covered both floors.

"Not a soul, sir," said Yokota as they regrouped in the kitchen.

"OK. Let's check outside," said Yamashita.

They opened the heavy storm shutters outside the living room, which led into the rear garden of the house, and stopped dead in their tracks.

Someone, presumably the absent Murakami-san, had erected a sizeable beige-colored tent in the middle of the small garden.

The tent was big enough for a man to stand up in, would probably have slept four adults, and had the word NORDEN, one of Japan's most popular camping gear makers, emblazoned on the side.

"Well, well…," said Yamashita. "It seems our Murakami-san was an outdoors enthusiast. Let's have a look."

Yamashita watched as his DS advanced on the tent, opened the flap, paused, and then reeled backwards away from the tent with a loud curse.

He stared back at his boss and pointed at the tent, and Yamashita saw his eyes were open wide with horror.

"What the hell…" he breathed.

Yamashita stepped forward and yanked back the tent's flap for himself, and then stood there for a moment, unable to really understand what he was looking at.

Inside the tent, strapped to an old iron cot, was the naked and emaciated body of a man. Attached to his right arm was an intravenous drip, the tube leading up to an empty plastic bag hanging limply from a metal post in the corner.

But the real horror was not this, but the manner in which this man had been killed, a method so bizarre that the people who witnessed it that day would remember it clearly for the rest of their lives.

At first glance, the man's body seemed to have a garden growing from it, a small forest of bamboo that reached almost to the top of the big tent. It was hard to see what had happened at first glance, but it was soon understood that the killer had planted bamboo underneath the strapped-down body, a well-known species that could grow explosively up to twenty centimeters a day. The ends of the bamboo spears had then been cut to razor-sharp points, and as they grew, the tips had pierced the man's flesh and then forced their way through his immobilized

86

body, finally exiting the other side and continuing their path towards the sky.

Later research revealed a story, long thought apocryphal, that this form of 'bamboo torture' had been used on prisoners during the Pacific War by the now defunct Japanese Imperial army, but it was something that had never been proven.

"Ambulance... now..." Yamashita whispered to the stunned Yokota as he stepped carefully into the tent and knelt at the victim's side.

Even for a veteran detective like the chief inspector, who had seen more than his fair share of homicides, the discovery of a body in this kind of shocking and emaciated condition was something that he had never witnessed before.

However, they soon discovered that there was one more surprise in store for them.

As Yokota crouched behind his boss and dialed the number for the paramedics, Yamashita, shaking his head in pity, reached forward and gently put his finger to the victim's throat to check for a pulse, an action which was standard procedure in the event of the discovery of a body.

To their absolute amazement, the victim's eyes flew open, and a single rasping breath heaved its way up from the bloody, perforated lungs.

"Holy shit..." breathed Yokota as he watched his normally unflappable boss almost fall over backwards. "He's alive!"

And Murakami-san was, indeed, still alive, despite injuries that would have killed a normal person long, long before. What he had suffered, though, in clinging to this life, no one could begin to speculate, let alone the doctors that had attended him afterward.

The killer had obviously intended for his victim to live through the most excruciating pain possible though, as was evidenced by the drip, which must have helped to keep him alive. Several discarded saline bags were later discovered lying on the floor under the cot, indicating that the torture had proceeded for some days.

The ambulance arrived a few minutes after the call had been made, but it had taken over an hour to cut away the bamboo from above and below the body in order to lay the incredibly fragile victim on a gurney.

He had then, to no one's surprise, died before he made it to the hospital.

Chapter 7

Vivien

Several days after the discovery of the missing engineer, and with their inquiries no further advanced, Yamashita decided to update his closest advisors as to the latest developments in the case away from the prying eyes of his superiors and the pressure of his position as chief inspector at the Kamakura police headquarters. He reasoned that if they could gain some fresh perspective on this case, one that was becoming more complex and nuanced by the day, then it would be worth their opprobrium if they ever found out.

The Japanese police was a very closed and ultra-conservative world, extremely hierarchical and where information was held tightly and rarely discussed with outsiders. Retribution against those who exercised any form of unauthorized initiative outside of the group was usually swift and quite often final, and the chief inspector well knew that he was not trusted by many of those in the upper levels of the force as a result of his unorthodox methods, but merely tolerated because he inevitably got results with them. However, he had no qualms when it came to seeking a solution to his case, no matter whom he spoke to. Particularly in respect of people like Penelope and the others gathered at his house tonight, he was well aware of how valuable they had all proved in other cases in the past and that he would have never been able to solve half of them without their help. This respect especially applied to Penelope, whom the chief inspector regarded as one of the sharpest minds he had ever met. Whenever he was stymied, he inevitably found himself sitting in her kitchen while she listened patiently to him and offered him her perspectives.

His guest list was basically the same people whom he had previously gathered at the shrine: Ran, the great expert on *Il Monstro* along with Sal Nakajima, Penelope, and this time also their friend Fei Chen, the official police coroner who had performed the autopsy on the latest victim, the unfortunate Murakami.

Both Penelope and Fei were surprised by the rare invitation to the chief inspector's house, which was a lovely old western-style villa set next to the famous Meigetsu-in temple and just a stone's throw from Engaku-ji where his older brother Dokan resided. Although these folk had been there several times before over the years, they were all a little aware of the intrusion they were making into the extremely private life of the inveterate bachelor, who, apart from his work, rarely left his home, which he regarded as an almost sacred place where he could be alone. Even Penelope, who thought of him as one of her closest friends, had always sensed a remoteness about him, like a carefully constructed wall, and she had long ago realized that she was never going to get to know him better than she already did.

With him, she knew, this was as far as the path went.

Penelope and Fei were even more surprised (but not disappointed) when they found Ran Maeda wearing an apron in the kitchen and preparing their meal again. Standing next to him at the sink was an unlikely sous-chef in the form of Sal, who was retrieving a tray of roasted vegetables from the oven.

"Wow, Eiji… I see you've brought in the catering staff tonight," said Penelope as the two women passed their coats to him.

The chief inspector, dressed casually tonight in blue jeans and a black turtleneck sweater which made him look vaguely like a professor of philosophy that Fei had once had a crush on, turned and ushered them into the living room.

Ran came forward in his apron and gave them a low bow.

"This man…" he said, waving a kitchen spatula at their host, "has no tools. I had to bring my own knives. And saucepans. This is possibly the worst equipped kitchen I have ever seen. I don't know how he can even fry an egg successfully…." he smiled.

Yamashita laughed. "I can't. That's why I asked you here."

Ran nodded ruefully and headed back to the kitchen, from whence Sal emerged to greet his friends, rolling his ever-present cigarette as he did.

"I've been learning at the feet of the master," he said, gesturing over his shoulder at the kitchen. I had no idea potatoes required such technique."

"That's quite apparent," came a voice from the kitchen.

Sal shrugged, Yamashita made them all drinks, and the women and Sal had a seat on his large sofa.

"It's nice of you all to come," said Yamashita as the doorbell rang in the hallway. "There's one more to join us... ah, there he is."

Yamashita went to the front door and returned with Detective Sergeant Yokota, also dressed in jeans and an open-necked shirt, which showed off his impressively muscled arms, honed from decades of *kendo*, in which he had a fifth *dan* license and where he was known as one of the most highly skilled men in the national police association team, which had won several national championships.

Yokota sat politely in the big leather armchair that he had been directed to by his boss, who gave him a glass of beer.

"Is this the first time you have been invited to the Holy of Holies, Sergeant Yokota?" asked Fei with a mischievous look.

"Er... yes," the big man nodded nervously.

"Well then... you must really be in the good books," said Penelope.

"Hmmm... that remains to be seen," said Yamashita, only half-jokingly.

The friends chatted amiably about a few different topics, and made Yokota show them photographs of his wife and young daughter, whom they had never met before.

When Ran finally joined them with the announcement that dinner would be ready in about thirty minutes, Yamashita broached the reason they were all here.

"So Fei, I read your autopsy report on the latest victim. Very detailed as usual… maybe you could bring everyone up to speed?

Fei took a sip of her white wine and, putting the glass on the coffee table, meditatively cast her eyes down at the floor.

"Well… as you probably suspected, neither I nor anybody I know has ever seen anything like it. Like *ever*…" she said, looking up at them sadly. "The victim had only been in that tent for about four days or so, but bamboo grows at a shockingly fast rate, and once the sharpened tips had penetrated the flesh, it literally ripped him apart internally. Massive organ damage, blood loss, trauma… you name it. I think if you had arrived an hour later, he would have been dead anyway."

"Jesus…" said Sal, who had already heard some of the story's details from one of his informants in the police.

The two detectives both shook their heads, and Yokota looked up at the ceiling.

"There were rumors, and that is always what they were, just rumors," Fei continued, "that the 'bamboo torture' had been used on allied prisoners during the war. But I, for one, had never heard of it. Nobody had ever seen it before, so it was a first. I checked it out on the databases… there is no record of such a method of killing anywhere in this country or any other. It's unique."

"At least, not in modern history…" Ran commented from his perch on the side of the dining table.

Fei looked over at him and nodded.

"That's true. There could be some historical records, I guess, that we don't know about."

Ran agreed. "Yeah, the Chinese had some pretty gruesome methods... as you probably know," he said, perhaps obliquely referring to Fei's Chinese heritage.

Fei smiled, and Penelope, who knew her well, wondered if Fei felt the same about Ran as she did.

"Well, I've never dispatched any of my previous boyfriends like that... although it is a thought..." she smiled wickedly and pulled out her antique pipe from her bag as Ran laughed.

"I should hope not... so, what else aren't you telling us?" he asked Yamashita.

Yokota leaned forward, and Yamashita gestured for him to speak.

"This time, he left us some souvenirs, it seems... inside the body."

Penelope raised her eyebrows, and Sal shot her a glance.

"What kind of ... souvenirs?" asked Sal.

"He had a roll of one-thousand-yen notes shoved in his mouth. And wrapped up in that was a small black crow's feather and several animal hairs."

"Fox, of course?" asked Ran, and Fei nodded.

"Yep, no surprise there," said Yamashita, sitting back and folding his arms. "We knew it was him already, naturally, but he just can't seem to help himself. You know, confirming it was one of his kills."

"So, it's *Il Monstro* again, that's certain," said Sal with a whistle. "This is going to sell a lot of books one day..."

"One day... not now though, please," said Yamashita with a terse look at the journalist.

Sal held up his hands in mock innocence. "Don't worry… I'm just making notes for the future. After you've nailed the bastard."

"That may be a way off, I'm afraid," said Yokota ruefully.

"Surely though…" said Penelope looking at him. "Each time he kills, we know a little more about him, don't we? He can't help that. Each kill reveals something more… we just have to figure out what that is. The fact that the method with which he dispatched his latest victim is so rare is actually revealing in a way. It may help us catch him."

Ran nodded. "That's right. But what he seems to be telling us is rather contradictory. All of these killings are staged somewhat theatrically - this we know. But each time, he seems to be referencing some different kind of, I dunno… theme."

"History seems to be the recurrent theme," said Yamashita.

Penelope agreed. "Yes, I was just about to say that. Many of his killings seem to be some kind of historical re-enactment. The shrine killing, of course. Betrayal was the theme. And this one, referencing the war perhaps, and again, betrayal. He sold his company's secrets, maybe for money. Hence the roll of money in the mouth…. You know…," she leaned forward and clasped her hands on her knees. "I would not be surprised to find out, once we eventually catch this creature, that *he* has experienced some sort of betrayal. Perhaps by a wife, lover, or somebody close to him… maybe he was even betrayed by his family. I think all of these killings are one big act of revenge projected onto others. There definitely seems to be an element of… I dunno… moral outrage. Anger at others…"

She leaned back, and there was silence for a moment.

"I'd agree with you; that makes a lot of sense, psychologically speaking," said Ran. "That's a pretty good profile if you ask me, Mr. Policeman. I'd definitely be looking along those lines," he smiled at Yamashita and stood up to return to his duties in the kitchen.

Yamashita and Yokota exchanged glances, and Yokota made a note in his pocketbook.

When it eventually emerged, the meal was one of the best any of them had eaten in years and certainly the best that had ever come out of Yamashita's significantly ill-equipped kitchen. There was a tender roast chicken done in herbs with a rich red wine sauce, a simple plate of roasted vegetables, and a dessert of *mouse au chocolat*, which had a delicious scent of mint. Both courses were served with different wines, and only Fei dared to ask how much they cost.

Ran, of course, told her that if he revealed that, it would spoil the taste.

"It doesn't matter what things cost. It matters if they work. That's cooking. My father taught me that."

"Wasn't your father a Duke or something?" asked Sal with a grin.

Ran made a face at him.

"That was my great-grandfather. And Japan has never done 'dukes,' by the way."

"Yes," said Penelope. "Duke is a weird translation of *daimyo*… feudal lord. I've always thought that. The

Japanese aristocracy was completely different from the Western kind."

Ran smiled and ran a hand through his long hair.

"Thank you, Professor Penelope. You understand me," he said with a smile.

"She's maybe the only one, then," said Yamashita, with a raised eyebrow at his old school friend.

Ran walked around the table collecting their plates.

"You know…," he observed. "Regarding *Il Monstro…* and this is just a thought. Hospitals and medical suppliers keep records of drugs. Very precise ones. And this guy must have used drugs on some of his victims, right?"

Yokota looked at Fei, who put down her napkin as she handed her plate to Ran.

"That was wonderful," she said. "Oh, and that's true about the drugs. He seems to have quite a sophisticated pharmaceutical knowledge. Perhaps a bit *too* sophisticated for a non-professional. I think you guys may already be thinking along the lines that this guy may be a doctor? Or at least a nurse?"

Ran leaned against the table with a tea towel tossed elegantly over one shoulder and his arm, perhaps deliberately brushed against Penelope. "You know… I think there was that case in Germany some years ago, where a nurse killed dozens of people. According to what I read, he knew far more about the drugs in the hospital than all the doctors put together. One of the reasons he got away with it for so many years…." He looked down at Penelope's face, smiled, and returned to the kitchen.

Yamashita confirmed that this was indeed the direction of the current profile he had received from

Tokyo and that a team of people was looking into the drugs that had been identified in the victims.

"We did find one common drug… in both the shrine victim and the latest one," Fei continued.

"What was it?" asked Sal.

Fei looked at Yamashita as if asking for permission to put forward this information, and the chief inspector immediately nodded his head.

"It was a form of tranexamic acid… used to prevent bleeding. Presumably to stop the victims from bleeding out before he had finished with them."

"That would make sense," said Ran, wandering back into the room with some dessert wine. "And it would also indicate he held them somewhere else before transporting them to the kill site. Somewhere where he could take his time with them, presumably. Especially the last one… I think he particularly disliked him."

"I'd agree, that did seem more personal," said Penelope.

"Wasn't Murakami killed at his home, though? In the tent?" asked Sal.

"Well… yes. That's where the final killing took place. But he seems to have been drugged up before that, maybe while the killer was preparing the other site. Everything seems to have focused on the display set up in the tent. So, we strongly suspect he was abducted, kept somewhere, and taken back there, maybe while the bamboo and the tent and other things were being prepared. Of course, as you know, the shrine victim was also drugged and held somewhere else before being transported to the shrine. He might even have been frozen…."

"So…" said Penelope. "Like Ran said, what all this means is that this guy's got a kill room."

Yamashita nodded. "Exactly. Some place, probably very well prepared, with surgical equipment and that sort of stuff. A quiet place where he can work undisturbed…"

"A real psycho then…" said Sal.

"Yep, I'm afraid so," said Penelope. "But maybe someone who doesn't come across like that. What we know is we're looking for someone in his fifties or sixties, someone with medical training, someone with a love of the theatrical, someone who loves Japanese history, and perhaps someone damaged. Someone with a grievance and a hatred of people."

Yamashita nodded. "That's pretty much exactly what the profile says. And following that line of thought, we will probably find that this guy, who is clearly a narcissistic sociopath, started his behavior at a young age. Killing animals, perhaps, and then working his way up the food chain. This guy has form, I suspect, in these areas of sadism. Most psychopaths develop; they're not born like that. They develop into their mature form as a result of deep experiences they had when they were young, and often where they had an unhealthy fixation with dead things. That's the classic profile anyway."

Ran nodded. "That is indeed the standard approach, I'd have to agree. Death, and in this case, revenge. To which we would have to add a level of detached refinement. This guy thinks of himself as an artist. That's why he puts so much effort into how he stages the kill. It's not just to send a message about the theme, whether it's betrayal or whatever. It's a piece of art for him. A new masterwork each time, for his audience to gawk at and admire," he said.

"Yes. Ran's right. You've got to respect this killer's mind and his personal discipline," said Yamashita. "This guy is *meticulous*. A planner... down to the very last detail. *Nothing* is left to chance. Nothing. The kill itself is the simple bit. It's the show, that's where all the details are. And he executes flawlessly. That's why he's going to be so difficult to catch. Your usual criminal makes mistakes, and as Penelope said, they reveal themselves with each succeeding crime. Not this guy, though."

"Yes, and *Il Monstro*, as he no doubt enjoys being called," said Penelope finishing his idea, "He's still telling us his story, and there are things in there that tell us a tiny bit more about him each time. But most of it, unfortunately, is the story he *wants* us to know. The one that leads away from him..."

Yamashita nodded and finished his wine.

"Into the darkness..." he said, staring at the empty glass. "Who wants more of Maeda-san's ridiculously expensive vintage?"

=====================

The next afternoon, Ran, who had been up quite late after the dinner party, made his usual scheduled visit to the Oyama Mental Hospital in the wealthy seaside resort of Zushi, about a half hour's drive from his old house in

Kamakura. This was the only job he did these days which required using one of his medical licenses, and he did it *pro bono* as he had always done in this case.

The hospital director, Dr. Yamaguchi, a kindly-looking man in his early eighties, looked up from the papers strewn across his messy desk at the sound of the knock on his door and smiled.

"Ah, Doctor Maeda. Welcome…. it must be Thursday," he smiled as he stood up and gave the younger man a short bow. "Please have a seat."

Maeda waved away the offer though, and remained in the doorway of his large office.

"I'm sorry, Dr. Yamaguchi. I'm really in a bit of a rush today. I think I'll just press on if you don't mind. Any news?"

Ran knew from long experience that accepting the director's offer of a seat would mean listening to a long expository on his family, his golf game, and the hospital patients generally, which usually took over an hour to complete.

The old doctor sighed and resumed his seat.

"Well… no, nothing to report, I think. She's the same as ever. I'm sure she's looking forward to your visit, however. Unlike me, she has a much better memory for the day of the week," he said with a self-deprecating smile.

"Oh, I dunno about that. You're still pretty sharp from where I'm standing, *sensei*," said Ran with a smile.

The older man chuckled.

"If only that were true. I guess you're up to your eyebrows in another book? I have no idea where you find the time to publish so much. I can't even remember the last time I wrote an article for the *Japan Psychiatric Journal*, let alone a book… are you still consulting with the police as well? What's that inspector's name?"

"Yamashita?"

"That's the fellow. Nice chap. You went to school together, didn't you?"

Ran smiled.

"There is nothing wrong with your memory after all, Yamaguchi *sensei*. I think you just fake forgetfulness so people don't bother you."

Yamaguchi laughed. "It's true, you've found me out. Don't tell my wife or daughter, though, or I'll be forced to sue you…"

Ran smiled. "Don't worry, *sensei*. Your secret's safe with me. Now, if you don't mind, I'll go and see her."

Yamaguchi gave him a short bow of farewell.

"Of course. Off you go. You know the way…" he said, returning to his papers.

Maeda wandered down a long corridor from the director's office, where the patient's rooms on one side looked out on the extensive gardens with their huge old zelkova and cherry trees and many flowering plants and shrubs. The place may have been a mental hospital, but it felt and looked more like a high-class resort, and the patients who stayed here generally came from very well-off families who footed, usually without complaint, the very large bills the hospital sent them every month.

He stopped at one of the rooms about halfway down the hall, knocked and opened the door, and, finding it empty, proceeded further along the corridor to the large and well-equipped lounge the patients often spent their day in, which had a very pleasant courtyard outside where he knew his patient particularly liked to sit. And indeed, there she was.

He pulled up an oversized wicker chair and sat down next to her.

She was a tall, elegant-looking woman with waist-length, completely white hair. She was only in her late fifties, and Ran knew her hair had turned from lustrous black to absolute white almost overnight due to a trauma she had experienced years previously. She had large, beautiful black eyes, which contrasted with the white of her hair, making her look like a mysterious visitor from some kind of spirit world of myth and fable.

She had been a resident of the hospital for over ten years now, and the staff regarded her as one of their family and treated her accordingly. Ran was her court-appointed psychiatrist and reported to her family as to her mental condition on a bi-annual basis, not that they had ever come near her after her diagnosis and later admission here with a progressive form of dementia and the memory loss that inevitably accompanied it.

Her name was Vivien, a Western name she now chose to go by, and she had originally been admitted with severe delusional bipolar disorder when she was forty-eight years old, which had led to increasingly disturbed behavior until she had been deemed a danger to herself and possibly others. Her wealthy family still picked up the tab for her, and were relieved to have nothing more to do with her.

She looked up and gave him a heartfelt smile as he sat beside her. There was no question that this bi-weekly visit from her psychiatrist was something she both looked forward to and found immensely pleasurable.

"Ah, doctor. You're a little late today…" she said, tenderly laying her soft white hand on his.

Ran looked into her lovely eyes, and did not move his hand away, allowing her to stroke the ruby ring on his finger.

She was fashionably dressed today in a long light-brown knitted dress, set off with an elegant gold chain around her neck.

"Hello, Vivien. How are we feeling today?"

Vivien withdrew her hand and leaned back comfortably into her chair, her lithe body resembling a cat making itself at home on a cushion.

"We? *We* are fine. That's the nice thing about being schizophrenic, don't you think? You always have company."

Ran laughed and pointed to the book that was open on her lap.

"So, what are *we* reading today?" he asked.

Vivien passed him the book, a hardback with a red cover. He knew she was a great reader, and often brought her books from his extensive library.

"Caesar. *De Bello Gallico*," she said as he examined it.

"Looks interesting," said Ran, passing it back to her. "I think I read this when I was in school. The Gallic Wars? It's a bit of a standard work for Latin classes…"

Vivien smiled.

"You're so well educated, Dr. Maeda. I forget sometimes… Yes. It's very interesting. You know, the professor who wrote the introduction says that Caesar was not a nice man at all. In fact… he was a sociopath! So, I guess we have something in common, don't we?"

Her eyes glittered as she spoke, and Ran wondered if she was feverish.

"He thought nothing of killing thousands, even less of enslaving a whole nation... Which he did, according to the Fourth Commentary, to one of the German tribes that had the temerity to invade Gaul when he was out of the country."

Ran nodded. "I remember."

She cocked her head at him, folded her beautiful long fingers under her chin, and looked at him, amused from under a long lock of white hair.

"Yes. Dr. Maeda remembers *everything*..." she said, somewhat drolly. "He even remembers to visit little old me. So sweet of him..." she smiled warmly again.

"Vivien... how could I not come and see you? It's the high point of my week. You know that."

"You're given to flattery doctor. You have a... *penchant* for it. That's a lovely old French word, isn't it? ... But, I'll take it. I don't get that much flattery in here..."

She leaned forward to him conspiratorially.

"You know, doctor... I think I would have quite enjoyed being locked up with Caesar. He *definitely* belonged in someplace like this too. Don't you think?" she smiled coquettishly at him.

Ran nodded. "I think a case could have been made, that's true."

Vivien stared out over the garden, and there was a silence between them for a few moments. A silence like two old friends have, and not like the one you shared with your carer.

After a while, she looked at him again.

"I can't remember my old life much. You know, before I came here. But I think I was happy. I don't remember why... but I just get the feeling... I had a happy life. Now, I have a peaceful life. But then... I had a happy one. What do you think, doctor?"

Maeda looked at her a long time, and then nodded.

=====================

Later, on the drive home in his large black antique Jaguar, he searched through his music files for an old recording of the cellist Vladimir Rostropovich playing the *sarabande* from Bach's first cello suite. The system having located it, he gave a voice command for it to begin to play as he waited at some traffic lights.

The music he had chosen was known as one expressing the most refined of emotions, and each time he heard it, Ran was always reminded of a story he had once read of the compassion extended by the great cellist to the famous sumo *yokozuna* Chiyanofuji.

The story went that on hearing of the death of the great wrestler's young daughter one evening, Rostropovich had been so moved by the tragedy that he had immediately cancelled his plans and taken the first flight to Tokyo. Upon landing, he had taken a taxi straight to the great wrestler's home, outside of which he had set up his beautiful old Stradivarius cello to play, just once, the Bach *sarabande*.

And then he returned to the airport, and left.

His compassion at that moment joined in Ran's mind as the music rose around him like a great sea of aching sadness, and he found it hard to breathe.

He soon arrived home, where he sat in the car for a while, allowing the music to cascade through him until it drew to its final, doleful conclusion.

A single tear rolled down his cheek, and he let it fall, his face frozen and immobile in the gathering twilight outside and the feel of the long-ago softness of someone's white hand on his.

Chapter 8

The Journaler

For over twenty years, each Thursday morning without fail, Penelope visited the ancient Zen Buddhist temple of Engakuji in Kamakura for a one-hour meditation class that was held, unusually, in English.

As a result of being held in a foreign language, which was a rarity, and the fact that the temple was one of the oldest Zen temples in Japan, the morning *zazen* session attracted people interested in Zen Buddhism from around the world, and most mornings Penelope found herself in the company of at least a few foreign visitors, usually tourists, and often had the chance to speak in her native language, which was a rare event for her these days.

Today's class followed the usual format: an explanation of how to meditate, the meditation or *zazen* session itself, and a short *dhamma* talk by one of Engakuji's resident monks who happened to be from Scotland, where his strong Glaswegian accent gave the whole occasion a decidedly non-oriental flavor.

After the class wound up, Penelope chatted with the other attendees, in this case, a couple of elderly Zen Buddhists from France, and then, as was her habit, wandered over to Dokan's office for a cup of tea with Chief Inspector Yamashita's older brother.

As usual this morning, she found the Head Monk in his tiny but immaculate little tatami mat office, sitting at his low table with his laptop engaged in one of his myriad administrative tasks for the running of the huge temple and its massive grounds.

She knocked quietly on the little sliding door, and Dokan himself opened it for her with a broad smile and ushered her inside for their weekly catch-up on the outside world, which often turned into a discussion about whatever case she was helping his brother with. Dokan himself would occasionally offer his advice on these things to Penelope, and she had always found him to be a man possessed of a broad and penetrating understanding of the human condition that far surpassed her own.

"So, you are no further along? I read about the murder at Hachimangu... awful. Now you're telling me someone else involved with that has died? The person who worked for the shrine's security company?"

Penelope told him the story, and the monk looked sadly at the floor and shook his head.

"You think he was killed to silence him? That this man knew the shrine killer?"

Penelope nodded. "Yeah, I think that much is obvious. But there also seemed to be an element of... I don't know, pleasure? I mean, I think he enjoyed killing him. It looked to us to be more than just killing him to silence him. Why go to all the trouble doing it in the rather elaborately sadistic way he chose? Why take the time? If you wanted to silence him, you could have just knocked him on the head and been done with it...."

Dokan looked at her carefully. He was a tall, thin man in his early sixties with deep-set dark eyes, the usual shaven head of an ordained Buddhist cleric, and dressed today in the traditional dark blue *jinbei* tunic and pants that monks wore when they were involved in manual work.

"Yes, I agree," he nodded. "All this scene-setting would indicate far more deep-seated motives. It would appear that with each crime, he is sending a message. But his timetable seems to be accelerating. I would expect him to kill again and soon. He's gathering speed as he goes along, like a stone rolling downhill. And two cases in Kamakura? There's something about this city that seems to draw him now. I have a bad feeling about it…"

"Why do you think he's suddenly chosen Kamakura of all places?" asked Penelope, who, like Dokan, had spent almost her entire adult life in the old capital, with its eclectic mix of ancient temples and popular seaside venues that had given it the name of 'little Kyoto.'

Dokan shrugged. "That I can't tell you. But I think you're right about the history thing. He seems to be interested in parodying key elements of the Japanese story. Yes, I think this man is very concerned with history. The shrine, the ancient murder of the *shogun* there… and the bamboo torture, reminiscent of the war… I think Kamakura has plenty of things for such a mind to work with. This place is all about history, let's face it. Otherwise, no one would come here," he smiled, and poured her some more tea from an old black teapot with a shiny glaze that he always kept on his desk.

"You could say that about a lot of places in this country," Penelope sighed.

Dokan smiled his gentle smile again, like he was listening to one of his young novices attempting to explain some arcane Buddhist concept they didn't really understand.

"Where else has he committed his crimes?" he asked.

She thought for a moment.

"Well, as you know, the Kiso region, the one I was involved in so long ago. Kyoto, Nara, Tokyo. Now Kamakura," she counted the places off on her fingers.

"All ancient or current Japanese capitals. The odd one out seems to be the Kiso Valley killing. But it is a place of long history, as we know…. That one is interesting, though." Dokan said as he took a sip of tea.

Penelope stared at him. Somehow this monk could always put his finger on something she had missed.

"Japanese capitals…. I never thought of it that way. I don't think any of us has…. I will mention it to your brother the next time I see him… which will be soon, I reckon. Why don't you come, and we all have dinner?"

Dokan smiled. "I would love to, but…" he waved his arms in the air to indicate his surroundings. "This place never gives me any rest. Let me know the date, though, I'll do my best to join you. As you know, my brother just loves receiving advice from an old monk…" he smiled mischievously.

Penelope laughed.

"Oh, and by the way, I met an old friend of yours. Do you remember Ran Maeda? He's helping us with the case."

The monk sat up straight and looked out the window at the temple gardens behind him. Penelope, who had known him for many years, thought he suddenly looked a little uncomfortable.

"You don't like him?" she asked, curious.

The monk was silent for a moment, as if choosing his words.

"Hmmm... Maeda-san. That's a name I haven't heard in many years," he said absently. "He was more a friend of my brother's than mine. They were thick as thieves in high school and later at Tokyo University... I remember him, though."

Penelope nodded. "He showed me a photograph. When you were all in some string quartet? I didn't even know you played an instrument. The viola, right?"

Dokan smiled distantly and nodded.

"Yes, that's right. I had almost forgotten that. Yes. I did play the viola. A long time ago."

"You gave it up?"

Dokan nodded. "Yes. I gave it up when I became a monk. Things like that are a... distraction, we find. My teacher thought it best if I gave up my worldly obsessions, so it was playing chess and the viola I chose. These things are not for monks... we have other things we should be concentrating on. But when I was young, they were very important to me. Of course, my brother still has his... interests..."

Penny knew she was referring to his brother's love of the Japanese game of *shogi* and his passion for music, which were still a very big part of his life.

"So... did you know Maeda-san's wife? Yuriko? She played violin, I think. Very pretty girl..."

Dokan stared out the window again for a long moment.

112

"Yuriko… yes… another name I haven't heard for many years. Yes. I knew her. She was, as you said… very pretty. Very bright too. Much smarter than all of us…"

"Didn't she come from some famous family? The Nakatome family? Aren't they big real estate developers or something?"

Dokan nodded. "I believe so. Yes, I think she was the younger daughter of the company's chairman. She was expected to join the family business… but instead…"

Penelope waited for him to finish his sentence, but it never came out.

"She married Ran?"

The monk smiled and took another sip of tea.

"I think it was something like that. It didn't end well for her, I think. Mental problems. She died, I heard…"

"By suicide?" Penelope asked, and Dokan nodded sadly.

"So I was told. Eiji knew her better than me."

"Wow… that's very sad. I didn't know. Eiji never mentioned the details…"

Dokan picked up the small ceramic pot and poured her some more tea.

"I think there may be reasons for that. Best not to mention her to him… if I were you…"

Later, in the bright autumn sunlight, as Penelope walked down the short flight of stone steps outside the temple that led to the road and the nearby railway station, in another place, a man found himself waking up in a darkened room he did not know.

The room was lit by candles, and the first thing he heard upon awakening was the faint sound of a piano playing in the distance.

Mozart? Something baroque perhaps, he thought vaguely.

He also knew, somehow, as people do, that it wasn't a recording. Someone was actually playing, though so perfectly, that it sounded like a professional recording. Yes, an authoritative hand, the hand of someone intimate with the music through long practice.

The man, who owned a small stationary business in Ginza, knew about classical music well, and had played the piano himself nearly all his life. This music, though, was to a standard that he had never approached.

No, the person playing now in that other room was a master. He could tell that much just from a few moments of listening.

And then the music stopped, and the man became more aware of where he was and that he was strapped down to some kind of table. He tried to move his legs, then his arms, and then to raise his chest against the straps he could feel binding him there.

It was to no avail. His body felt like it had been cemented to the metal table.

He opened his mouth, but discovered that it had been sealed tight with some kind of heavy tape.

All around him, shadows danced on the dark bricks of the walls, and although he had no solid idea of his whereabouts, his senses told him he was underground somewhere.

After a while, he heard footsteps and felt a soft presence to one side. He turned his head, which he found moved freely, but could see nothing in the shadows beyond the flickering light of the candles.

Someone was there, though, standing quietly in the darkness, watching him.

He felt eyes raking across his body, and a cool air on his flesh.

He realized he was naked.

How did he get here? What had happened to him?

Nothing came to him.

He had been in the back room of his store, looking at something he had just received… what was it? And then he was here. But how?

He wondered for a moment if this was some kind of dream. Would he wake up soon? He hoped so.

He felt the faintest of pricks from a needle going into his arm, and then he was drifting again.

He was so tired now, he could not even move his fingers.

He fell asleep, and never woke again.

The man standing beside him put the empty syringe on the metal table next to where the dead man lay, and surveyed the body carefully, like someone looking at a laboratory animal. He switched on the powerful overhead lights above the operating table, and loosed the straps one by one.

As always, when he killed, he felt nothing. He was completely unconcerned with the feelings of his prey, utterly removed from their fear and panic. Whether they screamed or sang a song made no difference to him or whether they lived or died.

It was always the latter if they found themselves in this room. Dead suited his purposes better.

Of course, the death had to be just right, with a victim and, more importantly, a method of execution that lived up to his meticulous standards, but he knew it wasn't always perfect.

He was, though, if nothing else, a patient man.

If things did not work out the way he wanted with this one, there would always be another. Thanks to his vast historical research, he had a long list of potential targets, so he could always afford to wait for the right one to make himself available.

As long as they all came from the right pool, he was largely unconcerned with who they were, unless, along the way, he could do the world and himself a small favor and remove one or two of the more disagreeable entities. And as his killings had continued, and in the fullness of his over-arching plan, the only thing that really surprised him was how no one, especially the police whose efforts he monitored closely, seemed to understand what he was doing.

How odd, he sometimes thought to himself. Could I *not* have made myself clearer?

Apparently not, though. They were still wandering around in the dark.

However, if someone *did* by some lucky accident stumble upon his real motives (and, he had to admit, that lately there were a few very bright people who had been brought on board to stop him) and if that person ever did manage to put two and two together, that also didn't matter.

He was packed and ready to go.

All he had to do was pick up a bag and simply walk out the door.

He was thus many miles ahead of any kind of punishment, and he had the discipline to leave at a moment's notice. His belongings prepared, his funds available, his next abode and identity waiting for him to slip into like one of his well-tailored suits.

Discipline and planning, and preparation.

And, of course, his specialty.

Execution.

Above all else, that was what separated him from the aimless herd of other serial killers. People might *think* that he was like the others, oafish Americans like the Green River killer, the gormless David Berkowitz, or even *Il Monstro di Firenze*, the latter being some pathetic Italian vermin whose moniker the Japanese press had lifted and bestowed on him.

But he was *nothing* like them.

He had an absolute reason, a complete clarity, about what he was doing with his victims. There was no randomness in his kills, no aimless wandering around hunting for someone 'likely' as they had done.

And also, and this was the critical point, these other killers made mistakes.

He *never* made mistakes.

Not with anything.

Finished with his afternoon's work, he walked back upstairs to his comfortable house, swung the heavy metal door to the basement shut behind him, punched the entry code into the keypad, and then slid the fake wooden door across it that made the entrance to his basement look like a cupboard.

The house was large, and no one ever went into this room. And why would they? He lived alone, and the cleaning staff had long ago been told that this room was just for storage and there was no need to enter it. He kept it locked, and they believed what he said without question. Even if they had been able to get into it, the panel to the secret room below was well concealed, and the room itself looked completely normal.

He paid them well, too.

The man they called *Il Monstro* blinked slowly in the sunlight that was streaming through his windows as he walked through the well-appointed rooms of his house, his eyes adjusting quickly from the darkness of the place beneath his feet.

It was quiet, and he decided to rectify that situation by playing some music while he worked.

He walked over to the room next to his study and spent a few moments inside, running his finger over his huge collection of vinyl records, many of them extremely rare recordings, until he found what he wanted.

His moving finger stopped on top of an album by Yehudi Menuhin, a 1960 recording of a concert given in Leningrad of Beethoven's Violin Concerto in D Minor, where Menuhin had been one of the first ever visiting American musicians to be allowed to play in what was then the old Soviet Union. It was not his rarest recording, nor even his favorite, but he had been listening to it ever since his late father had recommended it to him as a child, and he suddenly felt nostalgic as he remembered those afternoons after school when he had come home and listened to it, the volume up as loud as possible, which was a little pleasure he had allowed himself whenever his parents were out.

These days, he kept the volume at a more respectable level, and having placed the record on the turntable, he went into the study where he sat at his large antique desk and listened to the opening strains of the famous concerto with the Leningrad Philharmonic Orchestra, its members and conductor all long dead now.

From the drawer, he took out his black Moleskine notebook, a favored type of stationary which, somewhat ironically, he had often purchased from his latest victim's store in Ginza, turned to a new, blank, and unruled page, and began to write with an antique mechanical pencil.

This was his journal, his commonplace book, where he wrote down all his thoughts in his beautiful, if somewhat dated, handwriting and thought through all the details of whatever he did in life.

He knew he had long been afflicted (or was it gifted?) with what one writer had termed 'the Midnight Disease,' a mental condition sometimes given the term *graphomania*, which was a compulsion to write everything down. This compulsion, which he had known since childhood, was now so ingrained that it was the tool with which his mind worked best.

It was like the strings on a violin or the keys on a keyboard.

He thought best with a pen in his hand, and worked out every aspect of his life in writing both before and after he acted. He wrote down everything, whatever occurred to him, and without discrimination, laying out his mind upon each new page without filter or re-reading. It had always given him a physical pleasure somehow to see his own beautiful hand, making its way in words across the new page, and it was enough just to write whatever he was thinking, to be able to see it in physical form, to make it real.

He rarely looked at what he wrote a second time, as there was no need, and as soon as a journal was full, he would place it on a special hidden shelf next to a thousand of its identical relatives, and never look at it again. He was, had he known it, just like his distant ancestor, the famous Heian period courtesan Lady Murasaki Shikibu, the world's first novelist and the author of the enormous *Tale of Genji*. She had been just like him, uncomfortable without the brush nearby, constantly scribbling a new story or a letter, unable to sit still or concentrate without some means to write readily at hand.

He had the same gene too.

On this sunny morning, as the music poured from the recessed speakers around the ceilings of the old room, he enjoyed himself writing about his dinner plans that night (he had duck fillets marinating in red wine in the kitchen) and his online meeting with an amateur historian whom he was paying for some more research, and his plans for the following day, when he would be executing his next little performance at another even more public location, a site which he was well aware entailed a considerable risk to his freedom.

He wrote about the white van he had stolen some weeks previously, which now waited in his garage covered in a white sheet, and how he intended to change the plates before he made his 'delivery.' He also made a note about the World War II army uniform he had removed from a museum some years before and carefully stored for this occasion in an airtight plastic bag with its medals and short sword waiting in its sheath. And then his thoughts wandered, and his hand flowed over the page in a short description of his next victim's family, and how beautifully apropos his little show would be.

Almost like he was setting history right after so many years of it willfully heading off in the wrong direction like an errant child.

He would make the past right now and, for her, take the revenge that she could no longer take.

This, after all, was his calling in life.

Retribution.

Justice.

For both of them, and especially for her.

Righting things until they were the way they should have been all along, just like one would right a small boat that has blown over on a lake and then set the sails again so it could continue along its proper path.

Yehudi Menuhin had finished playing, but the last notes still lingered in his mind as colors, which was how he understood music and mathematics, another field in which he excelled.

He looked down at the page beneath him, and smiled his soft smile at his own beautiful calligraphy, appreciating the elegance of the characters as they moved gracefully down the page from top to bottom before him, each exactly and perfectly drawn and, in a way, almost pure.

Chapter 9

The Honorable Dead

The old Kasumigaseki area in Tokyo has, for hundreds of years, always been the traditional center of administration in Japan, reaching back to the early days of the Tokugawa *shoguns* in the seventeenth century, and is still home to most of the government ministries, including the Ministry of Justice and the National Police Headquarters.

The name *Kasumigaseki* is made from the words *kasumi* meaning fog or mist, and *seki* meaning a barrier or gate. Where this name comes from is a subject of some debate, but it is probably a reference to an ancient highway checkpoint on the road that became the *Oshu-kaido*, or the Oshu Road that led to the far north of the country.

The boundary also separated the ancient Yamato people from the 'Eastern Barbarians,' or the wild natives of the 'Eastern Country' as specified by the 'legendary' twelfth emperor Yamato Takeru. The implication here is that on the other side of this border, there was nothing but clouds and haze and barbarianism, and thus not a place you would venture lightly.

Kasumigaseki has always been just a stone's throw from the seat of power in Japan, whether it was the modern Japanese Parliament (or Diet) which is just up the road, or the adjacent Imperial Palace, which used to be the *shogun's* palace until the emperor moved there from the old capital of Kyoto in the late nineteenth century.

The Imperial Palace itself is ringed by a broad footpath that winds its way around its high white walls and moats, circling the huge green area at the very heart of Tokyo where the emperor and his family reside. This path is beloved not only by tourists, who are constantly walking around it, but by two other domestic groups – the local joggers and the local walkers, who both claim that the path is 'theirs,' hate each other vehemently, and live in a constant state of complaining about the other's 'rudeness.' As beloved for its scenery as it is disputed, this path is exactly five kilometers in circumference and is thus the perfect place for Tokyo's more athletically minded public servants to take a run (or walk) during their lunch breaks.

Of course, if you wanted to avoid the swarms of people who take advantage of the path at the most popular time of day, you could find more hardy souls, such as Harayuki Itami, an almost-retired veteran of the Kasumigaseki scene and a very senior public servant in the Ministry of Home Affairs, who preferred to do his running at dawn every day before he headed off to the showers in the basement of the Ministry building.

A veteran of several marathons in a number of different countries, the extremely fit sixty-four-year-old regarded the five-kilometer run around the palace as his daily warm-up, and could manage it in under twenty-five minutes without barely breaking a sweat, even in summer.

He usually started his run at the Sakuradamon Gate, one of the traditional eight gates that gave access to the palace, and proceeded after that in an anti-clockwise direction, enjoying the early morning air and the beauty of the traditional walled compound, with its impressive old stone walls and famous cherry blossom sites, its quiet green moat and the old white *yagura* watch towers. It always made him happy to see these things and proud of his heritage and his nation's culture as he jogged quietly past in the pre-dawn light each day.

On this quiet Thursday morning, though, he hadn't gone more than four hundred meters when he detected something odd just near where the path crossed in front of the Seimon gate, the traditional main entrance to the palace and the place from whence the emperor and empress usually came and went from when they left the palace on official business.

Just before this gate was an expansive lawn covered with elegantly cut pine trees, and as he approached these, stepping lightly and steadily on his run, he suddenly saw a white van pulling away rapidly up the road and the figure of a man kneeling on a white sheet facing the palace where it had been parked.

It was this sheet that the man was kneeling on that grabbed his attention at first, as he had seen enough 'samurai' dramas on TV to know there was only one reason that a person would be kneeling on a white sheet, and that was because they were committing the act of *seppuku,* or ritual suicide.

The second thing that surprised him was that the man on the sheet was dressed in the old green uniform of the now-defunct Imperial Japanese Army, replete with medals and the usual peaked cap.

Thinking he had stumbled upon some crazed right-winger about to kill himself, he approached the man at a run and shouted loudly at him.

"Oi! What do you think you're doing!!"

The man, however, did not acknowledge his presence in the slightest and remained absolutely still, staring at the high palace walls.

Itami approached him carefully until he stood directly before him, and his sneakered feet touched the edge of the white sheet.

This was when the full import of what he was really looking at dawned on him.

"*Shimmata*...." he swore softly, his eyes widening, while at the same moment, he started reaching for his mobile phone.

The man was clearly dead.

His green jacket was open from neck to groin, and a long slash of red showed where the stomach had been cut open horizontally just under the navel in the traditional fashion. The short sword with which this had been done was still grasped in the man's lifeless hand, a piece of white paper wrapped neatly around the hilt.

Even stranger was that the man's eyes were open, and he had a peaceful expression on his face, almost the faintest of smiles, as he looked past where Itami stood toward the object of his veneration, the home of the emperor, that lay beyond the white walls and the high trees.

As he looked at the man's tranquil face, a face he would never forget for the rest of his life, for just the briefest of moments, Itami felt something almost akin to envy at the unearthly calm that seemed to wrap itself around this figure like the ancient mists that had once given the area its name.

==========================

Just a few hours later, news of the latest killing exploded across the nation's television screens, and in no time at all, Chief Inspector Yamashita had been informed by his colleagues on the *Il Monstro* task force based at the Tokyo Metropolitan police headquarters, that the killer had, without question, struck once more.

Even more damning though, he was told, was that the killer had struck at the Imperial Palace itself, which was, needless to say, ground zero for national security as far as the Japanese state was concerned. *Il Monstro*, therefore, found himself immediately plucked from the lesser list of common murderers to the far more prestigious role of State Threat, and panic such has not been seen in the capital since the toxic gas attack on the Tokyo subway by the Aum Shinrikyo cult almost a quarter of a century previous erupted.

By midday of the next day, Yamashita and DS Yokota were being hustled into a large meeting room by the head of the *Il Monstro* task force, the dour and extremely senior police Chief Superintendent Tomaki, who opened the meeting by brusquely commanding one of his subordinates to describe the known facts about the latest killing. No one was unaware that the killing had, to the Metropolitan Police's profound annoyance, taken place less than eight hundred meters from the building they were now all sitting in.

"OK. Speak…." Tomaki ordered his underling, an officer by the name of Detective Sergeant Mitsunari, who had, like Yamashita and Yokota, only recently been granted the dubious and possibly career-ending honor of appointment to the group.

Mitsunari, a slight, bespectacled individual, who looked like he might have been more at home reading the evening news than being a policeman, looked up nervously at the officers assembled, most of whom outranked him.

"Er… Yes. Good afternoon, ladies and gentlemen… Um…"

The beleaguered detective sergeant picked up a small remote control and fiddled desperately with the buttons until a PowerPoint document appeared on the screen, which he then proceeded to read from word-for-word.

Yamashita sighed, rolled his eyes, and looked at Yokota, who also made a tired face. Neither of them was particularly enamored of this tedious method of presentation, extremely prevalent in Japan, and felt that if someone was just going to read verbatim from his slides, they should have just emailed the document to them and saved them the trip.

"Yesterday at 4.37 AM," said the detective, finally breaking from his prepared script and pointing to a new slide which was a timeline of events, "the body of the diseased was discovered by a jogger completing his usual morning run around the imperial palace. The body was sitting in the formal kneeling position…"

"Put up the photographs, dammit…" Chief Inspector Tomaki barked at the man, who hastily broke off what he was saying and complied.

There was an intake of breath around the room as the photograph of the dead man appeared on the screen, and Yamashita, Yokota, and many others leaned in to get a better look at it.

"Wow…" they heard someone whisper at the back of the room.

Yamashita found himself involuntarily nodding in silent agreement.

On the screen was a picture of a middle-aged man dressed in a World War II green army uniform and the standard peaked cap of the period. He was kneeling on a white sheet that had been spread underneath him and was facing towards the Imperial Palace when viewed from the rear. His jacket was open to the navel, and a long red slash showed where the man had cut with his short sword (still clasped in his hand) in what looked like the formal act of *seppuku*, or ritual suicide. Despite the gruesome manner of his death, Yamashita and the other veteran officers immediately noticed the absence of any significant blood on the white sheet and the position of the body, perfectly upright, where it should surely have been slumped forward over the knife wound.

In short, it was evident at even a cursory glance that the scene had been staged.

The bespectacled DS now continued.

"As yet, we have no idea who the victim is, as there was no documentation left at the scene, and of course, we are still waiting for the results of the autopsy, which is being carried out as we speak."

"How do we know it's our boy?" asked one of the officers at the back of the room, whom Yamashita recognized as being from the Nara police.

At this, Chief Superintendent Tomaki intervened.

"Black crow's feather taped to the handle of the sword under the paper, along with the usual fur, which I am sure will be fox unless we are greatly mistaken. It's our boy. No question," he said, nodding at the officer who had spoken.

"Is this some kind of, I dunno, war thing?" asked one of the junior detectives. Tomaki nodded gravely and got to his feet, where he snatched the microphone and the remote control from his subordinate, who hastily retreated to his seat.

"Yes, I would say that's pretty obvious. At first glance, at least to me, and I'm no historian, this seems to be some sort of reconstruction of the scene outside the Imperial Palace after the emperor broadcasted the surrender announcement in August 1945. At that time, as is pretty well known, I think, a number of soldiers and other patriots committed *seppuku* by *hara-kiri* on the grounds of the palace and in other places around the country. At first glance, that's obviously what this is about, so yes, this is some kind of 'war thing,' as you call it."

"I've never heard of it," said another officer, and Yokota, who was quite a history buff in his spare time, rolled his eyes at his boss.

"They're young," whispered Yamashita.

"He's the same age as me…" hissed Yokota.

There was silence in the room for a moment as the officers assembled absorbed the gruesome photograph and the information they had been given. Yamashita was well aware that the history of the Second World War was a subject that was only very selectively taught in Japanese schools, unlike in Germany and Italy. In these other Axis powers, people grew up with a comprehensive knowledge of their nations' atrocities during the war.

In Japan, however, the government had made sure that the whole matter, and especially the crimes against humanity the Japanese Imperial army had been guilty of as it had rampaged across China and south-east Asia in the thirties and forties, was very much downplayed and 'swept under the tatami' as the Japanese saying went. Most younger Japanese, and that included nearly everyone in the room with them, had absolutely no idea what their nation had done during the war, and therefore even less idea why the atomic bombs had been dropped and why their near neighbors like Korea and China often viewed them with a thinly veiled disgust. Most would have had no idea why anyone would have wanted to commit suicide outside the Imperial Palace, even though it had been widely reported after the war.

"Well, it's obviously staged…" said the officer from Nara, choosing to leave the historical discussion to others.

Tomaki nodded.

"Yes, that much is clear. Staged for effect. No one commits *seppuku* and ends up sitting upright like that. There was a stake driven into the ground at the victim's back to keep him propped up underneath the jacket. So, we know he was killed somewhere else, but that's all we know now."

"Any information from traffic about how the body got there?"

The still nervous DS Mitsunari now spoke up again.

"Traffic cameras show a white van delivering the body to the site at 4.31 AM. This van was also noticed by the individual who found the body driving away. The van was at the site for about three minutes, and then dumped nearby. We found it yesterday afternoon, parked with a set of false plates. The driver then must have walked away down a side street and vanished. There were no video cameras of the scene where the van was dumped, and we are still looking at all the available footage we can find, but he seems to have been aware of where all the cameras were in the area."

"Figures," Yamashita muttered.

"And the van?" asked someone.

"Reported stolen from a painting company in Ota ward a few weeks ago. Once again, no cameras, no information, no leads."

"What about the body? Has anyone been reported missing?"

Tomaki shook his head.

"Not as yet. We are looking into that too. Right… any other questions? Observations?"

Yamashita raised his hand. Most people in the room either knew him or knew of him, and that he had been responsible for solving some extremely prominent cases, including one recently involving a series of murders that had a major effect on the ruling political party in Japan. As such, heads turned when they saw his hand in the air.

They were not disappointed.

"Is there any sign the victim was drugged prior to death? Puncture marks or the like?"

There was a buzz of voices around the table at this unexpected question.

Tomaki raised an eyebrow. "We'll know more when we get the autopsy results. Why do you ask, chief inspector?"

Yamashita folded his arms and reclined a little in his chair.

"Well, we know that our boy *Il Monstro* has used drugs before, especially tranexamic acid and surgical-level general anesthesia. He does this because he keeps his victims somewhere prior to transport to what you might call the 'display site' to stop them from bleeding to death or struggling presumably. So it would seem likely that he has a kill room somewhere, especially in this case and in the Kamakura case. Probably not that far away, as otherwise the toxin levels in the other bodies would have been much lower. Also, I would be willing to bet the army uniform the victim is dressed in is probably an original, not a prop from a costume company. The Kamakura period clothes our boy dressed his victim in from the shrine killing were museum-quality originals from the thirteenth century, though we have received no reports of any being stolen from any collections. I would also be willing to put money on the authenticity of the clothing… this guy has a very strong eye for detail…"

There was a nodding of heads all around the room at these words, and many felt it was the first time anyone could say anything definitive about the series of killings they had been investigating.

Tomaki also nodded his head appreciatively.

"Those are good points, chief inspector… We will look into that, I promise you…. Right? Anything else?"

The hand of one of the female officers at the back of the room went up.

"Yes… the way of killing. The *seppuku*… I don't know much about that. Is there anything about that we ought to know? I mean… does it tell us anything?"

"Other than he's a nutter?" murmured one of her colleagues, to the general amusement of those assembled.

Tomaki scowled at them.

"The *victim*," he growled, stressing the word, "did not die from ritual suicide. He probably bled to death somewhere else. As you can see, there is almost no blood at the scene. So, get that out of your heads. This victim, like all the rest, was murdered somewhere else. Like the chief inspector here has just pointed out," he gestured towards Yamashita, who sat looking at the floor. "So don't be confused. This has been staged to *look* like *seppuku*. The details of this method of dying are fairly consistent with historical practice, by which I mean, the choice of weapon, the short sword, with the hilt wrapped in white paper. Also consistent. The white sheet he was sitting on, that's also common in this type of suicide, historically speaking. There are other things, though…"

"Like what?" asked the detective from Nara.

At this point, Yokota raised his hand, and Tomaki nodded that the floor was his. Yamashita also looked at him, surprised, as his DS was not much of a one for speaking in public.

"Yokota, from Kamakura," he said quietly, introducing himself to the assembled officers. "In cases of *seppuku* historically, there are a few other things which were usually done. One of the most important is a death poem. This was always part of the ritual, usually written shortly before the suicide either during or after a final meal which usually would include *sake*, which as you probably know, was seen as a purifying element."

The officers looked at the younger man with respect in their eyes.

"The other element, which is not always observed, is the presence of a second."

"A second? What do you mean?" someone asked.

Yokota nodded. "An assistant. After the person cuts open the stomach, it was common to have a second present to take off the person's head with a *katana*, or long sword. Obviously, in this case, that didn't happen…"

There was a hush in the room, and then Tomaki spoke again.

"Thank you, DS… Yokota. You never know, that could be relevant later. Anything else?"

Yokota again raised his hand, and the surprised Tomaki gestured to him to speak.

"There is one other point," said Yokota carefully. "You mentioned the reaction to the end of the war and the surrender among certain Japanese patriots… I think you may have been referring to the *Kyujo* Incident?"

There were confused faces all around the room, but the chief superintendent smiled.

"I was, but I have a feeling you know more about it than me. Would you like to tell us about it?" He gestured to Yokota to stand up and come to the front of the room, and the big man hesitantly came forward. But first, he bent down to Detective Sergeant Mitsunari and passed him a piece of paper with a name on it, and Mitsunari immediately started typing on his laptop.

Yokota turned to face his peers and took the microphone from Tomaki.

"The *Kyujo* Incident happened the night before the emperor went on the radio to announce the surrender of Japan to the Allies. Early that morning, before dawn, a group of senior officers decided that this had to be stopped at all costs, and decided to place the emperor under house arrest and stage a coup. This action was thwarted a few hours later that day when the military refused to support the action that was being planned. The coup plotters murdered a number of people to advance their plans, some of them senior officers, but in the end, they realized that they had failed, and several of them took their own lives."

Most of the room looked like they were hearing this piece of their own history for the first time, and looked genuinely surprised. One of the officers put up his hand to speak and Yokota nodded to him.

"So, do you think this guy was trying to stage a coup or something? I mean, our guy this morning?"

At this suggestion, there were immediate murmurs around the room, but Yokota shook his head.

"No, I don't think he had any such plans. But this *is* very reminiscent of the 1945 *Kyujo* Incident...." Yokota looked over at Mitsunari.

"Have you got it?" he asked.

Mitsunari nodded, and a second later, an old black and white photograph flashed onto the screen, which was greeted by an audible gasp from the people in the room.

The picture showed a man in an old Imperial Army uniform with a close-shaven scalp and some military brocades stretching across the uniform, indicating that the man was of high rank. He was staring straight ahead, and there seemed to be an air of both commitment and serenity about him. But what really caught everybody's attention, especially after Mitsunari uploaded a picture of the victim again side by side with the other picture, was that the two men not only bore an almost uncanny resemblance, but that their uniforms, right down to the brocade stretching from the shoulder and across the chest, were absolutely identical.

Yokota nodded toward the screen.

"This was Major Kenji Hatanaka, one of the main architects of the coup. He committed suicide that evening once he realized the coup had failed."

"Wow... they could be father and son..." said someone in the front row.

Yokota nodded modestly, handed the microphone back to Tomaki, and resumed his seat next to Yamashita without another word.

Tomaki got to his feet and nodded his appreciation to Yokota, and thirty minutes later, the meeting had broken up, and Yamashita and his DS headed on foot to the crime scene in front of the Imperial Palace, just around the corner from the National Police headquarters.

When they turned onto the long, straight road in front of the palace, they saw, off to their left, the wide gravel drive leading up to the Seimon gate, with its impressively huge wooden doors, and the famous Nijubashi or 'double bridge' behind it, while in front of them on the lawn with its elegantly cut pine trees that were so reminiscent of *bonsai*, there was a scene of frenetic activity. The entire area and the road next to it had been roped off and blocked to traffic, and perhaps a hundred officers were on the scene.

They showed their warrant cards to one of the nearest ones on duty, and were admitted to the area where the forensic tents and technicians were fanning out across the grounds in front of the palace looking for any clue to the murder. Of course, the cause of all this quite inordinate attention was not merely because murders were relatively rare in Japan, but that this was a murder in front of the Imperial Palace itself and, as such, represented a defilement of the most sacred property in the country. A murder *anywhere* near the Imperial Palace touched on the Japanese throne, and in this respect, it was just about as significant a breach of national security as it was possible for any police officer to imagine, and reflected on their ability to provide security and safety for the Imperial Family. As a result, the killing had been catapulted from a strange, if simple, murder to a major national security incident in one fell swoop, especially as far as the media was concerned, even though it was most likely nothing of the kind.

Inside the largest of the white tents, which was ringed with over twenty officers that were standing on guard while the forensic technicians worked inside, they found the white sheet where the man had knelt, the body having been removed for autopsy, and they were able to vividly understand the scene that the gentleman who had first discovered the body had witnessed.

The man had been kneeling in the formal *seiza* position on this very white sheet, and just a few feet in front of him was one of the small pine trees, looking very incongruous inside the sealed tent, like it had been brought inside as some kind of decoration.

Yamashita and Yokota looked at some photographs of the victim that had been uploaded onto a laptop on a table at the side of the tent, his old green army jacket opened to the waste and saw again slash of red just below the navel where the stomach had been opened, presumably by the short sword which still dangled from the corpse's right hand, clasping a sheet of white paper that had been wrapped around the hilt.

The face of the man in the photographs was the most interesting thing, however. There was an almost tangible air of tranquility about it, the eyes calmly staring toward the palace, like it was the place where his soul wished to fly. The act of *hara-kiri*, which was the procedure used in the act of ritual suicide or *seppuku* in Japan, literally means to 'cut the belly' and was a method employed because of an ancient belief that the soul resided just below the navel, and so opening this area of the body would allow it to leave.

And indeed, it looked like it had, and left in its place only peace.

Both Yamashita and his DS lowered their eyes and bowed towards the white sheet where the victim had been as a sign of respect, and after lingering for a moment to take in the murder scene, made their way back outside so as not to impede the work of the technicians who were busy gathering evidence inside.

"Well, I guess if you live long enough, you get to see everything…" Yokota commented to his boss as they returned to their car.

Yamashita nodded. "I think that's what he wants, though. The killer, I mean. I think he wants us to get all caught up in the drama, in the story he's telling. Maybe so we go chasing off down the rabbit hole of samurai and *seppuku* and swords and all that stuff."

"You don't think all that is relevant? I mean, we could find something in that, right? Something that leads us to him?" asked Yokota as they waited for the light to change at the bottom of the long hill that swept down from the Japanese Diet building.

Yamashita clapped him on the shoulder.

"No. I don't. I think it's smoke," he said bluntly.

"Smoke? Like it's not real?"

His boss nodded and gave a grim smile.

"Exactly. I think it's meant to lead us *away* from him, not *toward* him. Like Penelope said. It's a bit like watching a *kabuki* play or a movie and getting so caught up in the story that you forget where you are. You forget that the thing you are watching *isn't actually real*. That's what I think. But I do think one point is interesting, though…"

"What's that then?" asked Yokota.

"Well," said Yamashita after a pause. "History."

"History?"

Yamashita nodded. "Yes. History. Your favorite subject. All of these killings… they've all got a historical motif, right? The Heian Period spectacle at the shrine. These latest two killings referencing the war. The whole *tengu* and fox spirit stuff in Nagano and the other places all

140

those years ago.... It's all a reference to our history, our culture as a nation. It's all about the past, wouldn't you say?"

Yokota nodded.

"So, if this tells us anything about this guy, it's that he has a fascination, boarding on reverence, for our past. For our culture and our stories."

"He's a historian?"

Yamashita shrugged. "He could be. He could well be. Or he may just be a very well-informed amateur. A very well-read, cultured person, I would say, with a real respect for the past. Someone with an acute eye for detail, and a great gift for patience and persistence over a very long period of time. And that's what scares me most about our boy. That's what... bothers me."

"That he's patient?"

Yamashita nodded and sighed loudly.

"Yes. It's the patient ones you have to fear the most, Yokota. Not the smart ones or the rich ones, or the crims with the most resources. It's the patient ones. The methodical ones. The ones that won't strike until the odds are completely in their favor. Those are the ones that make the least mistakes. And in our job, a killer that doesn't make a mistake doesn't leave a trace. And those are the ones that you don't catch. Not unless you are very, very fortunate..."

Chapter 10.

The Spirit Hunters

Penelope watched Fei from the kitchen as her friend sat in her comfortable old armchair in the sunlit living room, absorbed in her usual newspaper and occasionally relighting the little antique Japanese pipe she loved to smoke.

The living room looked out over the vegetable garden, which was their joint passion, and the light was spilling across the floor to where Fei sat. Occasionally the quiet of the house would be broken by the rustle of the pages, as Fei was a voracious consumer of news and generally read her beloved Asahi newspaper from cover to cover every day.

She sighed to herself, and went back to washing the eggplants and other vegetables they had harvested that morning. Something in her heart told her that all was not as it should be, that her everyday quiet life was in danger of change, which was something she was loathe to allow most of the time, particularly if the cause of that was a man.

She had been suffering from what could only be called a feeling of confusion over the last few weeks, a cloudiness and a lack of clarity in her thinking, and a kind of numbness and wandering in her thoughts, which were usually so lucid and clear. She had begun to wonder what was the matter with her, but in her heart, she knew what it was.

She also wondered at her friend's almost stoic equanimity at times like this. Fei was always the same and seemed almost never to change, no matter what was going on around her. She lived with her elderly aunt, the feisty Auntie Chen, in the house next door, was completely absorbed in her work as one of the senior coroners for the police in Kamakura, and apart from these things and the news, her only other passion was the game of *shogi* or Japanese chess, which both she and Chief Inspector Yamashita played at a near professional level. Practical and down to earth, she seemed to move through her life unfazed, like a knife sliding through butter or a bird flying in an empty sky. Life, for her, it seemed, was always what it should be.

For herself of late, however, there had been an irritating feeling of distraction, and this feeling was beginning to bother her. Since she had retired as a professor of Japanese Literature at Kamakura's Hassei University while still in her mid-fifties, she had enjoyed a quiet and quite orderly life, with her house and her four cats and Fei for company, working in her vegetable garden, going to her tea lessons and writing her books. Of course, she had also been involved with many cases over the years, helping the police through her long friendship with the chief inspector, whom she knew valued her insights, but apart from this excitement, her life had been one of calm, and even boredom to a large degree, and she rather liked it that way.

And then, over the last few weeks since she had been involved in the *Il Monstro* case, she had met Ran Maeda, and this, she knew, was the cause of her problem.

Over the years, there had been a number of men in her life, but since her early love affair with Hiro, who had been taken from her by this same killer so many years before, she had never allowed anyone to come too close to her again. And she often wondered, now she was older and, like her friend Fei, still happily single (how they both hated the word 'spinster'!), if she had not been too fussy, too demanding of the male candidates that had presented themselves in the past and shown an interest. But then, at the same time, there had never been the chemistry between herself and these men that she had been looking for. There had never been one of them that she had not immediately forgotten about the moment they had parted company after an evening out, and she had never had the slightest difficulty refocusing herself on her studies or her teaching or her writing or whatever else had been occupying her attention at the time.

They were just there... and then they were not. Until they met up for dinner again or whatever other event was next on the calendar.

Basically, they just didn't really matter, and when they were out of her immediate presence, they just ceased to exist.

Standing at the sink now, she was aware of the sunlight reflecting off the water, and of her hands, and of the rich color and textures of the freshly picked vegetables as she gently washed them.

She looked at her hands and saw that they were still the hands of a young woman. The fingers were long and delicate, 'pianist's fingers' as her mother used to say, and she was careful to keep her nails trimmed and exactly cut and painted with a clear varnish most days, which added to their gentle elegance. When people watched her, they could sense the calmness and good manners in her, like when she turned the pages of a book and the tips of her fingers would caress the page, there was this certain refinement, a kind of precise and beautiful way of moving that only certain women had. And she had it. The way she folded her hands in her lap, for example, as she sat listening to someone, or how her index finger would chase an errant strand of blonde hair away from her line of vision as she looked at you... these things gave her a charm of which she was wholly unaware but quite struck the men that paused long enough to have an honest look at her, even though, if asked, they would probably have been unable to put their finger on precisely what it was that they found so pleasant about her.

Ran Maeda could though, and she knew it.

When she was with him, it was like he *saw* her, and unlike so many others, he was able to articulate exactly what it was he saw. It was like she was naked in front of him, and yet, somehow, she felt safe. He looked at her, not simply in a friendly or even in an admiring way, but in a way that made her feel known. When he spoke to her, he spoke to her not just as a friend or as a colleague, but as a woman and as someone he enjoyed exploring the world with, as someone he could challenge and whose perceptions he could stretch.

More than anything, it was his searchlight-bright intellect that drew her to him, perhaps as it was hers that seemed to attract him.

Penelope had always, and without any false modesty, realized that most of the time, the people she met were not anywhere near as clever as she was. She never made any show of this to them, and generally went out of her way to cover it up and to put others at ease. Yet she was an Oxford-educated PhD. with a first-class degree in Japanese literature, fluent in the language and with a shockingly quick mind, and she found herself often and sometimes frustratedly waiting for others to catch up to things that she had seen more or less instantly. Like Ran, she also had absolutely no trouble remembering things she had read or seen, even years before, and was able to use her memory and analytical powers to think widely outside the box and to make connections where others saw none. And it was this gift, particularly, which had proven so valuable and been so appreciated by Yamashita and her other contacts in the Japanese police.

But with Maeda, if anything, she got the feeling that it was he, rather than her, that was waiting for someone to catch up. His was a luminous intelligence, with a breadth of knowledge of so many different subjects from music to mathematics to languages, art, literature, history, and perhaps any number of other areas of intellectual interest that she was unaware of that left her feeling as she had just walked into the Louvre or some vast library for the first time. And despite what she felt was his obvious intellectual superiority, they had 'clicked' in a way that she had almost never felt before.

She felt appreciated by him, and in turn, she found herself thinking far too much about when the next moment would come when she would see him again, and feel his eyes, his unusual, prescient eyes, moving over her body and holding her own as they spoke.

She could never quite get him out of her head, which was a new experience for her, and something she found a little unsettling, like a vague cough that wouldn't go away, but vanished completely whenever they were together. She wanted the feeling, and at the same time, she wanted to return to how she had been before, unseen, unmoved - but tranquil.

She dried the vegetables with a towel and arranged them in a little basket on the dining table, and as she did so, she heard her doorbell ring.

Fei looked up from her newspaper and didn't move, but from the different parts of the room, as they always did, all four of her cats awoke from their afternoon siesta, stretched, and headed on masse in the direction of the front door to check out whoever it was that had dared to come into their kingdom.

Penelope followed them to the door, shooed them away, and opened it to find her old colleague and friend Machiko Tani standing on the doorstep, smiling at her as always and pushing a bottle of wine into her hands. They embraced in a most un-Japanese way, and she led her into the living room.

"Oh Fei!" said Machiko, "It's been forever! Nice to see you again."

Machiko threw her bag onto one of the dining chairs and herself onto another.

She was a large, ebullient woman with a loud voice, and a permanently cheerful disposition, a mother of three successful children who had all become doctors and lawyers and whose husband had just become the most senior bureaucrat in the Ministry of Economic Affairs. She also had absolutely zero patience with fools, and a merciless tongue. Penelope knew her well as Machiko was an Associate Professor of Japanese History at her old alma mater of Hassei University, and the two women, including Fei, had been friends for decades.

The three chatted happily for the next twenty minutes or so about family matters and various people they knew in common before the doorbell announced the arrival of the last guest, and a minute later, Penelope escorted Chief Inspector Yamashita into the room.

The veteran policeman was today dressed casually in a pair of old corduroy trousers and a dark green polo shirt, and took a seat on the other side of the dining table from Machiko Tani without further ado. He sat down with a happy sigh and accepted a glass of beer from Penelope.

"Ah… now I'm even more confused, Penny-*sensei*. Why is this nice policeman here? Is it about my overdue library books?" she said, smiling at Yamashita, whom she had also known for many years as a guest at Penelope's frequent dinner parties.

"That's right," said Yamashita with a polite bow. "I have an order for your arrest here somewhere," he said with a smile, and patted his pockets as if looking for the document.

"Damn," said Machiko. "I knew my crimes would catch up to me one day… Can I have a glass of wine, Penny-san?"

"I want one, too," said Fei, raising her hand. "It must be over the yardarm somewhere," she said in her effortless English, which she knew the others all spoke well themselves, even if they may not have shared her enthusiasm for offbeat English idioms like the ones she enjoyed.

Penelope opened a cabinet and put a bottle of Spanish rioja and four glasses on the table.

"Oh… that's more like it. A last drink before I'm taken off to jail, I guess…"

"Don't worry, Machiko-san," said Yamashita as they clinked glasses. "I have a very nice cell all ready for you…unless you can help me out, that is."

"Hmmm…" said Machiko. "Anyway, Penny-san will now tell us why she wants someone like me here for this meeting. Right, Penny?"

Penelope poured herself a glass of wine and smiled at her. "I want you here… *we* want you here, to pick your folklorist brain. If I'm not mistaken, you are the author of several weighty tomes on the subject of Japanese folklore, aren't you? You are, indeed, *that* Tani-*sensei*?"

"Guilty," said Machiko, looking at the floor in mock shame. "But why do the police want to know about Japanese fairy stories? Or you, for that matter?"

Yamashita and Penelope exchanged glances, and Fei gave a slight cough and applied her silver Zippo lighter to the bowl of her pipe.

Machiko looked from one to the other of her friends.

"Is this about *Il Monstro*?"

Yamashita gave her a slight nod in honor of her erudition.

"Yes, it is. How would you like to consult with the police?" he asked, tilting his head as he spoke.

"Hmmm… does this mean I can keep my library card?"

"Absolutely. No charges will be brought. If what you say is… useful… that is…" he smiled.

Yamashita opened his briefcase and took out several blue cardboard files, which he laid out on the table in order.

Before he opened the files, he sat back in his chair and folded his arms.

"As usual, this is confidential, ladies…" he said seriously. "That means you don't breathe a word of it. We've got to protect this information, especially so we can prevent copycat situations. I'm sure you all understand."

The women nodded, and Fei stood up at one end of the table.

"Fei already knows all this, I think, but some of it may be new, even to Penny-*sensei*."

He gestured towards the files.

"Basically, we are looking at seven murders, all committed by the same individual over a period of nearly thirty years. The first four victims, beginning in 1995 with Penelope's then-boyfriend Hiro Yamana, were killed in Nagano, Kyoto, Nara, and Tokyo at four to five-year intervals. Since then, we have had two more in Kamakura, and the most recent one in Tokyo. These last three were all in the last three months."

Machiko listened quietly.

"He's escalating, isn't he… something's triggered this…" said Penelope, and Yamashita nodded.

"Exactly. He's gone on a killing spree, something completely unlike his previous MO. Almost like it's a different person, only it isn't. It's him. But for some reason, now he seems in a hurry."

Machiko looked up from the folders he had spread in front of her.

"And you know this is the same creep... how?" she asked him, and her tone was like she was speaking to an extremely slow-witted student.

"We know this, professor, because he signs all his crimes."

"With what? What do you mean by 'signs'?"

Yamashita leaned forward and opened the sixth file to reveal a close-up picture of the victim at the Hachimangu shrine in Kamakura. He took out an old fountain pen from a leather case and pointed with the end of it towards the victim's hands, which were folded neatly on his chest like some old English effigy.

"You can just see the tip of a black feather here? Underneath the folded hands?"

He placed a second picture on top of the first one, which showed a close-up of the hands and the feather underneath it, and a third, which was just of the feather itself.

Machiko leaned forward and stared.

"Is that a crow's feather?" she whispered.

Yamashita nodded. "Very good. And then there's this..."

He pointed to an area on the victim's elaborate black Heian robes just underneath the hands where there was a small collection of what looked like hairs, and then showed her another close-up picture of them.

The woman gathered around the picture, and Yamashita produced a magnifying glass from his briefcase and passed it to Machiko.

"All of us detectives have one of these," he said with a smile.

Machiko accepted the magnifying glass and spent several seconds staring at the hairs before passing it to Penelope, who did the same.

"Animal hair?" she asked.

Yamashita nodded. "Care to hazard a guess now why we asked you here?"

Machiko stared down at the picture and then again at the chief inspector, who watched her reactions in silence.

"Are you suggesting that it's... no... no... it can't be that... fox fur?"

Yamashita broke into a wide smile.

"Well done, professor. That's exactly what it is— and not just *a* fox. *The* fox..." he said, opening some of the other files and pointing out photographs of the same feather and the same hair on the other victims.

Machiko nodded and stared hard at the photographs before sitting down again and folding her arms.

"What do you mean, *the* fox?"

Yamashita tapped on the cover of the first file and then on the covers of all the other seven spread out in a row.

"Because it's hair from the *same* fox. The first one nearly thirty years ago and the final one last week. We've had it DNA typed. It's hair from the same animal. That, professor, is how we know it's the same guy."

Machiko nodded, impressed.

"Wow... thirty years."

Yamashita put his old fountain pen away carefully in its leather case.

"You can maybe appreciate a little more now the problems we have catching this fellow. He is extremely disciplined. Careful…. meticulous. Which makes him, well… elusive, to say the least. All the murders were different. Victims dressed up in different clothes, mutilated in different ways, in different places. But a few things are the same. These two signatures… the black crow's feather and the fox hair. They're there in each and every case. And the other…"

Penelope looked up.

"History… There is always some historical connection. Some reference or story about the past."

Yamashita smiled grimly at her.

"Exactly. And so…" he looked inquiringly at Machiko, who suddenly smiled at him and sighed.

"I get it. Are you asking me about the *karasu-tengu*? The crow *tengu*? And… fox spirits? *Kitsune*?" she said with a curious look at the files.

"Now you know why you are here. The crow feather and the fox hair. These are references to classical Japanese folklore, are they not?"

Machiko nodded.

"They are indeed… they are very common stories in certain parts, particularly western Japan," she said with a serious air, as they had now landed on her life work, the study of Japanese mythology and folklore.

Yamashita leaned forward and clasped his hands together.

"What I want to know is, first of all, why is this killer referencing these stories? And also, why both of them? Why this juxtaposition? What does the crow *tengu* have to do with the fox-spirit legends? Are there any stories where they are together?"

Machiko flashed a look at Penelope and looked away for a moment out of the window.

"There might be one..." she said with a far-away look.

Yamashita leaned back in his chair and smiled.

"I was hoping you'd say that..."

Chapter 11

Dr. Inagawa

"Can you spare a sec, sergeant?"

Yokota looked up at the young woman, a junior detective constable assigned to Kamakura's *Il Monstro* team. Yokota had requested that she and another officer look at some of the details relating to the drugs found in the victim's bodies after the autopsies.

"Sure. Ishibe-san right? What's up?" he said, trying to remember the young officer's name. "You found something?"

The woman slid into the chair in front of Yokota's desk, and the big man closed his laptop, leaned back, and crossed his arms.

Kyoko Ishibe was in her early thirties and had only recently been appointed to the position of junior detective on the homicide squad, which was her first assignment since graduating from the uniform ranks just a few months earlier. She was slim, wore almost no makeup, as was standard for women in the Japanese police, had her shoulder-length black hair pulled back in a ponytail, and was dressed conservatively in a dark suit and white blouse with a small silver broach in the lapel. Yokota also knew she had a law degree from the prestigious Keio University in Tokyo and was rumored to be fluent in both English and French.

The young woman placed a file on top of Yokota's laptop and opened it to reveal a single document, which was a copy of an invoice that had been forwarded to her by one of the pharmaceutical companies they had asked to cooperate in their inquiries.

Yokota peered at the piece of paper.

"So, what am I looking at?" he asked.

Ishibe pointed at the recipient's name on the invoice.

"Takahiro-san, I mean, Detective Constable Nemoto and I," she said, correcting herself, "have been looking through all the sales of this particular drug, Sivorix 72R, which was found in the Hachimangu and Tokyo victim's blood. It's one of a bunch of drugs on the market which contains tranexamic acid, which inhibits bleeding. This one was developed in Japan about fifteen years ago by Pharmax, and is fairly common in surgical practice these days," she pointed with her pen to the company name on the top of the invoice.

"OK, yeah… we know that. What's this, though?" said Yokota, pointing to the invoice and hoping she would get to the point soon. Ishibe-san, however, was not going to be rushed.

"Right, well. We went through all the sales, like I said, for the last three years, which is the known product life of this drug, meaning if you bought it, you would have to use it in that period."

"Right…."

"Anyway," said the young officer, brushing a stray hair away from her face. "As far as we could see, nearly all of this drug was bought by hospitals and dental clinics. We've been checking their records as well. But we found a few cases where the drug was not delivered to a hospital or clinic when we went through the company's delivery records. Three, in fact. Two of them were dentists. They had the drug delivered to their houses, rather than their clinics."

"OK. How come?" asked Yokota, who was beginning to wonder where this line of inquiry was going.

Ishibe produced another piece of documentation and put it on the desk.

"These are the two dentists," she said. "Both of them live in apartments above their clinics. So, for some reason, both these guys had the drug delivered to their homes, so maybe it was just for convenience if the clinic was closed or something. We decided it was not relevant, given the fact that they just walked downstairs to their clinic with it… but…"

"But?" asked Yokota.

"This guy…" the young woman pointed to the original document in the file, which Yokota picked up and read.

"Keisuke Inagawa. Dermatologist. Works at Kamakura Memorial Hospital… That's a big place. What about him?" asked Yokota, peering over the top of the paper at the young woman.

"This guy ordered the drug and had it delivered to his home."

Yokota sat up straight.

"You mean he ordered it *personally*? Not going through the hospital purchasing department?"

Ishibe nodded. "That's right."

"Interesting... anything else?"

Ishibe pointed to the address on the document.

"Is this his home address then?" asked Yokota.

Ishibe smiled and shook her head.

"No, it's not. We checked it out. It was his parent's home. They both passed away some years ago, but he is the registered owner of the property. He lives on the other side of town, near Kencho-ji temple. My folks also live in the same area."

Yokota rose slowly to his feet and leaned over the table.

"So you mean, he had this drug delivered to... what? An abandoned house?"

Yokota felt the blood begin to pound in his temples.

Ishibe nodded. "Yes. That's what I'm saying... the house is abandoned. But there is one more thing," she said with a triumphant little smile and tapped on the copy of the invoice with her pen.

"What?"

"Dermatologists... That's what my auntie does. She works at a hospital in Osaka. Anyway, I gave her a call. She told me there was no reason a dermatologist would use a blood flow inhibitor..."

Yokota was already dialing his boss on his mobile phone.

"Good work, Ishibe. Bloody good work!" he smiled.

The young woman beamed.

==================

Several days later, Yamashita and Yokota were waiting outside a large, detached house near Yuigahama beach, a seaside area in Kamakura that had grown in popularity over the years with younger families.

The beach had been a popular place to visit since the Meiji period over a hundred years earlier and faced out into the broad Sagami Bay. It was a long, sandy beach and was popular not only as a safe place for children to swim but also for surfers, and there were several shops to assist people wanting to take lessons and rent wetsuits and equipment in what was a kind of boom sport in Japan recently, especially since it had been showcased in the 2020 Tokyo Olympics.

That afternoon, a little bit away from the beach, the two detectives waited in their car in a quiet little street full of older homes, several of which had unkempt gardens, their shutters down across the windows, and their letter boxes covered in tape, which generally meant the properties were no longer lived in. This was an increasingly common sight across Japan these days, where the super-aged society had now arrived in force and where at least a third of the population was over sixty-five. The way property taxation worked in Japan meant that once the children inherited their parent's properties, it was often cheaper to keep the house shut up than to sell it. As there was almost no demand for old houses anyway, this meant that the *akiba,* or abandoned house problem, had mushroomed, not just in the rural areas but also in the big cities.

The previous afternoon after Yokota had informed his boss about Kyoko Ishibe's discoveries concerning the dermatologist named Inagawa, who was a respected member of the medical community by all accounts, there had been an explosion of activity at the station and also at the National Police Headquarters where the *Il Monstro* case taskforce was based. The decision had been made at higher levels that, at this point, Yamashita would head the investigation into the new lead, and they would be kept informed of how things developed. This news, of course, meant that the Kamakura police could, in effect, have the first real chance at catching a killer that every police entity in the country had been focusing on for decades. It was not a chance that they were going to take lightly, and they trusted Yamashita, who had a well-earned reputation as a safe pair of hands when it came to a major operation.

Discreet inquiries had been made with Inagawa's bosses at the hospital where he worked as the chief of the dermatology department, and a profile had been hastily put together as to the man they were interested in. Yamashita had, quite naturally, given the gravity of the case, decided to proceed with caution, and they had spent the next several days gathering information and quietly checking out his parent's old, abandoned house in Yuigahama from the outside and speaking to some of the neighbors by pretending they were updating the local fire control protocols. It was vital, Yamashita told his enthusiastic troops at a meeting that first evening, that nothing be done to spook their man, and to make sure that all their T's were crossed and I's dotted before they made any move.

The plan they had come up with was simple and, they hoped, benign-sounding enough that the suspect would both invite them into the house and allow them to look around, thus dispensing with the need to go to a judge and get a search warrant on the back of the quite flimsy 'evidence' of the invoice which Ishibe had tracked down. After all, there *could* be some perfectly legitimate reason for this doctor to have ordered the drugs, which as a medical professional he was legally entitled to do.

While they made their plans, two teams of officers were sent out to monitor Dr. Inagawa's activities as he went to and from his home to the hospital where he worked every day, and also to follow him wherever else he went. At night rotating teams of officers watched his home in the neighborhood of Kencho-ji temple, one of the oldest and most beautiful Zen Buddhist temples in the city, where he had an elegant, modern home with a large garden and lived alone, his wife having died some years before. He had no family, no children, and did not seem to have any hobbies, at least not any that took him outside the house. He did seem to be quite a fan of classical music though, and the officers staked out outside his house in an unmarked car often heard piano music in the quiet of the night coming from inside.

One other thing that did set alarm bells ringing down at police headquarters was the discovery that Inagawa, whose family originally hailed from Hokkaido in northern Japan, had inherited shares in a family business now run by his cousins - a fox farm in the town of Asahikawa that was now a popular tourist attraction.

Between this information and the invoice, and the fact that Inagawa was a doctor and the right age for their killer, facts which Yamashita was the first to admit was not something he would like to take in front of a judge, the investigation felt on slightly firmer ground.

On the eighth day of the stakeout, a Saturday morning when they had established that the doctor was at home, Yamashita ordered the first contact to be made.

A group of six officers on their task force gathered in the conference room on the fourth floor while Detective Sergeant Yokota, who had recently been nicknamed 'Detective Professor' since his impromptu history lesson to the *Il Monstro* task force a few weeks previously, made the call to the suspect's home, while Yamashita and the others listened in.

The phone rang for a short while, and then a pleasant-sounding voice on the other end picked up.

"Inagawa," the suspect said, his voice booming in the conference room where it was on speaker.

Yokota introduced himself as coming from the Kamakura police and asked if the doctor was the owner of the property at Yuigahama. There was a pause on the line, and the officers in the room looked at each other.

"Oh… yes. That was my parent's house. Is there some problem? It's been shut up for several years now…"

Yokota said there had been a report from some of the neighbors about a very bad smell coming from inside, and one of the outer doors appeared damaged.

"Damaged? Oh… I had no idea. A smell, you said?"

162

Yokota said there had been reports of homeless people breaking into houses in the area and living there. When was the last time the doctor visited the property?

Another long pause.

"Oh… that was some time ago, I'm afraid. I think maybe a year ago, actually… last summer," the voice continued.

Several of the officers looked up at this. The package of drugs had been delivered only four months prior, so it looked like they had caught their suspect in a lie.

Would the doctor come to the house so they could investigate and check that everything was all right?

Another long pause.

"Er, well… OK. I guess I could meet you there."

Yokota asked him if one o'clock that afternoon would be suitable and was told it was.

The moment he hung up the phone, there were shouts as a couple of the officers high-fived him, and Yamashita then made calls to the crew staking out the doctor's principal residence to be on alert for the suspect to move and to make sure they tailed him to Yuigahara at a distance. They were also to be on alert for the suspect to flee, so they had orders to watch for this, maintain a discreet tail, and call for backup if needed.

True to his word though, at 12:30 that afternoon, the doctor emerged from his house, and shortly afterward, his large black Mercedes Benz rolled out of the driveway. The two officers waiting further down the tree-lined street quietly pulled out and began to follow the car down the narrow streets, and there was a sigh of relief as it seemed that after a short while, the suspect was indeed heading toward the beach.

Yamashita and Yokota were already parked outside the house waiting, and a S.W.A.T. team and at least a dozen other officers were also on standby, parked in a side street further away.

"You know, I'm wondering how we explain the 'damage' I mentioned on the phone? I mean, there isn't any…" said Yokota, keeping his eyes fixed on the end of the street where they awaited the arrival of the black Mercedes.

Yamashita nodded grimly. "Well, we'll just say the neighbor must have made a mistake. Stuff happens. Let's just see what he does…."

A few minutes later, as the tension reached a fever pitch among the waiting police, the radio in Yamashita's car crackled.

"Approaching," the voice said, and a few seconds later, the black Mercedes with their suspect driving turned the corner and made its way slowly down the little street to where they were waiting. The two men watched as the big car glided past theirs and had their first chance to observe the driver in the flesh, a man whom they had only seen in photographs before.

"OK.," Yamashita whispered. "Let's do this."

They got out, and Yamashita gave the doctor a cheery wave as he parked his car behind their own.

Dr. Inagawa also got out of his car and smiled at the waiting officers.

He was a tall, thin man in his early sixties, casually dressed in a pair of beige corduroy pants, a checked shirt, and a light linen coat. He looked like any average man his age, with thinning grey hair and silver-framed glasses, and had a mild-mannered, slightly academic appearance that felt quite in tune with his profession. He gave Yamashita and Yokota a polite bow and immediately apologized for causing them trouble.

"You know, I should keep a closer eye on the place, but I don't know, somehow I never find the time. These old places are quite a hassle. A lot of people my age have them on their hands now... Anyway, I'm so sorry if this has caused you any inconvenience. Or the neighbors. You say there may've been a break-in?"

Yamashita nodded.

"Well, yes. We're sorry to trouble you too, *sensei*," said Yamashita, using the polite title. "It's probably nothing, but there have been reports of break-ins lately in this area. Sometimes even animals have gotten into these old places and died there. We've seen it many times, I'm afraid..."

Dr. Inagawa nodded, and Yokota gestured towards the house.

"Would you mind if we checked out the inside? Just to make sure?"

Inagawa shrugged. "Sure. Please go ahead. It's been empty for years, as I said. I have the key somewhere..." he reached into his pocket and extracted a set of keys on a large ring.

"This is it, I think..." he said, handing the key to Yokota.

Yokota inserted it into the lock, and the door opened at once. With Yokota in the lead and Yamashita in the rear following the doctor, they entered the house.

They were first greeted with an almost overpoweringly sweet stench of mold, which was extremely common in old houses in Japan, where the humid rainy season and hot summers caused it to spread rapidly, especially in old buildings that were locked up like this.

They made their way into the darkened living room and then the kitchen next to it on the ground floor, and Yokota found the breaker box on the kitchen wall and asked if the power was still on.

"Yes, I think so. Please go ahead," said the doctor accommodatingly.

The lights came on, and the detectives looked around the rooms on the lower floor and then went to the upstairs bedrooms, where all appeared to be in order.

"My wife and I arranged for the house to be emptied after my mother died," said Inagawa, looking around. "I think it was about eight years ago now, so there isn't much left here. Did you say there was some damage?" he asked, peering around the doorway of the main bedroom.

"Ah… yes. I think the neighbor did mention something like that. Maybe downstairs. Let's go and check it out, shall we?" said Yamashita. "Everything looks normal here."

The three of them went back downstairs, and both detectives thought that if the doctor was nervous, he certainly wasn't showing it.

They went to the back door, which opened onto the large garden to the rear of the house, and walked outside. The grass in the garden was higher than their knees.

"Oh… is that another part of the house?" asked Yokota, gesturing towards what looked like an adjoining building tacked onto the back of the house but with its own separate entrance.

Inagawa nodded. "Yes. That's where my father used to paint. He was an amateur artist. Landscapes mainly. Quite good. I have a number of his paintings at home. Like I said, though, it's empty now, we cleared that out too…"

Yamashita nodded amiably.

"Mind if we look inside? Maybe that's what your neighbor was referring to…"

Inagawa looked perplexed.

"Um… to tell the truth… I don't know if I have the key anymore… Maybe it's at my home?"

The doctor started going through the other keys on his big ring.

"I'm sorry. I don't think I have it…" he muttered after a while.

Yamashita nodded to Yokota, who put his hand on the door handle and tried it.

To their surprise, it opened.

"Oh… my goodness," said the doctor in a surprised tone. "That should be locked. I wonder how long it's been like that…" he said wonderingly, and pushed his glasses further up his nose with his finger.

Switching on his flashlight, which he had been carrying, Yokota stepped into the room, and the others followed him.

Yokota swung the light slowly around the room, which, like the rest of the house, had its storm shutters tightly drawn so it was almost pitch-black inside, but

Yamashita quickly located the light switch on the wall next to the door and flooded the room with light. As he turned, he heard Yokota swear under his breath.

The room was anything but empty.

Shelves full of various bottles and jars and medical equipment ran all around the room, which at its center had a large surgical table of the type seen in operating rooms and from which hung various kinds of restraints used to bind a patient to prevent movement. Above the table was a moveable galley of surgical lights that could be swung into place like in most large hospitals. Next to the table was a tray of quite new-looking surgical tools, including a row of razor-sharp scalpels and other medical equipment, and another tray of syringes and a box of needles in their small plastic containers.

There was also significant blood spatter on the floor and on the walls, where their attention was drawn to a large cork bulletin board with rows of Polaroid pictures of what, at first glance, looked like patients that had been strapped to the table.

In the corner of the room was a large open garbage bin full of bloody cloth swabs, used green disposable surgical gloves, and other medical detritus awaiting disposal.

Yokota and Yamashita turned to the doctor, who was standing open-mouthed in what looked like amazement.

"Well, doctor. Looks like you missed a few spots," said Yamashita in an even voice.

The doctor started to stammer something incoherent, and Yokota turned and took him firmly by the arm.

"I think we can finish this discussion at the police station, don't you, doctor? Please just come with us for now."

The older man looked wildly around him, and then seemed to simply fold like a rag doll and let himself be escorted back outside and placed in the waiting police car without a further word being uttered or even the slightest hint of objection, almost like it had been something he had been expecting.

Yamashita followed them outside and swiftly made a call to the waiting head of the tactical unit.

"You guys can stand down, we have the suspect in custody. Get Morita-san to cordon off the house and have forensics meet me here ASAP. They are going to have a long couple of days…"

Chapter 12.

They All Make Mistakes

For the police involved in the arrest of Dr. Inagawa and his '*Il Monstro's* House of Horrors' as the Japanese media quickly dubbed it, the next few weeks were probably the most intense that any of them had ever experienced, and this was doubly so for Chief Inspector Yamashita and his staff, who found themselves at the center of a media firestorm the like of which they had never seen before.

The usually quiet little headquarters of the Kamakura police, a non-descript and aging building situated near Kamakura station, was now thronged by a veritable army of media vehicles, with reporters of every stripe from Japan and abroad milling around it hoping for even the faintest titbit of information. Another even larger horde had amassed itself in the streets bordering the crime scene, where they waited day and night outside the cordoned-off area, much to the annoyance of the local residents.

Following a press conference a few days after the arrest given by Yamashita and Chief Superintendent Tomaki, where Yamashita had spoken for a full fifty-seven seconds (somebody timed him) and then left without answering a single question, no further information was released.

A suspect was in custody.

Investigations were proceeding.

No, that was all.

Ten days later, at a similarly truncated press conference attended by hundreds of reporters in the largest room they could find, it was announced that Dr. Keisuke Inagawa had indeed now been charged with the three most recent murders in Kamakura and Tokyo.

Once again, investigations were proceeding.

No, he had nothing further to add.

Were more charges about to be laid? Was it true the doctor was *Il Monstro*?

Sorry, no comment.

Amid much screaming about 'the public's right to know' and outrage from the Fifth Estate, after a few weeks, the inevitable happened. The throngs of reporters began to dissolve like the morning mist, moved on to the next piece of 'news' by their sensation-ravenous bosses. After three weeks, only a few reporters and the odd photographer still hung around the parking garage in front of the police station.

Inside, Yamashita and his team proceeded to do exactly what they said they would do: investigate.

However, even the old veteran, dedicated as he was, found he could no longer refuse the temptation of a decent meal with his friends and finally accepted a repeated invitation from Ran Maeda to his house, which was as much to thank them all for their help as to enjoy some pleasant company and to have a rare few hours off.

And he found now that he wanted someone to talk to, and he was sure Penelope would be there.

On his arrival at Ran's old family home, it was Penelope herself who opened the door.

"Well now," she said as if he were one of her errant students, "It seems you are not just a figment of my imagination, Eiji. I was beginning to think you were. Since you never seem to answer my texts these days…"

She was elegantly dressed tonight in a dark blue one-piece dress with a pearl necklace and even had her shoulder-length blonde hair swept up and pinned with an antique lacquer comb which he had never seen before but decided he liked. She waved him into the house, where his old friends gave him a friendly and suitably low-key greeting.

Sal Nakamura was, as ever, propped against the kitchen counter with a bottle of beer in his hand, with Fei sitting next to him, while Ran busied himself behind them with the oven. He had been expecting Sal to be there as he knew that their publisher had now commissioned him and Ran to produce a sequel to their best-selling book on *Il Monstro*, and he was happy as always to talk about it with people that really knew the case well.

"You're late, Eiji… but I forgive you," Ran smiled as he advanced upon Yamashita and pushed a glass of red wine into his hands.

"Ah… I need this…" said Yamashita as he threw his jacket on the sofa and clinked glasses with them all.

"So… how are things?" asked Sal, as he rolled one of his perennial cigarettes. "And none of this 'no comment' stuff here, please… Maeda and I have a book to write, you know."

172

"Oh, God. Is that why you invited me?" he grinned.

"In part. In part…," said Ran. "You have to sing for your supper now. C'mon. Have a seat…" he directed Yamashita to the sofa where Penelope was already waiting with a glass of white wine in her hand.

"So… tell us. Are you sure it's him? I guess you must be. After all, he's been charged. Why didn't you charge him with the other four, however? That's what I'm wondering. Or is that coming down the line later?" Sal said, wagging his bottle of Czech beer at the policeman.

Penelope gave Sal a stern look.

"Let the man draw breath, Sal. He's just walked in the door."

Sal laughed. "What do you want me to do? Wait until after dessert? No rest for the wicked now, Eiji…"

Yamashita shrugged and patted Penelope on the hand. "It's OK. It would be good to discuss a few things with you folk, who are not just thinking about the case from a police point of view…. And you were all very helpful, you know. Anyway… to answer your question, the truth is that we are still working on the other four. Well, at least I am. Everyone else I know just wants to charge the guy with every unsolved case for the last thirty years. But the way things stand, I would say it's pretty likely that in the end he'll be charged with the others… the evidence does seem pretty compelling," said Yamashita.

Penelope threw him a serious look and placed her hand on his.

"Are you saying you found evidence about…." she let the unfinished sentence hang in the air.

Yamashita patted her hand, understanding she was thinking about Hiro Yamana, the first of the killings, so long ago.

He looked up into her eyes briefly and nodded.

"Yes. Including that…" he said quietly,

Penelope hung her head, and Yamashita felt her shudder. She quietly got up and went to the window momentarily, and Fei, noticing this, followed her.

Ran and Sal watched the women standing quietly together on the other side of the room for a moment.

"You're that sure?" asked Ran quietly.

Yamashita looked at the two men.

"Yeah… the evidence is there. I have to admit…"

Ran sat down next to him as Penelope, who had gathered herself now, and Fei rejoined the others.

"What kind of evidence are you talking about, Eiji?" asked Ran, nudging his old friend's knee.

Yamashita smiled and looked up. Something in his eyes seemed to be hesitating for a moment, like a diver contemplating his jump into the air.

"I know that look," said Penelope, returning to the sofa.

"Me too," added Fei. "That's the 'I'm not sure' look.

Sal raised an eyebrow.

"I thought you said the evidence is there?" he asked.

Yamashita paused and leaned back into the comfortable leather sofa with one hand behind his head, and the others waited for him to answer.

"There *is* physical evidence in Inagawa's parent's house linking the room we found to the last three victims, in fact, to all the killings," he began. "The Hachimangu shrine case, the killing of the engineer from ProSec, and the Imperial Palace case... They were either killed there, or their bodies were prepared for display there after their deaths," he said, raising his eyes and looking at them all. "Blood. DNA. Even photographs. It's incontrovertible. It looks like all of these victims were killed in that room. Probably tortured and drugged there. And, despite his protestations to the contrary, there is evidence that he was also in that room. There are surgical gloves with his fingerprints and other items with his DNA on them. So, we can place both the victims and Inagawa in that room. That's why he has been charged with those three killings."

"Wow..." said Sal. "Looks pretty damning for him. But... he hasn't confessed?"

Yamashita shook his head. "No, he hasn't. He keeps saying he hasn't been in the house for at least a year."

Ran shook his head. "Well... that's hardly going to fly, is it?"

Yamashita gave him a grim smile.

"What about... the other four, though?" asked Penelope, who was now sitting on the sofa next to Sal, facing the Chief Inspector. "You said you found evidence of them, too, though?"

Yamashita nodded. "Yes. We found a box of 'trophies' hidden in his bedroom at his main house. It had personal items from the other victims and things related to their killings."

"You found something belonging to Hiro?" she asked quietly.

"Yes. He had his wallet... remember, we never found that? And also his camera, which had pictures... of the shrine he visited. Pictures of you too..."

Penelope went white and looked away. Sal reached over and put his hand comfortingly around her shoulders.

"Jesus," said Fei. "What else was there?"

Yamashita sighed.

"There were similar items taken from the other victims in Kyoto, Nara, and Tokyo. We don't have Inagawa's DNA and prints on everything in the box, but we do have positive IDs from relatives of the deceased. And there were other things... even more damning, I guess."

Penelope looked up at him, and he could see the anger rising in her.

"You found the fox fur, didn't you... The fur that comes from only one fox... like you told Machiko..."

Yamashita nodded. "And the crow feathers. Also a DNA match to some of the other feathers. He kept them in the same box with the other trophies."

There was absolute silence in the room, and Yamashita reached over to his glass of wine and finished it in one draught.

Sal slapped his knee and stood up to get more wine from the open bottle on the kitchen island.

"What a ... monster..." he said quietly.

Ran nodded. "He does rather live up to his moniker, doesn't he..."

Yamashita sat back and accepted another glass of wine from Sal.

"Maybe..." he said. "That's certainly the conclusion everybody has drawn..."

Ran gave his old school friend a sideways look, and Fei sighed audibly from her stool in the kitchen.

"Here we go… "she said with a sad look. "The chief inspector here, whom I know well, by the way, is not telling us something."

Yamashita smiled at her, and Penelope leaned forward.

"Fei's right. And I know what it is too…" she said with a piercing look. "It's the drugs, isn't it? Or, to be more precise… it's the mistake with the drugs…"

Yamashita felt a chill run through him at just how sharp this woman was, and how closely they seemed to think about things.

He looked at them all calmly. "If you people breathe this to anyone…"

"Don't be ridiculous, Eiji. What's all this about the drugs? That led you straight to him. I heard that from Yokota," said Fei. "The whole station knows it… Don't forget, I work there too…" said Fei.

Yamashita nodded. "Yeah, I know. That's just the point. He ordered a drug, a rare one. A drug no one in the dermatological profession uses. He had that drug delivered to his parent's abandoned house, where he used it on his victims…"

Penelope looked up at him.

"He didn't have to do that," she said quietly.

Yamashita shook his head. "No, he didn't have to do that…. He had access to a hospital where he could have just taken it with no one noticing, especially as he knew their inventory systems. He didn't do that. He didn't even have to *use* that particular drug, the hospital several others more suited to his purpose."

He looked about the room at their expectant faces and then directly at Penelope.

"But he didn't," she said again in a matter-of-fact tone, taking a sip of wine herself.

Yamashita shook his head and sighed.

"No. He didn't."

He stared into his wine glass. "He made a mistake," he said.

"One that led you to him, though," said Sal brightening, and Penelope gave him a withering look like he was a child who had just spilled his drink.

"That's the point, Sal. He made a mistake," she said, patting him on the knee. "He made a mistake that led us straight to him. Don't you see?"

Sal looked around at the others, confused.

"So? He made a mistake. I thought all criminals made mistakes. That's what Sherlock over here and his friends are always saying, anyway...." he said, nodding towards the chief inspector.

"Yeah... I know. That's what we police always say," said Yamashita. "You're right."

Penelope smiled and shook her head.

"Look, Sal. Unless I am totally wrong, here's the thing that's keeping Eiji here awake at night. Has this guy *ever* made a mistake? In the *last thirty years*, ever since he started killing?"

"Well, there's always a first time... after all," said Ran, walking over to the kitchen to check on the food. "It's true. Killers make mistakes. And sometimes, they even do it on purpose. To challenge the police, or just because they've had enough and want to get caught...

there's plenty of precedent with serial killers doing that sort of thing in the US especially…"

"That's true," said Yamashita quietly. "But…"

"But…" echoed Fei.

"But… this guy doesn't do that," said Penelope in a quiet yet firm voice. "He just doesn't make mistakes. Especially mistakes as basic as this one."

Yamashita nodded. "Yep. And that's the problem… she's right."

Penelope nodded at him. "That is indeed the problem… Tell me one thing, Eiji. The good doctor you have banged up in the Kamakura nick. He hasn't confessed, has he? Even when confronted with all the evidence. And he has no alibi, right? For the dates and times of the killings?"

Yamashita shook his head.

"Nope. He has no alibi for any of the killings. He was either at home alone, or nobody knows because it was too long ago. If he *was* set up, then the planning for this could go back a long way. Decades even."

"But didn't you just say you can put him in that room? The room where he killed the victims?" asked Fei.

Yamashita wagged a finger at her. "Not so fast, my learned friend. I can put *his DNA* in that room. For example, it's on the surgical gloves that we found. It's on other things in the room too. Furniture and the like. But remember, he grew up in that house. His prints are everywhere. The fact that the gloves are there does not mean *he* was there. He uses the same gloves at his hospital. What if someone…"

"Oh, c'mon Eiji…" said Fei. "And the box of trophies? What about that?"

Yamashita nodded. "I know. What about that... it's just so damning. I know. There was DNA, prints, hair... He claims the box was left outside his door a week ago and that he opened it and handled some of the items, but had no idea what they were or who they came from."

Yamashita sighed and stared at the carpet. "You know, I've been chasing this guy for so long. My whole career, as a matter of fact. Following him around Japan. Reading all the reports. Talking to witnesses. Watching him kill, again and again. Always telling his story with each kill. And I kind of feel... I know him. I know who he is... I know what kind of person he is...."

"Go on..." said Sal. "What kind of person is he, then?"

After a brief pause, Penelope answered for him.

"He's a narcissist. A very smart, very bright narcissist. An artist..."

Yamashita was nodding as she spoke.

"That's exactly right. And I've dealt with these kinds of people before. When you catch them, they don't deny it. They *never* deny it. They can't wait to tell you about it. To rub your face in how long it took you to catch them. He's never done that. In fact, he seems horrified by the whole thing."

Fei shook her head.

"That doesn't mean a thing, Eiji. Jail is full of people who will tell you they didn't do it when they did and vice versa. You should just stick to the evidence, in my opinion. This is just barking up the wrong tree..."

"I have always thought Eiji was in the wrong job," said Ran, rejoining them. "He should have been a defense attorney. Dinner is served, folks."

They all stood and moved to the dining table, which was elegantly set with a starched linen cloth and Ran's best antique French cutlery. Ran lit some candles in two large silver candleholders and dimmed the lights as he brought out the first course.

"An amuse-bouche…" he smiled as he served the food, and Yamashita saw Penelope shoot him a look of real affection which he hadn't noted before, almost like they were a couple.

In fact, they looked exactly like a couple.

She sat beside him, and he poured her another glass of wine.

As they began to eat, Penelope looked over at Yamashita and smiled, and the chief inspector, ever observant, noted a happiness about her that was not usually there. Perhaps, he thought, the capture of this man had finally given her some peace and enabled her to move on.

But then she said something that made him wonder if that was the case.

"You know, Eiji, there is one other mystery about this case that I would like solved. I'm talking about Hiro now. There was always one thing I've wondered about…"

"What's that," said Sal, leaning over and taking some fresh herb bread from a silver bowl in the middle of the table.

Penelope looked at the policeman.

"Who was the girl with him?"

The silence that followed made everyone feel like they had just walked over someone's grave.

Chapter 13.

The Fox Spirit

As the detention of Dr. Inagawa entered its third month, and the police continued to slowly build their case against him, Penelope received a phone call from her friend Machiko, whom she had not seen since their talk with the chief inspector, and where they had spent the evening discussing old Japanese folklore, on which subject Machiko was probably one of the country's leading experts.

Unfortunately, even after they had both been deluged under Machiko's usual torrent of academic and anecdotal information on *tengu*, fox spirits, and all their spooky friends, almost nothing she had told them had proved of any use at all. Still, Machiko was a warm and very engaged friend, and Penelope had always welcomed her wise and down-to-earth council over the years on any number of other matters.

As usual, her voice thundered down the telephone that morning.

"Well darling, guess what? It's taken me a while, but I think I've managed it.... Are you free tomorrow night?"

Penelope, who had been watching the usual rather tedious NHK evening news program with Fei, wandered into the next room so their conversation would not annoy her guest.

"Sorry, Machiko. What have you managed?" she asked, somewhat perplexed.

There was a pause, and then her friend continued.

"To find a link. You remember?"

Penelope still had no idea what she was talking about.

"A link?"

"Yes, silly, don't you remember? The crow *tengu*? Foxes? I found one. That's what you pair wanted to know, right? I told you I didn't know of any off-hand, but I've stumbled on one. A very old story. Do you want to see it?"

Penelope, who had more or less completely forgotten their former conversation, now remembered that Machiko had sworn to continue her investigations and let them know if she found anything, which it now seemed she had.

"See what? Is it a movie?" asked Penelope.

"No, of course not. It's a *noh* play. At the National *Noh* Theatre. If I book now, I can get us tickets."

Like most people did when invited to a *noh* play, which was usually a very long and quite incomprehensible stage drama from several hundred years before, Penelope hesitated.

"It's very simple dear," Machiko continued. "This play has been rarely performed. And I mean *very* rarely. But it is the only version of the story I have been able to find, and so I am kind of interested. I thought you would be too…"

Penelope pulled herself together and realized that she was being rude.

"Oh, of course," she said quickly. "Sorry, you just kind of caught me off guard. Yes, let's go. It sounds interesting. Maybe it'll shed some light on things. By the way, what's it called?"

"It's called *Kitsune no Sei*. 'The Fox Spirit.'"

"Oh! Well, that does sound like it might be useful, I guess…" Penelope lied.

And so it was that after a long conversation that veered onto several other topics, they made arrangements to meet the following evening at a restaurant near the theatre in Tokyo's old Sendagaya district, not far from the busy Shinjuku area where they could have an early dinner and still get to the play on time.

Early the following evening, Penelope entered the little French brasserie that Machiko had selected, and as she pushed open the door immediately saw her friend waving at her from the back of the restaurant.

They ordered a set course, and as the waiter was pouring the wine, Penelope was given the full story about what they were going to see. Machiko, for her part, was in her element, as she was a great fan of traditional Japanese stage drama like *kabuki* and its much older cousin *noh*, and frequently went to the theatre with her friends and her husband, who was also a Japanese history buff.

"It was Yasu who told me about this," she said, referring to her spouse. "Apparently, it was his friend who found it. It's very exciting, actually."

Penelope found she was often exhausted after an evening with Machiko, mainly because of her habit of starting a story halfway through and assuming you were up to speed when, of course, you weren't and had no idea what she was on about.

"Sorry... found what? Who is Yasu's friend?"

Machiko rolled her eyes, and Penelope wondered if she left her university students as confused as her friends. She had a feeling she did.

"This play, of course. I told you, it's only recently been rediscovered. This is the first performance of it since the early seventeenth century! And it was Yasu's friend, Professor Suzuki, over at Waseda University, that found it. The only remaining copy of it. It was in the rare book collection in some library in Osaka, and it had been mislabeled back in the Meiji period or something as a different play. We had dinner with him recently, and he was telling us about it, and that's when I thought of you and your policeman friend. How is he, by the way? Such a nice man... are you going out with him?"

Penelope wondered what it must be like for her husband to be married to Machiko, and concluded that it was probably quite consuming. Tonight though, she looked as pleased as if she had found the manuscript herself.

"Well, that's wonderful. Thanks for the invitation. So... what's it about then?" she said, adroitly sidestepping the subject of her love life.

Machiko drained her glass of wine and ordered a carafe of the same, and Penelope remembered that she was probably the strongest drinker of all her friends, including Fei, who was certainly no slouch when it came to *sake*.

Machiko launched into her theme.

"Yes, Yasu managed to get me the synopsis. Here, I made you a copy," she pulled a few pages of closely typed foolscap from her voluminous black leather bag and passed them to Penelope.

"It's a very old story that allegedly occurred in the early Kamakura period, in the twelfth century. The story was part of a collection originally called the *Nishinokai Monogatari* for short, or 'Tales from the Western Sea' because it featured many stories from places on the Sea of Japan. Anyway, this particular story was made into a play sometime in the sixteenth century, and then it kind of faded from view and stopped being performed, and then, of course, it got lost, so… anyway. The original story is about a wealthy family in Kanazawa."

"Kanazawa?" said Penelope. She suddenly wondered if Ran was aware of it, as the great prefecture of Kanazawa on the western coast of Japan had been his family's hereditary fiefdom for hundreds of years.

"Yes. Anyway," Machiko plowed on. "The story goes that the family's eldest son, the heir to the family line, fell in love with a woman he met while he was out hunting one day, who was actually a fox spirit. You know, foxes often impersonated beautiful women. Anyway, the son was so enamored of her that he married her without the consent of his family. This enraged the family, who thought it was an inauspicious match. Of course, none of them had any idea that she was a fox, which I imagine might have complicated things as well…. So while the husband was away in Kyoto attending the emperor, the

186

family arranged an autumn leaf viewing party for her and her ladies at a famous spot deep in the forests of Kanazawa, where they were attacked by a group of men, who were all retainers of the groom's father. The other ladies all died, but their target, the bride, transformed into a fox and ran away. She ran from the lord's men for a night and a day, and then one of the retainers managed to shoot her dead with an arrow. And then, when her husband heard what had happened to her, he was so overcome with grief that he committed suicide. And now… the good part…"

Penelope was all ears.

"Which is?"

Machiko smiled. "She reappears with her husband, who is now transformed into an avenging crow *tengu*. And one by one, the pair of them hunt down the men and kill them. Very satisfying, don't you think? And more than anything else, dear, it's the *only* instance in Japanese literature I can find where the fox spirit and the crow *tengu* hunt together. The *only* one. So, I think that's quite fascinating, especially as you had specifically mentioned it, you know, in connection to *Il Monstro*. So pleased they caught that man, by the way. I heard our friend Yamashita was instrumental in that, too? You must be so proud of him."

Penelope took a sip of her wine and gave her attention to the very nice-looking plate of escargot which had just arrived.

"Yes, very pleased for him. It's a relief, I'm sure."

"I'm sure it must be…" said Machiko, giving her a sideways look, that clearly implied she was waiting for more information about their relationship, which Penelope did her best to ignore.

They finished their meal and headed for the theatre, where the play was just beginning, and took their seats. Fortunately, given that the language of most *noh* plays was an ancient form of Japanese that baffled even Penelope, there was a simultaneous electronic translation running on a small screen in front of their seats so that people could follow along with the story. A *noh* play can often run for several hours, but to Penelope's relief, this play was quite fast-moving and action-filled and only lasted a few hours. The plot was complicated, as was the language, but it was fairly easy even for a non-expert to understand.

As she watched, though, her thoughts naturally went to Ran Maeda. Even though there was no name given to the 'illustrious family' of the man who had married his fox sweetheart against their wishes, it was quite clear it was an important one, and so she found herself wondering if the story was not actually referring to the Maeda clan, Ran's ancestors and the hereditary feudal lords of Kanazawa. On the other hand, these types of *yokai* or ghost stories which were exceedingly common in western Japan often mentioned famous names and families where in reality, there was no connection whatsoever, simply because they were well-known. There was even, somewhat coincidentally, an attacker named 'Ina' in the story, which reminded Penelope of the murderous doctor, now sweating in his cell back in Kamakura. And the play itself had been violent as well, so full of death as the two supernatural beings tracked down the bandits who had attacked the fox spirit and caused her death. One by one, they met their bloody ends in different ways, always at the hand of the crow-*tengu*, who killed them as his wife looked on with a vengeful smile on her fox mask, which Penelope found quite chilling.

"My God," said Penelope as they exited the theatre and re-emerged into the cool night air outside. "That was quite something. I don't think I've seen a *noh* play before with so many killings. It was more like *kabuki* or one of those tv murder dramas. I'm surprised there is anyone left in Kanazawa after all that…"

Machiko laughed. "Yeah, it was pretty heavy on the gore. But interesting, don't you think? You know, we are the first people to see that play performed again for nearly four hundred years! I think that calls for a drink, don't you?"

They were just approaching Sendagaya station, and Machiko wasted no time dragging Penelope into the nearest *izakaya* bar where she could indulge her predilection for *sake*, a taste she shared with Fei. They were soon joined at the bar by several other people who looked like they had also just come from the theatre, some of whom were still clutching their programs, which were emblazoned with a dramatic black and white photograph of the crow-*tengu* mask and the fox mask side by side, as all actors in *noh* plays never showed their true faces and were always masked.

As the *sake* and a plate of octopus *sashimi* and *edamame* arrived, Penelope listened to her friend launch into a long story about one of their old colleagues at Hassei, whom both of them particularly disliked, who had been disciplined for engaging in an affair with one of his students. However, as Machiko talked on, and the effects of the *sake* became more pronounced, an idea floated to the front of Penelope's mind.

"By the way," she asked. Did you say there is an *older* story? You know… One the play was based on?" she asked.

Machiko refilled her little pottery *ochoko* glass, drained it in one hit, and looked up at the ceiling, trying to remember.

"Yes… er. I think it was in that old collection I mentioned, the *Nishinokai*. I may even have it at home somewhere. Or Yasu has it. I'll ask him. I know Professor Suzuki has a copy anyway… He knows the background. Why? Do you want to read it?"

Penelope leaned forward and refilled her friend's glass again.

"Actually, yes. Yes. I do…" she smiled.

Something, the very faintest whisper in the back of her mind, was attempting to take shape. She had no idea what it really was… but it was there nevertheless, and she decided that it wouldn't hurt to follow up on it.

As Penelope and Machiko were enjoying their drinks in the bar, some miles away, a telephone rang.

It was an old black bakelite telephone, and it was ringing on a small table in the hallway of an old wooden house in the same quiet street in Kamakura as the murders had taken place.

And at last, when it was finally answered, the case against the incarcerated Dr. Inagawa suddenly began to take a very dramatic turn all of its own.

==================

Yokota had been working late that night, following up on a list of statements from the residents in the neighborhood around Dr. Inagawa's parent's home, the abandoned house he had used for the killings. Nearly all of the neighbors had been visited and provided statements to the police, and none of these contained any useful information whatsoever. Still, Yokota was nothing if not as meticulous as his boss and was not going to leave any stone unturned when it came to this or any other case he worked on.

There had been one neighbor particularly, an elderly man who lived just opposite their crime scene, whom they had been unable to talk to as he had been overseas on an extended holiday in Europe. One of Yokota's young officers had finally tracked down the man's daughter in Chiba city to the west of Tokyo, who had informed them that her father would be returning very soon, and passed this information along to his boss in the form of a note that he had appended to their file of witness statements.

On the off chance that the man had finally returned from his travels, Yokota had decided it might be worthwhile to call and find out.

The phone had rung and rung, and he was just about to hang up when a voice answered.

"Osaki,"

"Osaki Jiro san?"

"Yes."

"Ah… I'm glad to be able to talk to you, sir. This is Detective Sergeant Yokota, from the Kamakura police…"

There was a long pause.

"The police?" said the startled voice.

"Yes, sir."

There was silence for a moment again.

"Is this about what happened over the road?"

Yokota was used to people reacting like this, as most people in Japan never had contact with the police other than to ask someone at the local corner *koban* for directions somewhere. They certainly were not used to having a murder committed across the road from where they lived and having to be part of a police investigation.

Yokota explained the reason for his call, and asked if it would be possible to come and get a statement. Would tomorrow morning be all right?

After a little pushing, Osaki-san finally agreed, and they made a time to meet the next day.

Yokota, with Detective Constable Ishibe by his side, duly arrived at the stroke of ten o'clock the following day and rang the bell of the old house, where they were soon greeted by Osaki, who looked like he had just gotten out of bed.

"Oh… hello," he said, opening the door and clearly not intending to invite them inside.

Osaki san was in his mid-eighties, thin and balding with a comb-over and wearing an old blue denim shirt and a somewhat ill-fitting pair of jeans, which looked like they were just about to slide off his bony frame.

Yokota and Ishibe introduced themselves and informed him they were there to gather witness statements from all the neighbors about any activity they had seen at the house opposite his own, which had been the scene of the recent murders.

"Oh… I thought it might be about that. Yes… dreadful business…" he said, scratching his head and looking over the low wall in front of his own house at the house of Inagawa's parents, which it faced. "Yeah. I knew the family quite well… you know. In the old days. Old Inagawa, the father, and I were quite friendly. Sometimes we went to the baseball together in Yokohama. He was a big Swallows fan, I remember. I always preferred the Tigers myself, but…"

"What about the son? Dr. Inagawa? Did you know him?"

Osaki gave them a vague look.

"The son? No, not really. By the time we moved here, he had grown up and left. We saw him around occasionally, you know, at New Year and such, he used to visit his parents now and again. His old man used to tell me he was pretty busy, being a doctor and all that. Of course, they locked up the house after the parents died, so I didn't see him again. That's what people do these days. When you get old like me… I guess my kids will do the same with this place. You can't sell these old homes. No one wants them…."

Yokota nodded, and Ishibe wrote some notes in her little black notebook. They talked for a few more minutes, and Osaki said that he had been overseas visiting his sister in Italy for the last several months, and so he hadn't been around when all the drama had happened.

"Just my luck, you know. Nothing much ever happens around here. And when it does, I'm away.... Typical," he smiled. "Anyway, sorry I can't be of much use."

Yokota and Ishibe both bowed and thanked him for his time, and had turned to leave when they heard the old man cough as if to draw their attention.

"You know, I guess you could talk to the builders, they were in and out. I suppose you have. Sorry…"

Yokota and his young constable both turned on their heels and looked at the old man just as he was about to close the door.

"The builders?" asked Yokota.

Osaki nodded.

"What builders?"

Osaki paused and looked at them oddly.

"Well… The builders. You know. Didn't anyone mention them? I guess they were builders anyway. Maybe Inagawa was getting some work done on the place. I don't know."

Yokota stared intensely at the man.

'You mean you saw people in the house? When was this?"

Osaki scratched his head. "Er… I'm not sure. They were in and out, like I said. It was a while ago, before I went overseas. I never saw anyone, but a black van was parked outside sometimes. It looked like a workman's van, you know the type. I never saw the driver or anyone, but they were obviously doing something inside…"

Yokota and Ishibe exchanged glances.

"Sir, I'm very sorry about this, but we need to talk to you. At the station. Now."

And with that simple statement, the case against Dr. Inagawa, once thought so airtight, began to slowly evaporate right in front of the bewildered eyes of both the police and the prosecutors.

Chapter 14.

Square One

The woman, who liked to be known as Vivien, appeared more and more agitated as the day wore on, but this was something the staff at the sanatorium expected.

It was, after all, a Thursday, and Vivien always interacted tensely with others on that day. She would sometimes refuse to eat, bite her nails or just stand outside looking at the high walls of the garden, like she could see through them. Sometimes the staff reported her slowly wringing her hands as if she were in some extreme state of mental anguish. On other days she would repeatedly change her clothes or comb her long white hair for hours.

It was always when she was expecting a visit from her doctor, something that seemed to weigh on her mind all week, the expectation and the agitation increasing gradually as the day drew closer. The staff had even taken to telling her doctor that it would be best if he visited in the mornings so she would not have so long to wait, and indeed he usually tried to do that.

Today, however, he was late, and Vivien had been wandering the gardens as she sometimes did, talking softly to herself. The staff nurse on duty was relieved to see him approaching the recreation room when he finally arrived a little after 3 p.m., and she watched as the woman came towards him from across the lawn with her soft smile and saw them sit together in their usual place on the sunny terrace overlooking the gardens.

The moment she saw him, she would noticeably calm down, like she had just been given one of the powerful narcotics the sanatorium used with its other patients.

The staff thought she needed routine, as many of their patients did, to see the world in a non-threatening way, but this wasn't true in her case.

She just needed to see him, to know that he was still there.

She needn't have worried, however.

Today Ran found her, as always, neatly dressed and showing no signs of undue stress. He found this comforting and took solace in the tidiness of her appearance, the soft beauty of her slender form in the ankle-length navy dress she was wearing today, and the carefully applied makeup. He knew she made an effort for his visits, and so he rarely, if ever, disappointed her. And even though her wealthy family provided for all her needs and more, he sometimes bought clothes for her or gave her other occasional gifts. The dress she wore today, which suited her so well, was one of these. He knew also that she had worn it just for him, as she always did when he had given her something.

"Hello, Vivien," he said gently as he sat in the comfortable wicker chair beside her. "How is Caesar? Or have you finished with him?"

Vivien turned her head and smiled, fixing him momentarily with her beautiful eyes. Then she looked away over the garden again.

"Caesar's gone to Gaul again, I think," she said happily. "Or perhaps to Britain. I guess there are plenty of things to burn and pillage there. Do you know he once enslaved whole nations?"

Ran smiled at her. "So I've heard. But the numbers are perhaps a little exaggerated." Ran, being well-versed in classical literature, was quite familiar with *De Belli Gallica*, as he was in so many areas.

Vivien continued to stare out over the gardens, and her eyes seemed to follow the flight of a crow as it crossed the horizon of the high wall. Ran watched it with her.

"Four hundred and thirty-thousand of one nation he decided to wipe out. Four hundred and thirty-thousand! He enslaved them all. It does sound like a bit of an exaggeration, though, I'll give you that," she said with a slow smile, and drew her legs up underneath her on her big wicker chair.

"We all exaggerate at times," said Maeda mildly.

Vivien nodded and looked at him carefully again.

"Would you like to be enslaved, Dr. Maeda?" she smiled, tilting her head.

Maeda stared at her. He was used to her odd questions, though.

"I think I would quite like it, actually," she said, without waiting for his answer. "You know, being someone's slave. As long as I liked them, of course. Being around them all the time. Looking after them... Yes. That could be quite nice."

"I guess when you put it like that, yes, I can see the plus side to it," said Maeda, casting a quick glance down at her file and noticing her medications seemed normal.

"How about if I was *your* slave, Dr. Maeda? Would you treat me well? Not beat me?"

She stared at him again, and Maeda felt like he was pinned against his chair like a butterfly in a specimen box.

"Of course, Vivien. We are old friends. And I never beat my slaves," he quipped.

Vivien nodded and gave the briefest of smiles.

"Yes, we are, aren't we... old, old friends. Do you still play the piano, doctor?"

Maeda started. This was a very old memory, obviously. An image she had never talked about before and something he had no idea she was still aware of. Was she starting to remember things? The subconscious mind never forgets anything, he reminded himself.

"Yes, Vivien-san. I do, actually. I like to play..."

Vivien smiled again and looked at her hands, which lay folded neatly in her lap.

"Vivien-*san*... that sounds strange when you mix the English with the Japanese like that..." she gave a little sigh.

"You know... I think I played something once...Yes, I know I did. I can feel it sometimes... here..." she said quietly, and held up her left hand and wiggled her fingers like she was touching an imaginary fretboard.

Maeda leaned forward. "Do you remember what it was you played?" Maeda, of course, knew exactly what instrument she had played, but waited to see if she remembered it unprompted.

Vivien was silent for a long minute, and then shook her head. A strand of long blonde hair ran along her cheek like a tear.

"I remember a big forest. And tall trees. Maple trees. They were beautiful... Do you remember? I wasn't like this then... was I? Were you with me? No... you were away that day."

Ran could tell she was struggling with a cascade of memories that she could not separate.

He sighed deeply and reached across to take her hand.

"The maples were very beautiful. Like you, Vivien..." he comforted her.

She grasped his hand firmly and looked him in the eyes.

"I wasn't called Vivien then, was I?" she asked.

Maeda shook his head.

"No. You weren't."

She fell into a long silence, and Maeda sat beside her and shared in it. At times like this, he felt, it was the only time he ever knew complete peace.

She's floating between her lives, he thought. She's not sure which one she's remembering...

He knew though, because he shared some of the same memories with her. Could she still change herself, he wondered? Was that something that was passed on, from life to life, down the long sun-dappled chain of days?

Perhaps she could, he thought, looking at her fondly.

They had known each other all their adult lives, and they had recognized each other from the first moment they had met, drawn together somehow like two planets

200

circling the same burning star. They had recognized each other across the misty road of time, and their dreams, their shared dreams, had at last made a kind of sense.

That was why he still came here, week after week, to see her, or what was left of her. To be with her as she slipped away.

After a while, he stood and put some of her usual sleeping tablets into the small leather bag she had lying on the table.

"For later," he said softly and turned to go.

He had just taken a few steps when he heard her speak again.

"Oh look… another crow…"

He turned and looked up at the deep blue of the sky.

It was empty.

=====================

Chief Inspector Yamashita sat down heavily in his comfortable leather chair in front of his immaculate desk and sighed. Outside, the traffic hummed as usual on National Route 21, which was one of the ancient roads built back in the twelfth century when the sleepy little city of Kamakura had been the country's administrative capital under the first *shogun*, Minamoto Yoritomo. It still had plenty of memories of its glory days, but mainly they took the shape of the city's many Zen temples, Zen being the favored Buddhist sect of the Kamakura *shoguns,* who had built many of them during their nearly two centuries of rule from the little seaside town. Now though, the old Kamakura road was just another two-lane highway running south to the town of Ofuna and usually packed with traffic, especially on the weekends.

Outside his office window, a large Japanese flag hung limply on its flagpole in the noon stillness.

Yamashita was still sitting there quietly contemplating the old road when Detective Sergeant Yokota entered, threw himself onto his boss's large black sofa, and let out a sharp expletive.

Yamashita looked up at him and drummed his fingers on the desk.

"Yeah, that's how I feel too, if it's any consolation," he said, aware that it wasn't.

Yokota nodded, put his hands between his knees, and hung his head. The two men sat silently for a while, aware that they could do nothing now, before Yamashita spoke up.

It had been a long morning, and they had just finished working to confirm the details that their interview with the elderly Osaki had produced over several hours of interrogation. The old man had patiently answered all their questions and even surprised both of them with the sharpness of his memory as to certain specific times and events.

Yes, he had said, he absolutely remembered seeing the black van several times, as he walked his dog twice a day and at precisely the same times each day, seven in the morning and seven in the evening. His dog, a cream Pomeranian called Chi-chan, and he would walk, without fail, rain or shine, and he had seen the van several times when he had opened his door for the evening walk. Never in the morning, though. It was always gone in the mornings.

Had he ever wondered what the van was doing there?

Of course, he said. But it was an old house, and he knew Dr. Inagawa was a good neighbor, so he assumed he was just having some work done to keep the house in good order. These old places sometimes went to wrack and ruin, fell apart, and became fire hazards, he said. Especially the old wooden ones like his and the doctor's. You needed to keep an eye on them, otherwise, something could happen, and if there was a fire or something, then the whole street could go up. He'd heard of that happening, and so, as it turned out, had the police. Yamashita and Yokota were well aware of this problem with old wooden houses in Kamakura.

The old fellow's other theory had been that maybe Inagawa had been fixing it up inside so he could sell it, which was why he had the workers in. If so, that was fine by him. So why would he worry about a workman's van?

Yamashita and Yokota had nodded. It was a perfectly reasonable deduction to make. In any case, old Osaki had no reason to question the good intentions of his neighbor nor of whoever owned the black van he had seen parked there of late.

Didn't he think it a bit strange, though, they asked, that the van was parked there at night?

Yes, he had. But his son-in-law was an electrician who worked for a big construction company in nearby Chiba, and he was always complaining that he had to work overtime, sometimes till late. That seemed to be the lot of tradesmen these days, Osaki thought. The poor devils were constantly being hounded by their bosses to get things done to tight deadlines. No doubt that was why the van was there, right?

Had he ever seen anyone getting in or out of the van?

No, he hadn't. Not a soul.

And with every question they asked and with each reply the old man gave, the two policemen had felt their case, their meticulously built case against Doctor Inagawa, which they had been so painstakingly constructing over the past several weeks, begin to slip away from them. Yokota said it had felt like those times when the fish you had been patiently reeling in towards the boat suddenly slipped its hook just as you saw the flash of the scales in the water in front of you. All of a sudden, it was just gone.

Yamashita looked over at his exhausted-looking comrade.

"Fridays…." he said plainly.

"Yep…" echoed his deputy. "Fridays…"

The old man had been very insistent on this point. He couldn't remember all the dates that he had seen the black van there, but one particular day had stuck in his head.

He had seen it on Friday, March 18th, the day before he had flown out of the country for his trip.

There could be no mistake about this, as he had mentioned it to his neighbor, who had so kindly volunteered to look after Chi-chan while he was away. That evening he had taken the dog and all its food and bowls and other paraphernalia around to his next-door neighbor's house, an elderly lady named Sachiko Terasaki, as he had to leave early the following day for Narita airport, and while he had been discussing things with her on the doorstep of her house she had mentioned to him that it looked like the Inagawa's were having some work done on the house. She had pointed to the black van parked in the driveway, and Osaki had agreed and told her he'd seen it frequently lately.

It was this very important point, and one that Yokota had then confirmed with the old lady herself, who, when prompted, had also remembered the conversation too, as well as seeing the black van herself on various occasions.

What this meant, of course, were two things,

Firstly, on the evening of Friday, March 18th, Dr. Inagawa had been at the monthly meeting of the Kamakura Haiku Society, a club he and his late wife had been instrumental in founding some thirty years previously. The club always held its meetings on the third Friday of each month, and multiple other members who had attended the gathering in the back room of the old Japanese restaurant where they held these meetings had adamantly attested to his being there, and that he had been there all evening as he always was as he now served as the Association's vice-president. He'd even been remembered as having read some of his own poetry at the meeting, which had been printed (with the date) in their monthly *haiku* magazine.

Which all meant, of course, that he had a rock-solid alibi and had not been at the house when the black van or whoever owned it had been there.

Secondly, it meant that *someone else* had been in his parent's old house.

Were the people in the house his accomplices? The police had not a shred of evidence he had any.

Whoever had been driving the black van was someone they didn't know, nor could they identify. The neighbors had no idea what the license plate had been, all they knew was that the van had been black. Yamashita had been willing to bet anyone at the station a case of Kirin beer that even if they had taken down the details, that the plates would have quickly been found to be fake.

"We're screwed," said Yokota briefly. "We'll have to let him go…he's got an alibi, and someone else was in that house. Someone else who might have done the killings there…"

Yamashita raised his eyebrows, sighed for a third time, and nodded.

"There's something else about this I'm wondering too, you know…"

Yokota stood up and reached for his cigarettes in his shirt pocket, and then realized, to his dismay, that he had quit again a few weeks before.

He looked over at Yamashita, who was rocking back and forward in his chair.

"What?" asked Yokota.

Yamashita stopped his rocking and sat still, folding his arms.

"Don't you think it's possible the good doctor was set up?"

The question hung in the air between them like a thundercloud.

"Set up? You mean… the killer… *Il Monstro*…sent him the box of trophies, as he said… got hold of those gloves we found from the hospital where he worked…" Yokota sat down again on the sofa as the implications of his boss's question reverberated around his head. "You mean, he's been playing us? He wanted this guy to go down for it?"

Yamashita leaned forward and drummed his fingers on the desk again.

"What's the point, though?" asked Yokota in a confused tone. "I don't get it. He's never done that before, you know, tried to blame the killings on someone else. He's more than happy to claim them as his, which is why he leaves the feather and the fur, right? He was just using the old, abandoned house, maybe… you know, as his kill room. Why would he want to set up Inagawa in particular?"

"Well… I can think of a reason," said Yamashita meditatively.

"Seriously?"

His boss nodded.

"Simple. He wants to stop."

Chapter 15

The Old Sakura

When Penelope informed Maeda that she would be unable to come to dinner that week due to a regularly scheduled tea lesson with her old teacher, Fujimoto-*sensei*, and some other things she had to do, Ran was disappointed.

They had been making it a practice to meet either at his place or hers for the last several weeks as their relationship deepened, and today were sitting in his library on his comfortable sofa, with Penelope stretched out with her head on a pillow positioned on his lap. They had been talking about the *noh* play she had seen a few days before with Machiko that had been set in Kanazawa, but Ran said he had never heard of it, nor had he ever heard the story about the crow *tengu* and the fox spirit. What seemed to be more on his mind was that she was not coming to dinner.

"So, you are skipping dinner with me because of the tea ceremony?" he had asked quite incredulously. "I had no idea you were such a serious *chajin*… I have a lot of tea people in my family, actually. My mother, for example, and her mother were totally into it."

"Well, yeah. Maybe there are a few things you still don't know about me?" she smiled, looking up at him. "Maybe that's good. A woman likes to have some mystery, you know," she said and felt herself blushing slightly.

"As usual, the more I know about you, the more I'm er… well… never mind…." he said. "You know, I have a lot of tea stuff here. It's been in the family for centuries. Would you and er… Fujimoto-*sensei* like to see it? Maybe we can do tea together? I'm a bit rusty, but…and that way I can see you too?"

As it turned out, Fujimoto-*sensei* was more than a little curious to meet this man that her old student Penelope had been taking an interest in and had been easy to persuade. So instead of their regular lesson at her house, she and her elderly teacher had arrived by taxi at Ran's old house in the Kamakura hills that afternoon to participate in a rather impromptu tea gathering that Ran had cobbled together.

Both the women were dressed in kimono, as they usually did for anything connected with the ancient practice of tea, and Penelope was quite shocked to see that Ran, too, when he opened the door to them, was also dressed in a very elegant silver-grey *kimono* and dark green *hakama* pleated skirt. As he turned around to lead them into the house, Penelope noted the small crest on the back of the kimono's neck that belonged to his family, the mark of the once mighty Maeda family, who had been among the leading feudal powers in the nation.

"You look lovely…" she whispered to him when Fujimoto-*sensei* was out of earshot.

Ran beamed. "Well, that's only fair. You *always* look lovely…" he said as he offered her his arm and escorted them through his impressive library and into another room that Penelope had never seen before, but which turned out to be a *chashitsu,* or tearoom, that looked out on his garden.

"I had the *tatami* mats changed recently," he explained apologetically to Fujimoto-*sensei,* who was admiring the room from the doorway. "I hope they don't smell too much. New *tatami* can be a bit strong…"

The older lady waved the problem away, and they sat down on the matted floor in the traditional *seiza* position, and Ran began showing them some inscribed wooden boxes containing various tea utensils that were obviously of great age.

"Penelope tells me that you are descended from the Maeda of Kanazawa?" asked Fujimoto-*sensei* politely.

Ran nodded and explained a little about his family and their connection to the tea ceremony.

"Yes, I'm afraid the best stuff got sold off yonks ago,' he said, gesturing to the row of small boxes that were lined up against the wall behind an old kettle that was set on an inlaid hearth on the floor between them, "But my mother and grandmother were quite fond of the tea ceremony, so I managed to inherit some of the remaining family treasures through them. I thought you could have a look anyway, you probably know more about them than I do…" he said modestly, as he set down one of the boxes between them and gently untied the traditionally knotted cord.

He slowly and carefully removed the lid, and the women saw that inside there was a tea bowl in an old dark blue cloth which he removed and unwrapped on the floor in front of them.

Fujimoto-*sensei*, a veteran of many decades of the tea ceremony, took one look at the bowl and let out a small gasp, raising her hand as she did so to cover her mouth. Penelope shot a look of surprise at her.

"Do you mind if I touch it?" asked the older woman in an awed voice.

"Of course," Ran said, gesturing to her.

Fujimoto-*sensei* very carefully picked up the bowl, and turned it gently in her hands, then turned it over to show Penelope a tiny maker's mark etched into the bottom of the bowl.

"I've only seen these in museums... This is an Ogawa... Made by one of Rikyu's old disciples after the master's death. Probably early seventeenth century...." she said, referring to Sen-no-Rikyu, the founder of the Japanese tea ceremony.

It was common knowledge that anything from this period, especially if directly connected to Rikyu, would likely be nearly priceless.

She slowly put the bowl down again on its blue cloth, and stared at Ran.

"I'm so happy to have seen such a .... thing. And to have touched it...Thank you so much..."

Penelope sat, quietly shocked. She had rarely seen her old friend so emotional.

Ran smiled. "I'm glad you like it. Let's use it, shall we? It's no use sitting in a box. Here... I've got some other stuff you might like..."

Ran opened the boxes one by one and showed them a series of very old and rare items. There was a bamboo tea scoop made from wood from one of Rikyu's tea rooms, another that a dowager empress had made in the eighteenth century, several other bowls and vases made by extremely important potters in Kyushu and the ancient capital of Kyoto, and a variety of hanging scrolls, one of which was by Sesshu, one of the greatest artists of the Zen school.

After looking at all of these things, he served them some sweets from one of the oldest shops in Kamakura that catered for the tea ceremony and which both the women knew well, and then asked Fujimoto-*sensei* to make them tea with the old Ogawa bowl and some of the other rare implements.

The older woman traded places with Ran in front of the kettle, where the host traditionally sat, and Ran and Penelope were her guests as she expertly drew the water from the steaming kettle and whisked the tea in the old bowl made by a man who had personally known and served Sen-no Rikyu himself five hundred years previously.

As Penelope raised the bowl to her lips and took a sip of the delicious, bitter tea, her hands trembled slightly, and she looked at Ran, who smiled calmly at her.

"Don't worry. Nothing lasts forever. Rikyu and Ogawa meant for tea things to be used. The fact that they can break is how they represent impermanence…" he said, and Penelope could see he meant it. She felt her heart open towards him in a way that it had not for many years. Fujimoto-*sensei* seemed to sense it too, and smiled at both of them.

As they left the house an hour or so later and walked down the hill to where they thought they would probably be able to find a passing taxi to take them home, the older woman touched her student on the long sleeve of her pretty light-blue kimono.

"You know, I didn't like to say anything up there in front of your friend, in case it was a painful subject or something, but I used to know his wife…"

Penelope stopped and looked at her like she had just seen a ghost.

"You *knew* her?" she whispered.

Fujimoto-*sensei* smiled and nodded. "Yes… she was a friend of my niece, Emiko. They went to university together. She was a Nakatome. You know them, I guess?"

Penelope shook her head. "Not really. Just that they were something to do with real estate… Are they important?"

Fujimoto-*sensei* shook her head in bewilderment at her.

"Important?" she said, giving her a reproving look. "The great-grandfather founded the Nakatome railroad and had a huge real-estate company. They built an early railroad in the western area of Tokyo and then bought up huge areas of land around it, which the grandfather later developed. As Tokyo expanded in the Taisho and early Showa periods before the war they became immensely rich. And I mean *immensely*… I'm surprised you've never heard of them…" she said.

Penelope rolled her eyes. "Oh well, you know me. I don't really follow the business news. So, what do you know about the wife?"

Fujimoto-san smiled sadly.

"Oh yes…Yuriko. A very, very pretty girl. A gifted musician, too, I hear. My niece studied music at the same university as her. She was a violinist, I remember…"

"Yes… Ran said they used to play together in a group. That's how he met her, I think he told me."

"Ah, I see. Was that how it happened? I wasn't aware. Such a shame, though…"

"Yes… she died fairly young, I think about ten or fifteen years ago now."

The older woman looked at her, confused. "Ah, yes, I think Emiko told me she had died. Actually, I was referring to the other thing…"

"Other thing? What other thing?"

Fujimoto looked ahead towards the bottom of the road, where a taxi was driving slowly down the hill, and waved at it, managing to catch the driver's eye.

"Oh… I don't know. My niece told me she went mad. Some kind of schizophrenia thing. She got committed to a mental hospital, I heard…a pity…"

Penelope looked at her friend, surprised.

"Really? I didn't know that…." she said quietly.

And then she began to wonder what else she didn't know about this man, who had so taken control of her heart in recent weeks.

=====================

Even since his very earliest years, Ran had always had a feeling that there was something unusual about his sense of time.

214

The past, it had always seemed to him, seemed to unravel behind him in a way that it did not do for others, like it was an open road and not simply something that disappeared the more he tried to think back to his early life. Unlike others, there did not seem to be a fixed starting point, an 'earliest memory' for him. There were just other memories, blurred shapes like people moving in and out of dense fog.

He had kept this to himself as he had grown older, not understanding what it all meant. But one day, the day he'd met the girl for that very first time, he had finally understood, and at first, it had shocked him, until he realized that he was not alone.

He hadn't been the only one to notice it, however.

His mother had also suspected something about him, something that had been quietly discussed with close family members now for some years, until he was old enough to grasp what he had heard whispered about him for so many years.

The first ones to notice it had been his grandparents. And in particular, it had been his grandmother who had witnessed a strange scene one day at the family home along the windswept Eastern Sea of Japan, and had sought out her daughter-in-law, Kayoko, to talk to about it.

It occurred when he was about five or six years old, and they had been on one of their infrequent trips to his father's old family home.

One morning the older woman had found her daughter-in-law sitting on the verandah of their old villa, looking out on the huge gardens and the blue hills beyond them that surrounded their ancestral home and reading a book. Next to her was a small wooden tray with a glass of tea in an old silver Russian holder that she liked to use, which had beads of water running down the side, as the day was already warm.

The older woman, dressed as always in a plain dark kimono as women of her age usually did in their old and rather conservative family, pulled up a small *zabuton* cushion from a pile in the corner of the room and came and joined her as she enjoyed the gentle morning light of early autumn.

Kayoko and her husband now lived in one of the family's other homes on the other side of the country, and her visits here since the boy had been born were rare but very welcomed by her husband's parents, who now lived alone in the rambling old samurai mansion of their ancestors.

Her mother-in-law made herself comfortable, and Kayako could tell she was here for one of their chats, and closed the book on her lap.

"You know… I think my grandson is a very clever little boy…" her mother-in-law began, smiling and taking a sip of tea from her glass.

Kayako, who was now an artist of some reputation and who had always been very clever academically herself, lifted her beautiful dark eyes to the older woman and smoothed away a long lock of her long black hair.

"Hmmm… what's he done now?" she said with an arch look.

Her mother-in-law shook her head and smiled.

"Oh! Nothing… he's been as good as gold… it's just that he says the oddest things sometimes. I mean…the *oddest* things. Have you been telling him about our family?"

216

Kayako looked confused and shook her head. Her husband's was a very old family, and there was a lot of history to know, and even her father-in-law, in his rather august position as head of the family often said he was always coming across new information about their clan that historians frequently dug up about them.

"No, not really. I figure Father can educate him on all that stuff in the future. I mean, he's the expert. Besides, history has never been my thing, you know that. Maybe Ryosuke's been talking to him," she said, referring to her husband, who had opted to stay in Kamakura this time due to his work.

Her mother-in-law nodded.

"Oh well… I guess so. I was just wondering…"

"Why?" asked Kayako.

She looked out across the garden.

"He just seems to know things… that's all. But not like he's been told them. I mean, like he was there. He's only five years old…, it just seems, I don't know. I don't know what I am trying to say, really. I just don't know how he's aware of some things. Do you know the old *sakura*?"

Kayako nodded, and remembered her husband had told her about the old tree once.

"We were walking in the garden the other day. He pointed to it, and told me he used to sit underneath it for *ohanami* cherry blossom viewing parties…"

"Sorry? What?" asked Kayako, even more confused. "Cherry blossom parties… that's weird… We've only done that once with him, and it wasn't here…"

The old *sakura* was the name given to an ancient tree in the corner of the gardens that had been over a thousand years old and still bloomed fitfully even when Ryosuke was a little boy. However, it had rotted to the point where even the best tree surgeons from Osaka had been unable to help, and the final blow had been when it was knocked down during a typhoon over twenty years ago. Currently, the place where it used to stand and which the child had pointed out was simply the remains of a blackened stump.

The older woman cocked her head to one side and looked carefully at her daughter-in-law.

"I've never mentioned that tree to him, and neither has your father-in-law," she said. "I asked him this morning. So how did he know that? Oh, and another thing. Something even I didn't know. You know the glass cabinet in the study?"

"Yes, of course. You know you shouldn't let him play in there. He could get up to mischief. He's always into Father's books and things. I never let him near that cabinet, you'll be pleased to know."

The big glass cabinet she was referring to stood against a wall in the study. It was where some of the family's more important historical heirlooms were kept, including some ancient black lacquer women's combs that dated to the late Heian period in the tenth century.

Her mother-in-law nodded and tapped her on the knee as if to get her attention.

"Well, this was something he said to his grandfather the other day... they were in there together, and apparently, he went over and pointed at one of the women's combs. You know the one with the inlaid mother of pearl?"

Kayako nodded.

"He told him that 'Mother wore it at her wedding.'"

Kayoko smiled.

"Well, that's interesting. Seeing I never had a wedding ceremony…"

Kayako and her husband had insisted on a simple signing of the marriage papers at the city hall in Kyoto, followed by a small party for the family only. The family had tried to talk her into a 'proper wedding,' but the couple had been adamant.

"No… you didn't. And did you know he points out buildings that are no longer there and tells me who used to live in them when we go for walks sometimes?"

Kayako's eyes opened wide.

"No, I didn't know that."

"Well… now you do. I have to confess, it's kind of creepy. I guess he's just making stuff up, however. You know… kids. Your mother told me you did the same kind of thing. You had an imaginary family of dolls… remember?"

Kayako laughed, and took a sip of tea. "Yes, the Takeuchi Family. I remember them. They still live in a cupboard in my old room…"

Her mother-in-law nodded. "Of course! You should never get rid of your old friends… but with your son… hmmm… it's a bit different. He says these things like he *knows* them… like he *knows* the people personally…"

"Wow… maybe he's been here before…" said Kayako musingly.

Her mother-in-law turned and looked her full in the face.

"That's *exactly* what I think, too," she said in a quiet, serious tone that the younger woman had rarely heard her use before.

Chapter 16

Tales from The Western Sea

As the plane approached Osaka's vast urban sprawl, Penelope looked out fondly over the familiar city beneath her. Coming back here always felt like coming home somehow, as she had visited many times even though she had never lived here. Gazing out the window now, as the aircraft drifted gently downwards, a shaft of pure white light pierced the grey morning clouds and fell upon the city below, almost as if it were showing the way to a secret treasure.

Penelope had always liked the Kansai region, and particularly this great city, with its raucous and friendly people, so different from the much more conservative and reticent gentlefolk of Tokyo. She had often thought that if she had not been given her position at Hassei University in Kamakura long ago, where she had enjoyed so many happy years and where she had made so many friends, and had eventually even bought the old wooden house she now called home, that she would have enjoyed living here, particularly in the old capital of Kyoto which lay just to the north.

Those were thoughts she knew belonged to another life, however. It was sad, she sometimes reflected, that you only had one life to spend in these islands. She would have liked to have had more.

She felt somebody move next to her, and Machiko peered over her shoulder and whispered loudly in her ear.

"Ugh… it's sooooo concrete, Osaka. Hideous. Not a park to be seen. I don't know how people put up with it…"

"Well, I like it. The food's better for a start…" said Penelope giving her a reproving look.

Everyone was well aware of the hostility between the two cities, one that reached back centuries to when upstart Tokyo in the east of the country, then called Edo, had been chosen as the seat of the military government under the *shogun*, and then continued its duties as the capital city when the Emperor had moved there from Kyoto in the 1880s, a fact that the people of Tokyo still tended to laud over their 'country bumpkin' cousins to the west.

"Hmmm… you foreigners all say that…" her friend sniffed. "Is Enrico meeting us at the airport? He's a real *kansaijin,* just like you…" she teased.

Penelope poked her in the ribs as she heard the wheels lower and thud into place beneath them. "Yep. He's going to be at the gates, he said. God bless him…"

The reason for their hastily arranged trip had been exacerbated, at least in Penelope's mind, by the sudden release of Inagawa from detention, an event that was being played out on every TV set in the country even as the two women descended from the clouds to their destination that morning. With the case against him in grave doubt and the real killer still at large, she had decided to act on whatever clues she had, if only to try and save another life.

Penelope had become convinced that the only line of thought they had left that led to some connection with the killer and the calling cards he left behind now lay in exploring the story they had seen in the *noh* play of the relationship between the crow *tengu* and the fox spirit, which as Machiko had pointed out, was the only one in existence that had made use of such an unusual storyline. If there was some kind of link, or even just something which may help in throwing light on the mystery, then it was worth looking into, as far as she was concerned. She was also very conscious of the pressure her friend Chief Inspector Yamashita must now be under, and felt that if there was anything at all she could do which could help, then she was going to do it.

Since seeing the play a few weeks previously, she had discussed the matter with both Ran and Sal, and even brought it up with Yamashita in a hurried telephone conversation the previous evening. All of them thought it was worth looking into, but Ran was the lone voice urging caution, and had stressed to her that even if there was something in it, there were probably a lot of old stories of a similar vein that had no doubt been lost over time, and this one could be just one of them and therefore lead them up a blind alley.

Also, as it seemed to her, by the rather sad-looking expression on his face when she had announced her trip to him the week before, she had wondered whether he might just miss her. He had openly questioned whether she might be better off waiting to see what happened rather than 'running off to the other side of the country' as he put it. As a long-term singleton, she had to admit that thought made her feel rather warm. The only people that missed her when she traveled were Fei and her cats, and even Fei she had some doubts about.

Penelope had initially asked Machiko to contact her friend Professor Suzuki, who had been the one to find the original play, to send them a copy of the *Nishinokai Monogatari*, which had been the original document that the later play had been based on, and which Machiko knew he was using to research his latest book.

But then disaster had struck.

The good news was that the professor did indeed have a photocopy in his possession of the original pages from the *Nishinokai*, which he said he would be happy to share with them, as the only extant copy of the document was in the rare books department in the library of Osaka University.

The bad news was that the professor was now on holiday in Greece, and would not be returning to Japan for at least a month. Undaunted, Machiko had tracked him down at his daughter's house on the outskirts of Athens and spoken to him, but the professor had been unable to give them any help in finding the document in his office files while he was away, which was something that Machiko had been loath to do anyway. It had then been the professor himself who had suggested that the quickest way to access the document in question was probably just to go to Osaka and have a look at it themselves, and it was this route that they had now chosen to take.

They had no luggage, and so they were quickly outside the baggage area of the Kansai International Airport, and there, waiting at the gate for them as promised, was one of Penelope's oldest friends, Enrico Monte, a now-retired professor of linguistics whom

Penelope had consulted about another case the previous year and whose advice had been instrumental in helping her and Yamashita in solving.

He was, as always, an elegant figure, dressed in a well-cut Italian suit with a large flash of purple silk protruding from the breast pocket like a wilted orchid and a jaunty-looking panama hat which he was rarely without when outside.

He greeted the women as effusively as ever and escorted them to the car park, where his old black Fiat awaited them.

Whereas he had known Penelope for years, he had also met Machiko once or twice before at conferences where their fields of ancient Japanese language and folk history had overlapped, so he was delighted to be able to take his two old friends to his university, whose library, especially the rare books section, he knew extremely well.

As they drove onto the expressway that led from the new airport on the outskirts of Kobe and headed to the university's main campus, they caught up on the subject of old friends and, of course, Enrico's life in the rambling old house he shared with his Japanese wife, whom he said was looking forward greatly to seeing them for lunch later.

"Oh, she was most adamant about lunch when she heard you were coming, Penny. I think she likes to have another woman to complain to about me… c'est la vie, though. You women don't know how lucky you are to have us," he noted with a smile and a wave of his hand as he merged lanes at his usual high speed and possibly forgetting that Penelope, at least, had never married.

"I think she knows how lucky she is to have you, Enrico," said Machiko jokingly. "Is it going to be a problem to get a look at this thing today? We don't need to make an appointment or anything, do we?"

Enrico shook his head vigorously.

"Absolutely not, *senora*. This is not Tokyo, you know…" he said, giving her a cheeky smile in the rear-view mirror. "We are not troubled by things like the bureaucracy you so love. And the head librarian and I… we are like brothers. I was in and out of his department like a rabbit every day for many years. And I play golf with him. He said he would be there in person to get you anything you need. So don't worry. You'll have whatever you want in no time. And, by the way, I want to see this thing myself. It sounds very interesting. In fact, before today, I had no idea it existed…"

Penelope thanked him happily.

"Yes, I had never heard of it either," she said. "The *Nishinokai* is really just a fragment, not a very long history or anything. It just happens to have the original story of this old play that Professor Suzuki discovered."

"Really? Well, it sounds very interesting. Is there anything particular you ladies expect it to reveal? You said it might have something to do with the *Il Monstro* killings?" he asked.

Machiko gave a non-committal shrug, but Penelope seemed more optimistic.

"What I think it may have… what I'm hoping it has…is names," she said. These old Japanese stories often identified the characters in them clearly. That's what I really want to see. Who were these guys that were sent to deal with the fox-spirit lady? I want to know if any of them were connected in some way to a family or some kind of feudal institution. And also, I want to know exactly what the relationship between the crow *tengu* and the fox spirit really was, and if possible, how it came about. You know *noh* plays, Enrico. They are as long on drama as they are short on details. This document may just have more information. And perhaps if we have that, then maybe we'll know something that up till now only *Il Monstro* knows, and has been keeping hidden from us… that's the really interesting hypothesis, at least. Not that it's likely to happen, but… at this point, anything is worth a shot. The guy they thought was *Il Monstro* just walked out of prison a few days ago."

Enrico nodded and followed a sign to a turnoff to the district where his university was located.

"Yes…" he said. "I heard about that. I was watching the news on TV last night. And, of course, I knew when these things happened in Kamakura that you would doubtless be involved… At least that's what my wife said at the time, and as we all know, she is never wrong…" he said with a desultory smile. "Anyway, let's go and test your theory. We are almost there…"

A half hour or so later, they were standing at the entrance to the Osaka University library, a huge modern building that was surprisingly bright inside due to its large windows, and where they were quickly found by the head librarian, Minami-san, a slight, academic looking man in his late fifties with a bright yellow cardigan under his tweed coat and an extremely polite air.

He did indeed greet his friend Enrico like a long-lost brother, and bowed deeply to both Penelope and Machiko before escorting them to the elevators which would take them downstairs to the Rare Books section of the library, which was a place that housed some of the nation's most important documents.

As they went downstairs, he and Enrico began to wax lyrical over some of the latest acquisitions.

"You may have read, Professor Middleton," the librarian intoned solemnly, "about the handwritten copy of *Oku no Hoso Michi* that was discovered last year in that second-hand bookshop in Osaka?" he said, referring to the miraculous find of a handwritten copy of the poet Matsuo Basho's *The Narrow Road to the Deep North*, a diary of the poet's epic journey to the north of Japan in the 1680s.

"Oh, yes… you have that?" she said.

The librarian nodded like a gleeful child. "We have. I curated it myself, actually…. Would you like to see it?"

"Oh…" said Penelope, thinking they were about to be waylaid, "I would very much love to see that… but you know, this trip we have so little time…" she said as politely as possible, and the librarian nodded sadly.

"Well, don't worry. Another time, eh? I asked one of the research students to bring you the document you were looking for. We have a room set up for you to use…"

"That's very kind of you, Akira-san," said Enrico with a bow. "We're sorry to put you out…"

The elevator doors opened, and Minami-san led them down a short corridor to the doors of the Rare Books section. As they approached, they found a workman in white overalls up a ladder, changing some of the fluorescent lights in front of the door, and he politely got down and moved his ladder for them so they could enter.

Inside was a little room to the left-hand side set aside for their use, and a pretty girl in an orange sweater and jeans was waiting for them inside with a large dark box on the table.

"This is Ishiura-san, one of our post-graduate students in the Librarianship school. We asked her to bring the document you were looking for to save you some time," said Minami.

Ishiura-san stood and bowed, gesturing for them to sit around the table, and then, handing them each a pair of white gloves, carefully opened the box for them.

Inside was a large air-tight bag containing a very old and very faded set of loose documents. The student opened the sealed plastic and carefully took out a set of perhaps fifty unbound pages that she laid on the table in front of Penelope to see. Each of the faded yellow pages was covered with an extremely fine brushwork, which reminded her of many similar documents she had seen in the past belonging to the Heian and Kamakura periods of a thousand years ago. The characters used in this document were particularly clear and well-written though, and not the large, flowing, and highly artistic brushwork of some of the more important women writers of the great tales and essays of the period. For some reason, Penelope instantly had the feeling that these pages were written by a man.

Enrico, who was an expert in ancient Japanese linguistics, put on his gloves and carefully moved some of the pages.

"Fascinating," he murmured. "You know, this kind of looks like a monastic hand… I would almost venture to say that I've met the writer of this before…"

Minami-san nodded. "Yes… you may be right. These were found, as you know, by Professor Suzuki. He found them sewn inside a scroll from a later period. They were used as backing paper. But the scroll was found in one of the Kyoto monasteries… so you may be right. It could have been written by one of the monks. After all, it was only the very top of society and the monks that could read and write during this period."

Penelope peered at the documents and sighed.

"I'm going to need your help with this, Enrico… I'm not that great at reading this kind of script."

Although Penelope, as a professor of Japanese literature, was familiar with the ancient Japanese employed a thousand years before, even the most talented of scholars like Enrico struggled to understand these complicated and highly idiosyncratic forms of brushwork that were used, as well as some of the archaic characters that were no longer a part of the modern Japanese language.

"Oh… don't worry about that. Have a look at this…" Minami san handed her a sheaf of closely typed documents in a clear plastic file. "One of the professors in the Department of Japanese Culture has been looking at this document. He made a transcription. He said you were welcome to use it…."

Penelope and Enrico looked up and smiled broadly.

"Oh… that's wonderful," said Penelope. "Please thank him. You don't know how much time that's going to save us…"

Minami and Enrico laughed. "Oh… I have some idea. Probably a couple of weeks, at least," said Enrico. "Let's have a look."

Enrico took the documents out of the file, and the two women came and sat on either side of him to read over his shoulder. The transcription was still in the ancient Japanese, but at least they knew what characters they were looking at.

They quickly read through the beginnings of the document, which talked about the different types of spirits that were to be found in the far-western areas of Japan and how they were to be dealt with, until they found where the document began to speak of a strange story that was immediately familiar to Penelope and Machiko, the story from the *noh* play it was so clearly related to.

Enrico began to read it slowly aloud, translating some of the ancient language into the more familiar modern Japanese when necessary and sometimes into English when he could not think of the appropriate language.

And like all good ghost stories, the effect was chilling.

Chapter 17

A Love Letter

The old Italian's beautiful baritone softly filled the little room as the others sat listening to the lilting words of the ancient tale, which seemed to have a music and a rhythm all of its own. And in the very first line, Penelope heard a familiar name:

> *Of all the strange tales that have come to pass in the western lands, perhaps the saddest befell the great House of Maeda, Lords of the land of Kanazawa, bestowed on them by the Grace of His Majesty the Emperor in perpetuity for their services, and later vouchsafed by the shogun appointed by him.*
>
> *For it came to pass in the spring of that year, the 4th Year of the Emperor Go-Sano, and just as the cherry blossoms of Yoshino were reaching their peak, that the first son of the Maeda, a princeling by the name of Tadayuki, was hunting in the great forests by the sea in the lands to the south of his family estates when he was overtaken by a storm and took shelter in a simple house of thatch by the Shinagawa river, which was then in full spate with the spring rains.*
>
> *The young lord was welcomed inside the house by the local ferryman, who introduced him to his daughter, a beautiful maiden of fifteen years. Little did the boy know, though, that in reality, the farmer was not a man at all but the River Spirit of the Shinagawa,*

who watched over the waters there, and the girl he saw, whose beauty he was immediately entranced by, was a fox-spirit that stayed with him. And not just any fox spirit, but the spirit of an ancient nine-tailed fox, a beast over one hundred years of age and possessed of great powers, such as being able to see into past lives and be in different places at the same time.

The old man told the young lord that the girl possessed the gift of sight, and indeed, in this respect, she told the young man that they had once before been lovers in another life, and to this end, showed him many proofs and astounded him with her knowledge of his ancient family.

This fox was, however, it must be said, genuinely taken with the young princeling, and before the dawn of the next day, she had sworn herself to wait for him to return and to take her to his parents as his bride, which the boy had promised to do.

The young man, Tadayuki, was a valiant and headstrong youth, and when he saw the maiden, even at first glance, he knew that he wanted her and no one else. It would also be right to say that the fox herself was in love with him and used none of her many powers to entertain him as she could so easily have done. And what she had told him was the truth, that theirs was indeed a love that crossed the starry sky of time, a love of two souls who found each other over and over in the great river of lives.

A few weeks later, the youth returned as he had promised. After giving the man that he thought was her father a large sum in gold, he also brought the maiden many sumptuous gifts of fine clothing, as well as two servant girls who would accompany her to his province, where he planned to introduce her to his parents as his intended bride.

And so it came to be that a few days later, the girl proceeded with Tadayuki to the great estates of the Maeda, which grew more rice than any other area in his Majesty's kingdom and had given them such exceptional wealth. There the girl was presented to the Great Lord Maeda, the father of Tadayuki.

The family feigned to welcome the girl and told her that they accepted their son's decision that she should be the first among his wives and that should she bear a male heir, the boy would, in time, follow his father as the Great Lord. Yet secretly, the boy's father, and particularly his first wife, were greatly displeased, and after a time, unable to control his impatience any longer, the Great Lord gave orders to eight of his most trusted liege men, ones who had been in battle with him and his most loyal companions, to arrange to have the girl quietly killed.

These eight men swore that all would be done as he had said. To this end, they met in secret and made plans to carry out the crime as soon as the autumn leaves began to change.

And these were the men entrusted with the dread command of the Great Lord Maeda. They were led by Ina Yasuhisa, his companions Hiraga Tomonori and Nambu Masahide, their uncle Murakami Shigemochi, and two of his loyal friends, Nose Tokiharu and Hatakeyama Kenetsugu. In addition, they were aided by the Great Lord's distant cousins, Yamana Takemori and Hatakeyama Akimitsu. Together these men conspired together, and soon they found an opportune moment to strike.

As it happened, the young bride and her two ladies-in-waiting and some of their friends had decided in Lord Tadayuki's absence (he had been called on to attend his august Majesty at court in Kyoto) to visit the maple groves of Asahina, just near the village of Koma, which were famous for their beauty in this season.

Hearing this, the eight liege men of the Great Lord followed them into the forest. They watched from a distance as the ladies found a place to spread their silken blankets under the gold-red trees in the bright light of the autumn afternoon and listened when one of the ladies began to play beautifully on the zither and the others sang old *songs that were greatly loved by all and recited poems fitting to the season as people do on these occasions.*

And this is when the cowardly attack began.

Led by Ina Yasuhisa, the men surged onto the defenseless women, and cut them all down in a moment. However, as they approached the bride of Lord Tadayuki and raised their swords, they were astonished to see before their very eyes that the girl had transformed herself into a beautiful white fox. The fox, still dressed in her kimono of autumn leaf pattern, and with her nine tails clearly visible under her robes, fled swiftly into the forest and disappeared in front of the men's terrified eyes. Fearful of failure though, they pursued her for a night and a day, hunting her throughout the great forest, until they finally tracked her down and then one of them, the master archer Hatakeyama Kenetsugu, the son of Hatakeyama Kiyomori, shot her dead against the wall of a cliff, the arrow piercing her heart as she turned to flee. Even then, as the men came upon what they thought would be her lifeless body, they found that the fox spirit had again eluded them, and nothing was found other than her empty robes. Angered, they brought back her robes to the Great Lord Maeda and, prostrating themselves before him, presented him with her bloody robes as proof that she was gone.

This, however, was not the last of the story, nor of the terrible retribution which would now befall this house.

When the young Lord Tadayuki returned from his attendance upon the Throne of His Majesty and was told what had happened and the truth concerning his bride, that she had been a fox and not a woman at all, the young man was bereft.

For a hundred days and nights, he searched the whole of the western lands, calling for her and speaking to everyone he found, yet it was no use.

And at the end of these one hundred days, outside the house by the Shinagawa River where they had first met, he took his own life, assisted by the River Spirit, who, after the boy had cut open his belly, quickly beheaded him, and then vanished, never to be seen by man again.

However, there was more to this story.

For generations afterward, the House of Maeda was cursed by the Spirit of the Fox, who visited it with the bleakest form of dark magic, cursing it and all the generations of those that had killed her in perpetuity, and who now returned in the company of another spirit, a crow tengu that was said to be the spirit of the young Lord Tadayuki, who followed her wherever she went, and together they took a terrifying vengeance on those that had done her such injustice.

And so the lands of the House of Maeda became forever unsafe, and people feared to travel, particularly at the time of the crescent moon, and dared not venture outside after the sun had set. And one by one, starting with the eight liege men that had taken her life, vengeance was in turn taken upon them and their children, and they were found, their bodies desecrated and scattered to the winds by the crow tengu and his mate.

Even to this day, when the crescent moon is in the sky, people say they have seen the fox spirit and her mate abroad on the quiet roads. She, walking quietly beside him, her nine tails trailing behind her under her robes, which are the color of freshly fallen snow, and he, clothed in a long black robe, his crow face hidden under a low hood.

Walking together, they make no sound upon the road, and leave not a single trace behind.

The enormity of what she had heard read out by her friend caused Penelope to struggle for breath, and she leaned back in her seat, her hand grasping at her chest and her face white as a sheet.

Machiko and the others stared at her in surprise, and then Enrico stood up and knelt at her side.

"What is it, Penny... are you all right?" he said, concerned, as Penelope quickly pulled herself together with a supreme effort.

"Yes... I'm OK. Oh my God..." she said breathlessly.

"Would you like some water?" asked Minami-san. "Ishiura-san, please get the professor some water."

The girl immediately scooted out of the room, and Machiko took her place opposite her friend on the other side of the table.

"What's the matter, Penny? You look like you've seen a ghost..."

Penelope's mind was racing, and as it did so, the facts began to present themselves to her, falling into place like jigsaw pieces and instantly forming a picture in her mind so horrifying in its logic and clarity that she knew its truth immediately.

"I'm so sorry... I just... I don't know. I just understood something... maybe for the first time... Can I see the documents again? The originals?" she asked.

Taking the ancient papers gently in her hand, she slowly leafed through them, then placed them one by one on the table and gave a long sigh... and then something in the corner of the box suddenly caught her eye.

It was a small piece of handmade paper, folded into a strange knot and with a tiny red flower protruding from the folds of the knot.

She carefully took it out of the box and laid it on the table.

"Well… I'll be damned…" said Enrico. "You know what that looks like to me?"

Machiko and Penelope both nodded.

"*Koibumi* …" Machiko said softly. "What's it doing here?"

"A love letter?" asked Minami incredulously.

"In the Heian period," said Enrico, "lovers would write poems to each other, and tie them up like this, usually with a sprig of some seasonal flower inserted into the knot. I recognize this, it's *higanbana*, the red spider lily. We have it growing in our garden…. it's a fall flower," said Enrico.

"This is most irregular," said Minami-san as the young student returned with the water. The head librarian pointed to the piece of paper they had found in the document box.

"Do you know anything about this, Ishibe-san? Who could have placed this here?"

The girl stared at the little slip of knotted paper and shook her head.

"No… I'm sorry. I haven't seen it before. Where did you find it?" she asked as she put the bottle of water and a glass in front of Penelope.

"Well… it was in the box. With the documents."

The girl shrugged.

"Has anyone else requested to see these documents?" asked Minami.

The girl nodded, clearly confused by all the fuss.

"Yes, there was a gentleman in here a few days ago. A researcher from Tokyo. I forget which university he said…"

Penelope opened her mobile phone and began swiping through her photographs.

"Was this him?" she said, holding up the phone so the startled girl could see.

"Oh! Yes…" she said, nodding. "That was him. Why?"

Penelope put her phone down face first on the desk and, without a word, picked up the slip of knotted paper and carefully opened it to reveal the tiny note written inside.

There were only two words.

I'm sorry.

It was in Ran's clear, unmistakable hand.

=====================

As Penelope and the others investigated the box of documents in Osaka, Ran Maeda parked his old black Jaguar XJ12 in the car park of the hospital and sat quietly for a moment to listen to the ending of a Handel aria called *He Was Despised.*

The piece was from *Messiah,* which was still one of his favorites, and a piece he had sung himself as a boy soprano in a choir when he had been at school in Britain as an exchange student for a year. The music sounded beautiful and clear from the very expensive Swedish sound system he had ordered specially fitted, as Ran enjoyed driving, and found listening to music as he drove passed the time in the best of ways.

This particular piece, an aria for alto often sung by a male counter-tenor, never failed to move him, sometimes even to tears.

The counter-tenor was the rarest of all voices, exquisite and clear in a way that the female voice could not match, and capable of a range that seemed almost out-of-body. These highly-trained singers were the descendants of the Italian *castrati*, an experience of pre-pubescent boys in the Renaissance period who were operated on to ensure that their vocal cords did not mature so they could continue serving in church choirs. Some of them had found their way to London in the 1700s, where Handel and other composers had employed them to take parts usually sung by young boys, the presence of women performing on stage in the period being something that was still frowned upon.

Ran, who hated blind prejudice and stupidity above all things, understood how the women must have felt but still found his soul soared at the sound of a man's voice as it gave the inherent sadness in Handel's lamentations about Christ's death on the cross an almost inexpressible poignancy.

Yet, time pressed on him now.

There were now only a few last important things he had to do, and they were things that he had long prepared for. Now that the day he had hoped to forestall indefinitely was upon him, he could not but think that it was something he had brought upon himself.

As he sat listening to the music, he felt himself slipping away, almost like the sand in an hourglass.

The music rose and fell, and Christ hung on the cross.

Despised.

Rejected.

And for Ran, his plans began to slide into effect, like a bolt being drawn across a closed door.

The music finished, and he pushed an image of Penelope's face to the back of his mind. This was something he was profoundly disciplined at doing, compartmentalizing the various segments of his multifaceted life.

Plenty of time to think about her later.

Now, there was something far more pressing to do. Something that had to be done and which he had kept until this final moment.

But now, at long last, that moment had arrived.

He stared up at the low brick building, and his eyes traveled along the row of windows, each with their small, white, wrought-iron balconies on the uppermost floor until they came to her room, where he knew she would be at this time, perhaps sitting quietly in her armchair with a book and maybe even thinking of him and wishing he was there.

Yuriko, his wife, lay just inside these walls, a woman who now preferred the English name she had found somewhere in the many books she spent her days reading. Vivian, the enchantress of Merlin in the Arthurian Romances. Vivien, in Tennyson's poem *Idylls of the King,*

Viv*i*an was the male spelling, she had explained to him once in one of her pedantic moods. Viv*i*en was the female.

Vivien, from the Latin 'vivus,' to be alive.

"I'm alive, and I have always been… alive. With you…" she used to like to say when they were young, and whenever she did, she would reach out and grasp his hand, and entwine her soft fingers with his as if to prevent him from slipping away again.

And he would nod and kiss her and feel the rareness and eternal beauty of the bond between them, just like they had both felt the day they had met so many years ago on the old campus at Tokyo University.

He had often revisited that first moment in his mind.

It had been a beautiful, clear autumn day, he remembered. He had spent the afternoon writing yet another essay for yet another professor and had just walked out of the library into the soft sunshine, when he felt something move in the back of his mind, almost like the sudden twitch upon the line when a fish bites.

Something he had no control over suddenly took him over, and he was helpless in its grasp.

He looked up and scanned the people around him, somehow conscious that something profoundly familiar was moving among them, something he *knew* in a way that he could never explain. Just as he had known the old *sakura* as a child, or his long-ago mother's comb.

Then, just a little way away from him, in a crowd of other students that were leaving a lecture hall, she had felt it too.

Yuriko always said it was like someone had called her name from far away, and she had looked away from the girl she had been chatting to as they headed towards the library steps and moved her eyes over the crowd of students.

And then he saw her.

Walking towards him, her long black hair moving gently in the cool breeze that sprang up in the afternoon. And she had suddenly looked up at him, like something had startled her, and stared straight at him.

Both of them now stood motionless before each other and had the eerie feeling that time had suddenly and inexplicably ground to a complete halt.

They looked into each other's eyes for a long moment, and recognized each other in an intimate and utterly final way.

Yuriko's friend also stopped and stared at her, somewhat bemused, as her companion stood silently staring into the eyes of some boy they had never met before, like they had some strange bond between them.

And that was exactly what it was, because finally, they had found each other again, as they always did, life after life after life. This was something that both Yuriko and Ran knew in their very bones.

It was always there, always present. An unbreakable cord between them, always with the same instant and unfaltering recognition, a little like the moment two magnets that come into each other's range will snap together as one.

"You," the voice inside each of them said. "It's you…"

They both knew it at once. And even though they had no understanding of what had just happened as they stood looking into each other's eyes, they could hear this word in their minds, ringing clearly like a bell in the morning air.

"You."

He remembered he had taken a step towards her, and she had allowed him to reach out and touch the little silver fox's face that hung from her necklace.

She remembered his fingers had felt cool and instantly familiar, like they were her mother's hands.

And he had smiled at her and let the necklace fall.

And she had smiled at him too, a quiet, almost conspiratorial smile, that told him she knew their secret.

And after that, they were together again.

Yuriko Nakatome, the most beautiful girl in the university, the scion of the vastly wealthy Nakatome family, a brilliant mathematical prodigy, a consummate violinist, a deeply sexual and passionate lover, and a woman who could kill, like him, without the slightest qualm or regret.

A woman that needed, just like he did, to take life.

Over the years since their 'reunion,' as they called it, they had cut a bloody swathe together, bathed themselves in red death, and taken exquisite pleasure in the agony of their victims for nearly three decades.

Going from place to place, and always at the time of the waning moon as they had of old, they had found the ones they wanted, a process which had often taken years of painstaking research, and finally tracked them down. Then, with much joy, they had planned their demise together in sumptuous detail.

Then, they had taken them… one by one, until the list was once again almost complete.

But then their perfect life, their intimate, consuming world, had begun to change, little by little, but with a deadly certainty.

Of course, Ran, ever attentive to her, had noticed the symptoms of her dementia early. The slight forgetfulness. The way she would sit for hours looking out at nothing. The quick outbursts of temper that suddenly appeared and disappeared like a summer storm… as a trained psychiatrist, he knew what these things meant.

Helplessly he watched them build, looked after her as best he could without saying anything, taken her around the world for the most expensive and exotic of cures… but in the end, he knew he would have to face the sweet agony that came when she would forget who he was… and then remember, and then forget again as her memory phased in and out of coherence like a guttering candle.

And then, one day, just like that, she had gone.

He knew that deep inside her, somewhere, the recognition of him was still there, embedded in her soul just as it was in his. Their terrible bond was, it seemed, made of an iron that knew no form of rust. And yet, how she struggled now to remember him whenever she saw him, like a bird with a broken wing trying to fly.

He pitied her, almost as much as he loved her. That was why he had hidden her here, with the blessing of her family, who had been desperate to keep things quiet, in this silent place where she could live out her days and where he could still watch over her, and, importantly, where anything she said would not be believed.

Because now she spoke, without filter, of their many lives together.

And this was a danger to both of them.

Chapter 18

The Final Victim

Yamashita had immediately done what she had asked.

The moment he had hung up the phone, he had ordered Yokota and three other uniformed police to find Dr. Inagawa (he had been quickly located at a restaurant having a celebratory lunch with his *haiku* friends) and to both escort him home under guard and to place a watch on both the front and rear of his property.

No one was to enter.

Only Yokota was to answer the phone or the door, and absolutely not the doctor.

Very few people in this world enjoyed the level of trust that would make a seasoned policeman like Yamashita take this sort of action without a full explanation, but Penelope Middleton was one of them, and perhaps the only one.

If she thought Dr. Inagawa was in danger, then he almost certainly was, and he would wait to find out the reasons later. In the meantime, Penelope had made it clear that there was not a second to lose and that, for all she knew, he was already dead.

Yamashita had been greatly relieved when the man had immediately answered Yokota's urgent phone call and even more relieved when he had quietly acquiesced, as was his way, to the imperative command to stay right where he was with his friends until a police escort would arrive to take him to a safe place, which in this case and for lack of anywhere better, was his home.

Meanwhile, Penelope had informed him she was on a flight leaving now, and would meet him at the doctor's house in the next few hours.

"You're not going to tell me what this is about, are you?" he had asked rather lamely.

"No. I need to do that face-to-face. Believe me, you're not going to like what I've got here. You need to get to Inagawa, however. Immediately. I'll tell you everything in a few hours, don't worry. And get Sal. I want to talk to him too. OK?"

"Didn't you say you were going to Osaka to look at some old document?"

There was a long silence on the other end of the line.

"Must have been some book then, was it?" said Yamashita.

"You could say that…" said Penelope quietly. "Now, stop talking to me. Get to Inagawa. Understand? Oh… one more thing. Under NO circumstances contact Ran Maeda. Do you understand? We need to talk about this. My plane is leaving now, I have to go…"

And with that, she hung up.

As the afternoon wore on and the doctor was safely escorted to his house, Yamashita felt he could not stay in his office waiting for things to happen. He texted

Penelope the address and asked her to meet him as soon as she could at the doctor's house, and then he rounded up one of the uniformed officers to get a squad car for them.

A half-hour later, he headed to Dr. Inagawa's home nearby to check on things with Yokota, who had been ordered to remain inside the house with the doctor while the other officers patrolled outside. On his way to the house, he got another text from Penelope to say she had arrived in Kamakura and would be with them in the next few minutes.

As Yamashita and the squad car pulled up outside the house, where a young, uniformed officer was standing in the driveway, he noticed a taxi heading down the street, and seconds later, he saw Penelope walking swiftly towards him.

"So, this is where he lives?" she asked.

Yamashita nodded.

"Poor devil," said Penelope. "He didn't deserve any of this. But still, he's lucky to be still breathing," she said bluntly, and marched up to the door in front of her confused friend.

"You know, I'm dying to know what all this is about…" said Yamashita in a slightly irritated tone.

Penelope turned and gave him a grim smile.

"Let's go inside and sit down first. I have a lot to tell you… and none of it is nice."

The door opened, and Yokota gave Penelope a slight nod and silently escorted them inside.

"Where is he?" Penelope asked straightaway as she sat herself on the living room sofa.

"He's in the kitchen making us some coffee. I thought you might like some..." said Yokota.

Penelope nodded. "I would. For God's sake, do NOT take your eyes off that man. I think he is in very real danger."

Yamashita sat down opposite her.

"OK, talk. What's going on?" he ordered her.

She was just about to begin her story when the doctor arrived in the sunny living room with a tray of coffee mugs and some biscuits on a plate, and Penelope stood and introduced herself.

"Doctor, I'm so sorry about all this and what's happened to you..." she began.

Inagawa, surprised at seeing a civilian woman in his house instead of the usual police, nodded sadly.

"I understand... thank you," he said briefly and without emotion, as Yokota took the tray of coffee cups from him and put them on the table.

"Doctor... could I speak privately with these officers for a moment? Do you mind?" she asked politely.

The doctor nodded. "Of course..." he said simply, and with that, he turned and walked into the adjoining dining room, where he opened his laptop to continue writing an email to a friend.

Penelope turned to the two detectives.

"Right... look. I'm so sorry about all this. You don't know how relieved I am to see him safe..." she said, nodding toward the doctor in the other room.

She took her glasses from her bag and looked up at Yamashita like a teacher about to give bad news to a failing student.

"I'm so sorry, Eiji… but what I am about to tell you is going to be painful. It's about Ran, I'm afraid…"

Yamashita picked up one of the coffee mugs and poured some milk into it.

"Ran? What about him?"

Penelope opened her mouth to speak, then stopped herself and began staring intently over the chief inspector's shoulder at the wall behind him.

Without a word, she stood up and went over to the small security panel on the wall and scrutinized it carefully.

Suddenly she wheeled around and whispered in a hoarse voice.

"Oh God…" she pointed at the coffee mugs the two policemen were holding. "Don't touch that! Look!"

Yokota, understanding her immediately, put down his mug and rushed into the next room to the doctor, whose coffee was still sitting untouched next to his laptop.

Yamashita went over to the security keypad Penelope was pointing at.

On the front cover of the panel in sharp blue letters was one word.

ProSec.

Yamashita's eyes opened wide, and he stared at Penelope, who walked quickly into the dining room where Yokota was standing with the startled doctor.

"Doctor, have you eaten or drank anything since you got home?" she asked.

The doctor shook his head.

"No, nothing. I just made the coffee, that's all. And I put out some water for Tama...

"Tama?" asked Penelope.

"Yes... my neighbor's cat. I'm looking after her..."

"Where is her water?"

The doctor pointed.

"In the kitchen. Why? What's this about?"

Penelope and Yamashita turned sharply and walked into the kitchen. A large black and white cat was lying unmoving on the floor beside a water bowl.

Penelope rushed over to the stricken animal and touched its soft fur.

It wasn't breathing.

She looked up and shook her head at Yamashita, who was already dialing the police station.

===================

It had taken several hours, but at last, the forensic department confirmed that the water supply to the kitchen had been contaminated, as Penelope had suspected.

"We dunno what it is at this moment, but my guess would be it's some kind of homemade nerve agent. Very clever and highly toxic. We found this inside the water purifier on the kitchen tap...."

The technician, a middle-aged man who had run the forensic laboratory in the nearby and much larger city of Kanagawa for several years, was an old friend of Yamashita's and someone he occasionally met to play *shogi,* as he did with Fei.

"I think you guys had a very close call," the technician intoned seriously as Yamashita, Yokota, and Penelope all looked at the little brown vial in the small plastic evidence bag. "This stuff would kill you stone dead in under five seconds... seriously nasty. But anyway, we'll know more when we have had a chance for a full analysis. I suggest you all get the hell out of here and let us inspect the rest of the place. It's going to take a while, I think..." he said, looking around at the large house.

Penelope and the others took his advice and went outside, and Yamashita asked one of the officers on duty to drive them all back to the police station in Kamakura. The shocked Doctor Inagawa had already been taken to a hotel in Tokyo, where he was being kept under armed guard until a decision could be made as to whether it was safe for him to return to his house.

Thirty minutes later, they were all gathered in Yamashita's office, and Yokota closed the door behind them.

"So... ProSec again... Thank you, Penny-*sensei,*" said Yokota with a slight bow. "We all owe you... I never spotted that panel myself when we went in. To tell you the truth, it wouldn't have occurred to me even if I had. ProSec does half the security alarms in Japan, and I think they have about sixty percent of the market for domestic alarm systems. It never crossed my mind..."

Penelope smiled and waved away his thanks.

"Don't worry about it. It just hit me when I saw it. If he had access to the shrine through a ProSec employee, he could have breached their security completely. He could probably get into any home that has one undetected," she said, momentarily reflecting on the fact that not only did she not have an alarm system, but that she didn't even lock her doors unless she was away on holiday somewhere.

Yamashita nodded. "Right, well... don't worry, I'm not going to offer you any coffee." he quipped. "So, tell me, why was this guy trying to kill the doctor? And what has all this got to do with Ran?"

Penelope looked at the floor for a moment.

"It's not just Ran, Eiji. It's not just him..." she said, and when she looked up, Yamashita could see the trace of a tear in her eye.

"It's his wife too... Yuriko."

"His wife? What do you mean?" said Yamashita staring at her in amazement. "Yuriko died years ago. Ran told me. The family buried her somewhere in Kansai..."

Penelope shook her head.

"I don't think so. I think she's alive. I think he put her somewhere... maybe some hospital. He mentioned to me once that he still did one job as a psychiatric consultant. He just didn't say where. Anyway, what you need to know, gentlemen... is that Ran... is *Il Monstro*."

There was a dead silence in the room for several seconds as Yamashita and Yokota stared at her dumbstruck.

"That's not possible, Penny..." said Yamashita with a horrified look at her. "I've known him all my life... he's ... just not capable of this..."

Penelope stared at him thoughtfully and shook her head.

"Not only capable… more than capable. He's taken us all in, Eiji. All of us. Especially me," she said as she looked around the room helplessly.

"We've been totally played, which is why the doctor is in such danger. He was never the killer. In reality, he was *the last victim*. Ran set him up to be that, and for the courts to later execute him. It killed two birds with one stone. It satisfies the police, as they think they have caught the killer, plus it achieves his final goal."

"His final goal?" said Yamashita, standing up and leaning against his desk with his arms folded.

Penelope nodded. "Yes. His final goal. Inagawa was actually the last of eight planned killings. The final victim, who served the purpose of allowing Ran to stop his killing spree and retire to a quiet life… He fooled everyone for so long…"

She looked at the floor again.

"But when you put it together," she continued, "it's all there as plain as day. But as I said, it's not just him. *They were are pair*, he and Yuriko. Don't you see? She's the fox spirit… the other half of the pair. And I think she was the driver in all this. The real motivator… Ran allowed her to select the victims, and they both executed them… Here. Let me show you something…"

She rummaged through her oversized black bag, produced a clear plastic file full of papers and handwritten notes, and took out a small piece of paper which she laid on Yamashita's desk. The document had eight handwritten names, which she had copied down from the ancient document they had seen in the library in Osaka:

Ina Yasuhisa,

255

Hiraga Tomonori
Nambu Masahide
Murakami Shigemochi
Nose Tokiharu
Hatakeyama Kenetsugu
Yamana Takemori
Hatakeyama Akimitsu

Yokota stood and peered at the list over her shoulder.

"Those look like old Japanese names. Where did you get this?" he asked.

Penelope nodded.

"You're right. This list of names is from an ancient historical record detailing a series of killings done to avenge the death of Lord Tadayuki Maeda, the heir to the Maeda feudal fief of Kanazawa, and his bride, who was, according to the legend, a fox in disguise, back in the twelfth century. Tadayuki was a direct ancestor of Ran Maeda, by the way. The story of her killing was later made into a lost *noh* play, only recently discovered by a friend of Machiko's. The play was based on *this* document which we found in Osaka, or on another perhaps that has been lost. Still, this document is the only one with the names of the men sent out that day by Tadayuki's father to kill his young bride. After they killed her, the spirit of the fox cursed the whole Maeda family forever and promised revenge, and afterward, she and Lord Tadayuki, who had returned in the form of a crow *tengu*, murdered all of these men one by one."

"Now, I know this is only an old legend, a story that was made into a play. But, real or not, doesn't this sound familiar to you?" she said, tapping her forefinger on the piece of paper. "Because it sounds to me a lot like the killings we've all witnessed here over the last thirty-odd years…"

"Oh, come on, Penny…" said Yamashita. "That's *eight hundred years ago*… I mean, yes, you may have tracked down the original story, and there may be some link to Ran and his family… but…" said Yamashita, but he no longer sounded very sure of himself.

"It might be eight hundred years ago when it *started*, but don't forget, I saw *both of them* with my own eyes. We know it's them. In all the killings, we have the fox fur, and we have the feather. It's all pointing back to this story. Don't you see? They wanted us to know that it was them. That they had returned, and that they were still carrying out their promise to the old Maeda family."

The two detectives exchanged glances, and Penelope could see they were still unsure.

"OK, guys. Let me put it plainly… You know we could never understand how he, or rather they, chose their victims?"

Yamashita nodded. "Sure… that never made any sense…." he said, staring at the document she had placed in front of him. "But I'm kind of wondering, how does this list of names from eight hundred years ago help?"

Penelope shook her head at him in frustration.

"Don't you get it? In the story, the historical record in Osaka said that the fox spirit had cursed the Maeda family and the men that had killed her *for all their generations*. All their generations… don't you see? Look at the top name on the list."

Yokota took the piece of paper from the desk.

257

"Ina Yasuhisa," he read aloud.

He looked at Penelope and shrugged.

And then he looked at his boss, who suddenly let out a long sigh and looked around the room wild-eyed as the truth of what Penelope had found suddenly dawned on him.

"Ina…" Yamashita murmured. "Oh my God…"

He reached out, took the paper from his Detective Sergeant's hands, and pointed to the surname. He tapped his forefinger on the name and stared at Yokota.

"Ina…" he said forcefully.

"Ina…" Yokota repeated slowly, and then suddenly, his eyes opened wide. "Inagawa? The doctor?"

Yamashita pointed at the fourth name on the list, and Yokota read it aloud too.

"Murakami Shigemochi…." he paused. "*Murakami*? The engineer from ProSec?

Penelope and Yamashita both nodded slowly at him.

Penelope took the piece of paper out of Yamashita's hands and, holding it up, ran her finger down the list of names.

"And Yamana… Yamana Takemori…" she said sadly. "That's what this is about, gentlemen. They weren't killing just *anyone*. This *wasn't random*. They were killing these people's *descendants*. The descendants of those that murdered Tadayuki's bride. It was the curse. A curse on the house of Maeda, *for all time*…"

Chapter 19

The Waning Moon

That evening it was the night of the Young Moon, or the *wakazuki* as it was called in the old lunar calendar, the night when the *Nishinokai Monogatari* claimed that the fox spirit and her mate would hunt together in ancient times.

On this particular evening, with the crescent moon rising over the Kamakura hills behind them, Penelope and a large group of policemen led by the chief inspector, once more entered Ran's house, whose owner, just as she had predicted to them, would not be there.

The front door was unlocked, and they had walked slowly and carefully into the familiar kitchen, with its heavy Italian marble island and black slate floors.

It was, as always, spotlessly clean.

Then they had drifted from room to empty room, but there was no sign of its former inhabitant, nor any indication as to where he might have gone. The books still stood quietly on their shelves, the tearoom where Penny had been so recently with her teacher was clean and empty, the sofa where they had lain so many evenings in the past, all were silent and the same, just as if nothing had ever happened there. Penelope even began to wonder, as the weeks deepened into months afterward, if she had not just dreamed the whole thing.

In the months to come, and despite the mobilization of the entirety of the nation's police and the posting of Ran's face on every international wanted list in existence, not the slightest trace of the man had been found. As they had discovered on that first night, his large black Jaguar was parked in the garage of the house, his clothes still hung in the various wardrobes on neat, color-coded hangers, his desk and his computer records, which were minutely assessed, also contained nothing that could help them. Many of the records had been wiped with a high-end hardware cleaner, and the police techs had been unable to salvage anything of any use.

The house had then been pulled apart minutely by teams of forensic specialists and investigators.

The kill room in the basement had soon been located, and a set of stairs to it had been accessed, locked behind a hidden steel door in the spare bedroom, and this room had finally confirmed everything that Penelope had warned them they would find, and provided absolute proof that their friend and colleague of many years was indeed the serial killer known as *Il Monstro*, and that they had all been completely deceived.

Sal, particularly, had been so shocked by the discovery that the man he had written books with on the subject of *Il Monstro* was actually the killer himself, he had been unable to work for months afterward and had to be coaxed back to life by Penelope, Yamashita and his other friends, who had their own reasons to be distraught.

However, if they had hoped to find more information about Ran's motives and what had really happened, they were to be disappointed. Behind one of the bookcases in the study, they had found a series of empty shelves, which they suspected had once contained Ran's journals, and in the back gardens of the house, they had also discovered an industrial-level incinerator, which was where they conjectured that these and other records had ended up.

Not a trace of them remained in it, however.

It was as if the man known as *Il Monstro* had turned into smoke and vanished, just like the spirit he had pretended for so long to be.

Yuriko, the wife they had all believed dead, was found in a well-heeled mental hospital in the seaside resort of Zushi just a few miles down the coast from Kamakura. Relying on the advice of Penelope, who insisted that she would not be far away, inquiries had been made about a patient whom a Dr. Maeda was supervising, and she had been located in a matter of hours.

The staff had found her dead in her room the previous evening, and the cause was later confirmed as stemming from a lethal injection of a cocktail of powerful drugs. She had died instantly, according to Fei, who had been put in charge of her autopsy at Yamashita's insistence, and as they had known each other well at university decades before, he had been able to make a positive preliminary identification himself. This was later confirmed by her sister and other members of her family, who had kept the secret of her whereabouts for many years at her husband's request, and also out of a desire to avoid any scandal attaching itself to the prestigious Nakatome name.

Mental illness was not something any good Japanese family wanted to be aired publicly, and hers had the means to ensure it wasn't.

At the same time, they had no idea, as did anyone else, as to the things she and her husband had done before her madness had claimed her, if, indeed, that madness had not simply been lurking inside her all the time as Penelope, for one, suspected.

Yamashita had asked to be alone with her at the identification, and after some time had passed, Fei had knocked on the door of the room and found him sitting next to her body with her hand in his. Tears had run unnoticed down his face, and he had struggled to compose himself, grateful that the only person who had seen him in this moment of complete weakness was one of his oldest friends.

Fei stood behind him in silence for a moment, then gently put her hand on his shoulder.

"She didn't suffer, Eiji," she said quietly. "She was gone before she knew it."

Yamashita nodded and wiped his eyes with a handkerchief. The two stood looking at the silent and beautiful face of Yuriko Nakatome, framed in her long white hair, and at the tiny silver necklace that lay on her unmoving chest, which bore an elegantly wrought fox's face, with eyes that were dark blue sapphires.

"She used to wear that necklace when we were students…" he said, with a choking voice. And Fei realized that this woman had once meant something very personal to him, just as she also knew that he would never divulge to anyone what exactly that had been and that he would soon wrap himself once again in the protective blanket of his privacy.

That was who he was, she knew, and she respected it.

So she simply nodded, and when he had managed to pull himself together sufficiently, they had left the room and the body of the woman he had loved, and closed the door.

======================

Some time later, Penelope poured them all some of her best chablis and touched her glass to Sal's, who was sitting next to her. Chief Inspector Yamashita, Machiko, and Fei passed some plates around, and they were soon enjoying a *bouillabaisse*, which Penelope had been simmering for almost the whole day.

Once again, they had gathered in the living room of her old wooden house, where apart from the seafood, they largely dined off the produce of her vegetable garden, which, during the summer at least, made her and Fei well near self-sufficient.

After they had all eaten, Penelope, who had grown up with a father who loved a glass of port after a good meal, poured them all some vintage Australian tawny port, that he had been particularly fond of, and then the conversation, inevitably, turned to that of Ran Maeda, and the book that Sal was planning to write about it.

It had been three months since Ran fled, and the mystery of his whereabouts had still not been solved, and perhaps, they all feared, might never be.

Sal had not given up, and was still investigating his old writing partner, despite the shock and the sense of betrayal he and the rest of them had felt at the duplicity of a man they had all admired and even loved.

"The only thing I don't get is this…" said Sal, emptying his glass of port in a single draught. "Why was there such a long gap between the first murders and those in Tokyo and Kamakura? I mean, your friend Hiro was killed in the 90s," he said, gesturing towards Penelope, and then there were three more in the 2000s, and then these three all of a sudden. Why such a long gap?"

Penelope nodded and poured him another glass.

"I'm not sure, to tell you the truth, but I have a theory…"

Yamashita smiled and nodded. "Well, out with it then…"

"Yes, I was wondering this too… Why not just kill all of them once they got started?" asked Machiko.

Penelope looked around the room at her guests.

"Well… I think it may have been two things. First of all, I think they had trouble locating the correct people. We know they employed at least one genealogist, a woman in Osaka who specializes in this, you know, recreating family trees, tracking down relatives… that sort of thing. She told me, and I know this is a fact, that genealogical records can be very, very scarce in Japan, especially before the Edo period in the seventeenth century. She said that it would have taken considerable time for them to track down the descendants of these people, and the task would have been well-nigh impossible. Japan never had a proper registry of people, that kind of thing was mainly left in the hands of local temples before the 18th century, and people outside the monied classes never even had family names. Knowing your lineage was more a matter of oral tradition, names passed down through the generations and through families that kept their traditional Buddhist altars in their homes with records of their ancestors' names. Anyway, I think that was the first hurdle. Both of them wanted to kill the right people, to revisit the curse that the fox spirit had placed on the families of the men that had killed her back in the day, and to revive the legend, so to speak. I think they felt, or particularly *she* felt, that it was a kind of divine mission that united them across time. That's my first theory anyway."

"And the second?" asked Fei.

The second, I think, was Yuriko..." said Penelope, with a sigh.

"Yuriko? How so?"

"Well, I think Yuriko's illness flared up from time to time. That's what her outside medical records show. I think she had good and bad periods, and her psychological condition gradually worsened in the 2000s. As I told you, she was the driver behind this, not Ran. Most of all, he just wanted to be with her, to satisfy her."

She looked down at the floor for a moment, and then continued.

"She was convinced that she was the reincarnation of the fox spirit of the story, and that Ran was the reincarnation of Tadayuki. Now, I have my suspicions that Ran may not have ever totally believed this, but I do know he loved her, and would do anything for her happiness.

And we both know that neither of them had the slightest problem with killing people. This was something they shared, and this discovery of their joint psychosis bound them together in a way few other things would."

"Wow… so this is a love story? Two murderers finding each other?" asked Machiko.

Penelope nodded.

"Absolutely, it's a love story," she said. "Imagine finding someone you could share your darkest passions with…. It must have been, I don't know, very special for them. And I think that both of them had killed before, too. You don't just get together and start doing this. I think Ran killed his family for a start. Both his parents died in a boating accident, right?" she said, turning to Yamashita, who nodded.

"Yes. As I remember. Their boat's engine exploded while sailing on Lake Ashi, right next to Mount Fuji. There was no real investigation into the cause as the wreckage all sank," he said. "It was called an accident, and there was never any reason to think it was something else…"

Penelope smiled grimly. "There you go then. And Ran inherits all the estate and can do what he wants the rest of his life."

"That would seem to be the case," said Machiko. "So you think they had to stop their little quest to attend to Yuriko's mental problems?"

Penelope nodded. "Yes. There are records showing she spent time in two clinics in Europe in the 2000s before the illness progressed, and then afterward, he arranged for her to stay in the hospital in Zushi. At that point things stopped, and they had only five of their intended victims accounted for."

Sal shook his head. "So why start again? If the wife was bonkers... sorry," he looked apologetically at Yamashita, who said nothing and waved him to continue. "What's the point of starting again?"

"Well... I think he felt he owed her something. To finish their work, *her* work before she died, maybe so he could tell her he had completed that. Maybe it was a cause of distress to her somehow. And I also think he wanted to stop, I'm sure of that. He wanted to stop, and to forget about the whole thing and live like it never happened. But he couldn't do that to her. It was something they had both committed themselves to, something which had bound them together in the first place. And so, he decided to finish the job..."

"And in that sense, I wonder if perhaps he wanted to stop so that when she died, he would be free to be with someone else..." said Machiko, looking pointedly at her friend.

Penelope looked out the window at the gathering autumn sky, where the first stars had just come out above Fei's house next door.

"I do have one question myself, though," Machiko continued. "Call me a curious old witch. But I was wondering how she knew about this story in the first place. She must have known about it *before* she met Ran, or maybe he told her later. But then the chief inspector here said that, according to Fei here, she had worn that fox necklace they found on her body *before* she met Ran. Is that just a co-incidence?"

"Good point," said Yamashita. "Except for one thing."

"What was that."

Yamashita picked up his port and twirled the reddish-brown wine in the little antique glass.

"I gave it to her," he said, looking at Machiko, whose eyes opened wide.

"You? You were dating her?" asked Machiko, surprised.

Yamashita nodded.

"Yes. Believe me, every guy at Tokyo University wanted to date her. I was the lucky one, however. We met in our first year, but it was never more than... how could you call it... a very intense friendship. I was head over heels, though. I gave her that necklace for her birthday. She was eighteen, like me...."

"Wow... aren't you the dark horse," said Machiko with a smirk.

Yamashita looked up and smiled at her.

"But here's the thing... *she chose it.* We went to a jewelry store in Ginza together, and she chose it... and she told me she had a collection of fox things. I saw them once at her house. She had hundreds of little glass foxes and necklaces and fox knick-knacks and things in her room."

"You went to her room," said Sal with a knowing look, clearly enjoying the chief inspector's discomfort.

Yamashita cleared his throat.

"Yes, well... but then she met Ran. And that was that..."

Penelope offered him the last of the port.

"There's one more thing though, Machiko... maybe you didn't notice..."

"I bet *you* did, though," laughed Sal. "You notice everything..."

Penelope turned to Machiko, who was leaning forward in anticipation.

"Do you remember when we went to the library? When Enrico and Minami-san took us downstairs to the Rare Book Room?"

"Yes, of course. Why?"

Penelope smiled at her.

"Do you remember the electrician, the one that was changing the lights in front of the main door to the reading room?"

Machiko sat back in her chair and looked at the ceiling as if trying to coax a memory from it.

"Oh... yeah. Vaguely. I remember now. We had to get him to move his ladder so we could go in, right?"

"That's right," said Penelope. "And that made me look up and see the name of the room above the door."

"The name of the room?"

She nodded.

"It said *Nakatome Rare Books Collection*."

Yamashita started in his seat.

"You mean, Yuriko's family?"

Penelope nodded.

"Yes. Yuriko's grandfather donated the family document collection there in the 90s before he died. He was, among other things, a major collector of Japanese antiquities, particularly rare documents. The *Nishinokai Monogatari* that we saw there had previously been kept at their home in Tokyo, where Yuriko grew up and where

269

she obviously was familiar with it. That document was *never* in the possession of the Maeda family. It belonged to Yuriko's family, and so…"

"So, when she met Ran…" said Yamashita.

Penelope touched his hand.

"She already knew the story of the fox spirit. And of course, she knew who *he* was. Or rather, who she thought he was… just like she knew what she was, the fox spirit, reincarnated. And he was her lord…"

Yamashita gave out a long sigh.

"All these years… I always wondered why she had such a huge thing for him. It was like the moment she met him… there was no one else for her."

Penelope rose, and as she did so, her large black tomcat slid appreciatively into her chair.

"We all have our place in life, it seems…" she said, gazing affectionately at the cat, who looked up and purred loudly from its throat.

"Well… that may be so," said Sal. "But there is one thing I've been kind of wondering. You know, it's clear he loved his wife, and I think he probably killed her because he could no longer be with her, and he knew this was something she would not be able to understand or bear…"

Penelope stood and looked at him. "Yes, that's what I believe too. He knew their time together in this life was over. So he ended her, rather than let her suffer without him."

Sal nodded. "You can probably guess my question then. Do you think he took his own life?"

There was a long silence in the room, and Penelope looked around at her guests.

"That's a very good question. What do you think?"

Chapter 20

Mr. Lee

Long ago, way back in the fifth century BC, Fuchai, the King of Wu, had ordered a great canal to be begun in his lands for trading purposes, his idea being to link his kingdom with the other commercial centers and trading routes, and thus bring prosperity to his people, one of the most powerful in ancient China. Over the centuries, this canal, known today as the Grand Canal, became the longest artificial river in the world. Starting in Beijing, it passed now through Tianjin to the south and then made its winding way through a dozen provinces and cities to the city of Hangzhou, and on the way making a link between the mighty Yellow River and its equally lengthy counterpart, the Yangtze.

The canal also passes through many of China's most picturesque 'water towns,' small and very ancient places like Tongli and Wuzhen, which are quite rightly compared to Venice and thus treasured by the whole nation and the throngs of tourists that visit them each year to glide along their waterways and snap pictures of their well-preserved old architecture.

Of all these lovely old towns, Wuzhcn is one of the oldest and most beautiful, where the old buildings have been scrupulously preserved and where the weeping willows lower their long fronds to trail in the waters near the many little bridges that cross the canals.

In such a charming place, where there were many tourists and people from different places, the man known to his neighbors as Lee Qiang hardly stood out at all.

He had been visiting the place for many years, and now he had retired, he had bought one of the larger old homes, an old *siheyuan* with an enclosed courtyard garden and a grand tiled roof in a quiet back street near one of the canals. It was a sumptuous old home that had belonged to the Gong family of rice merchants for many centuries, before it had fallen into disrepair when the last of the line had died, and it had only recently been put up for sale.

Inside its large wooden doors and high, meter-thick mudbrick walls, there were many rooms, all with pretty windows and views from the upper floors, and all of these faced into the large inner courtyard garden, which the new owner had lovingly restored over the past few months. Now, once again, the smell of orange trees wafted from the grounds, and the climbing roses had been replanted on the newly built trellises that ran along the huge old red walls of the compound, which gave the place the feel of some of the best of the old Chinese summer palaces. Mr. Lee had even excavated the old pond, which had been covered years ago and filled it full of colorful orange and black carp, and had put in a water wheel at one end where a little stream from the river flowed through a part of the property, but it was more for the pleasant sound it made than for any practical purpose.

The neighbors had also been both impressed and startled by the delivery, one bright morning, of a very fine, brand new Steinway grand piano, which had to be craned with great care and much shouting into an upstairs room, and which they now often heard being softly played at night. The local carpenters and other workmen had also been kept busy with a wide variety of different restoration works, and much to their delight, Mr. Lee always paid in cash, and seemed to have no shortage of it.

What had especially got their attention, though, the Chinese being an intensely literate people with a profound respect for scholarship, had been the extensive amount of shelving the men had been charged with putting up, using only the best quality of hardwood (at the insistence of the owner), in one of the largest of the upstairs rooms, which they were told was for the new owner's library.

Not long after they had finished this task, a great many boxes of books started to turn up, and the shelves began to fill with hundreds of meticulously arranged volumes in many languages. Another tale came to them from the local woman he had hired as a maid to keep the place clean and dusted, that the workmen had installed a large and very beautiful antique Chinese desk and chair that looked like it had come from one of the imperial museums, and that this room was where he liked to spend most of his time.

Along with all the other work, there was one area of the house where Mr. Lee had shown that he, like most other Chinese these days, was quite willing to forget the old ways completely, and that was in the kitchen. The workmen claimed that this ancient, dark, and dirty room at the back of the house had been completely gutted, rewired, re-plumbed, and newly fitted with a skylight. The walls were now covered in shiny new white tiles, and it was further graced by a fully-fitted Italian oven, along with rows of the best brand of French copper pans that now hung from the ceiling and the walls, and knives and other cutlery that were of a quality you usually only saw in five-star restaurants in nearby Shanghai, not that they had ever been in one.

Mr. Lee, it was now claimed, must also be a first-class gastronome, an accolade that only added to his reputation and the warmth of his welcome among his new friends in the town.

Although the new arrival had let it be known that his great-grandmother had come from Wuzhen and that he was happy to be returning to his roots, no one had any memory of his illustrious ancestor, which of course, was only to be expected after the chaos of the cultural revolution and the various iniquities the Red Guards had visited upon the town in the bad old days, where many people had been forced to uproot themselves and leave their ancestral homes. Mr. Lee maintained that after his father's death, his mother had been one of these, and that, coming from a family of respected scholars, she had been put to work at a pig farm on the outskirts of Shanghai to be re-educated as to the virtues of the working peasantry.

Mr. Lee claimed that he had been a good student, a fact no one doubted, and that he had been able to get a good education and as a result had been many years in the north of China near Harbin as a representative of a textile firm, and had later spent a lot of time in Europe as an executive with a trading company. Because of his many years away living in places like London and Germany, he spoke a relatively flat, accent-less form of Mandarin, such that it took a lot of work to tell where he came from.

This, however, soon changed, and added even more to the qualities that he was so much admired for.

In Wuzhen, the locals all spoke the *Ningbo* dialect, a form of what is known as Wu Chinese, which is generally understandable to Shanghainese speakers, but not even vaguely comprehensible to the rest of the country. Mr. Lee, however, and in a matter of months, soon spoke it so well that people meeting him for the first time thought he had been born there, a fact which soon enabled him to make many friends and to be completely accepted by the local community as one of their own.

Mr. Lee often took a walk in the mornings or early evenings, and soon became well known in the local markets and side streets, where he was frequently seen buying fresh produce, chatting with his friends, and sometimes even playing cards with some of the older men, although he generally eschewed the alcohol they pressed on him on these occasions in favor of the delicious local bean tea, which he claimed he was almost excessively fond of.

The only slightly strange thing about Mr. Lee, a man of slight build with shoulder-length grey hair he wore pulled back in a ponytail, were his eyes, which were a deep shade of indigo blue. This was not a completely unheard-of thing in China, where there are many ethnicities and where blue eyes were quite commonly seen, but it was something that you noticed when you spoke to him.

If anybody mentioned it, Mr. Lee told them that one of his ancestors had come from Liqian, a place well-known for folk with blue eyes and, even more strangely, blonde hair.

Whenever Mr. Lee told this story, nearly everyone believed him.

Did you enjoy the book?

If you enjoyed the book, please take a moment and write a short review on Amazon.

This would be most appreciated by the author!

About the Author

Ash Warren is an Australian author who graduated with a degree in medieval history and English literature from the University of New South Wales in Sydney.

After a period of roaming the world with a backpack, he settled in Japan, where he has lived since 1992.

During that time he has written and published widely on language and Japanese culture, and teaches at a university in Tokyo.

He is the author of The Penelope Middleton series: *Dark Tea, The Quiet Game,* and *The Singing Blade* and also of *The Way of Salt: Sumo and the Culture of Japan* (Silman-James Press, Los Angeles), *The Language Code: How to Effectively Learn Foreign Languages* and *Mastering the Japanese Writing System.* (Also available at Amazon and elsewhere.)

He lives with his family in Tokyo with one dog, two cats and has a penchant for chess, sumo, classical music, long walks and talking about politics over too much sake.

The Penelope Middleton Series

The Fox Spirit is the fourth book in the Penelope Middleton series and follows:

Dark Tea
The Quiet Game
The Singing Blade

If you would like to be updated about further books in the series and other books by the author, please go to:

www.arwarren.net

and subscribe!

If you would like to contact the author directly, please write to:

wslc2000@hotmail.com

Printed in Great Britain
by Amazon

WING

OVER

MALAYA

by

GEORGE RICHEY

Editor: Mike Willmott

Artwork: Gerald Newton

BISHOP STREET PRESS

**8, Bishop Street, Shrewsbury, Shropshire
SY2 5HA Phone: 01743-343718 Fax:01743-231826
E-mail: michael.willmott@ukonline.co.uk
website:www.bishopstreetpress.co.uk**

ABBREVIATIONS/LOCAL TERMS

AFC	Air Force Cross
Amah	Local domestic help
Basha	Either a barrack hut or a wood-and-leaf hut built in the jungle
CT	Communist Terrorist
DZ	Dropping Zone
IO	Intelligence Officer
Kampong	Malay Village
Kiwi	New Zealander
KL	Kual Lumpur
Ladang	Area in the jungle cleared and cultivated by the Aboriginals
LZ	Landing Zone
Mossies	Mosquitoes
NCO	Non-Commissioned Officer
RAA	Royal Australian Artillery or Royal Artillery Association
RAAF	Royal Australian Air Force
RAF	Royal Air Force
RASC	Royal Army Service Corps (part of Logistics Corps)
SACEUR	Supreme Allied Commander Europe
Sakai	Aboriginal
SAS	Special Air Service
Sprog	Inexperienced beginner
MIO	Malayan Intelligence Officer
Padang	Public playing area usually in centre of town
Pangy	Sharpened stick placed at bottom of concealed pit
PR	Public Relations
WO	Warrant Officer

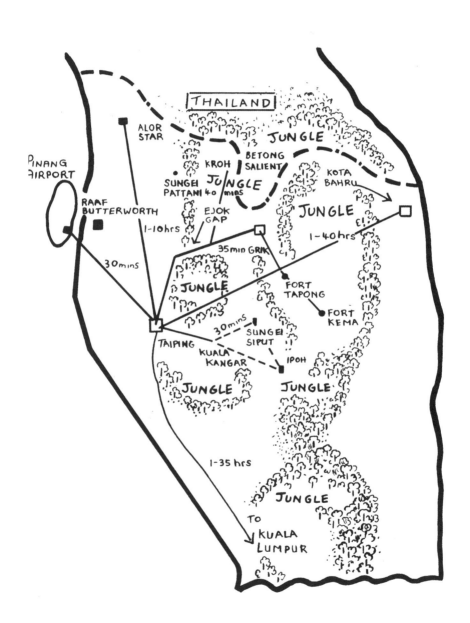

INTRODUCTION

This is a personal story describing my experiences as a light aircraft pilot during the latter stages of the Malayan Emergency. That started soon after the Second World War, and continued until 1960. It was politically and militarily successful. Indeed, it was the only example in continental Asia where the Communists were defeated. This story will not deal with the political and military strategy adopted so successfully, except in so far as it directly affected me. However, the strategy and tactics of the Malayan Campaign were used with equal success in the Borneo and Timor Campaigns. The so-called 'Emergency' lasted from 1948 until 1960, and even after. Then, in the far north, particularly in Perak State, operations continued. The mainly Chinese Malayan Communist Party found that a political solution would get nowhere. They decided on military means, and the hard core under Chin Peng went into the jungle, from whence a long campaign of terror and violence was started.

The importance of the *'Malayan Emergency'* as it was called to the future of Southern Asia cannot be emphasised too much. It was both a military and political victory over Communism. In 1958, the time that I went out, the final demise of the jungle war was in sight. Nevertheless, operations continued, especially in the northern Malayan States, even after the Emergency was officially declared over in 1960.

MIDDLE WALLOP

I volunteered at the age of twenty-six-and-a-half for flying duties. At the time, as a young captain, I was due for my third posting. My first three years after Sandhurst were with a heavy mobile anti-aircraft regiment, and I was well into my second tour with a field regiment. Now was the time to branch out. Having passed the interview and medical, I was posted to Middle Wallop, where all army pilots received their initial flying training. I was a member of 126 Course which was unfortunate to start as an Air Observation Pilot Course, but to end as an Army Air Corps Course. This meant, that whilst we attended the "Wings" parades of those courses that preceded us, we never had the opportunity

2

to receive our Wings in front of those following behind, as we didn't have a Wings Parade.

On going back, having retired, I found that for some reason Course 126 has no photographic record. We started with thirteen students, but there was a fair attrition rate, and only four of us actually passed out.

The course started on 27th May, 1957, with Elementary Flight. The aircraft used for this initial training was the well tried Chipmunk, a sturdy aircraft which could practically fly itself, if one removed hands and feet from the controls. The first hurdle was to go solo. At least one of the students failed to get that far. It was made clear that there was no disgrace in failing at this point, nor indeed at any subsequent time. Some people could not judge height, and tended to "round out" consistently too high. The Course was very high intensity, and time was simply not available to allow students to fall behind. They departed.

My first instructor was Flight Lieutenant Corbin, who saw me through to my first solo after 6 hours 10 minutes. Thereafter, I found myself in the hands of a Captain Waddington, a fellow gunner. Elementary Flight ended with a final handling check by the Chief

Flying Instructor, an experienced RAF officer.The hours flown by students at this stage were in the order of twenty-six hours solo, and thirty five dual.

The second part of the Course which started on 26th September,1957, was Intermediate Flight. We were introduced to the Auster Mk 7, a high-wing monoplane with good all-round view, especially downwards. I went solo after four hours forty minutes dual on the Mark 7. From this point, the flying became more military-orientated, and included netting in the air, cross-country navigation, low flying, and night flying.

Auster Mark V1

4

There was a 30-hour flying check, and a couple departed at this point. The culmination of this part of the Course was the final handling check again by the CFI. This sortie lasted for an hour and a half, followed by a comprehensive debrief.

The final six weeks of the course was with Exercise Flight. This required the introduction to the Auster Mk9. This had different characteristics to the Mark 7. However, the transition was easy, and my solo took place after about forty-five minutes dual. Thereafter, the course became much more interesting, as flying was almost all geared to the type of flying that an operational pilot would need.

Virtually all the flying was tactical and most of it was solo. It not only involved flying into and out of short strips, but the observation of artillerty fire on the ranges at Larkhill.

The Course actually ended on 31st January,1958. There were by now only four of us. Then came the matter of postings. One volunteered for Northern Ireland, another, with a family and a child due, opted for the UK. There were two other postings, one to BAOR, the other to Malaya. On the toss of a coin I got Malaya. I now had 177 hours' flying time under my belt, of which 98 were dual.

Apparently pilots were required urgently, so I and my family, wife, and two children flew out in a Hermes aircraft. Our dog Rupert, an Alsation, went out by boat with the *Ben Line*. This flight took two and a half days, with stops at Rome, Basra, a night stop in Karachi, and a final stop in Bankok, before arrival at Singapore. We spent a hot night in a hotel, before boarding the train to KL. This was the first time that I had been in the Far East, although my wife Barbara, a daughter of a soldier, had remembered the hot smell that had greeted us when the doors opened at Karachi. The children (3 and 1) were fascinated by the scenes which passed as we were carried up the Malayan Peninsular to KL. On arrival we were met by the Adjudant of the squadron. He was an RAF officer, the last from that service to hold that appointment, as by now the Army Air Corps was in existence. We were put up in the Service Rest House in the middle of KL. The next morning, I reported to HQ 656 Light Aircraft Sqadron, AAC at "Noble Field". This consisted of an airstrip, the normal HQ buildings and hangers with workshop facilities for the six or so aircraft based there.

START OF THE MALAYAN TOUR

The Squadron had four flights, one stationed at Taiping in the far north, another at Ipoh also in the north (both in Perak State), a third at Seremban, the location of HQ 17 Gurkha Division, and the last stationed in Singapore. I had relatives in KL but this was not sufficient reason for me to be stationed there. I was to go to Taiping to join 7 Recce Flight, AAC under the command at that time of a Major Clive Russell, DFC.

First, though, I had to undergo familiarisation training. The gap of a month and a half together with the apparent different landing speed of Mk9 in a hot climate was interesting enough. What made the introduction to flying in Malaya more interesting was that the landing technique was quite different from that I had been taught at Middle Wallop. There, we did nice three-point landings. Now, one was introduced to the two-point landing at what, initially, seemed to me to be done at a significantly higher speed. However, Captain Southall, the Chief Flying Instructor (CFI) and a gunner, let me go solo after one hour ten minutes' dual.

Having gone solo, much of the next three weeks was spent in familiarising oneself with the two-point landing on the various strips in the southern half of Malaya. One also became familiar with the air traffic control system operating in the country at that time.

The squadron was equipped with the high frequency (HF) 19 set, common to most units in the British Army. There was a dedicated frequency, one which all the squadron's aircraft operated. This was tuned with a crystal. The drill was simple, as the aerial had to be 'let out' once the aircraft was airborne.

The length of aerial needed was indicated by a dial which showed the amount of power being transmitted on the crystal frequency. If one required to talk to troops on the ground who were also on HF, one followed normal netting procedures and adjusted the amount of aerial required. This was a simple procedure. The drawback was that sometimes before landing, pilots could in the early days forget to take in the aerial with the result that the drogue would be lost. A fine usually helped the memory.

There was also a very high frequency (VHF) set with some ten channels, all pre- set. One was the international distress frequency. Others were tuned to frequencies used by the civil airfields. When flying on any sortie, one kept in touch with the squadron or flight bases on HF, and with the civil network using VHF. Communication with RAF, Royal Australian or Royal Malayan Airforce pilots was also by VHF.

During the next fortnight whilst the family had a pleasant, *amah* (servant)-assisted, stay at the very comfortable hotel, I flew both dual with the squadron CFI, or solo to Seremban , KL main, where the second line servicing squadron workshops were, and Simbawang, the airfield at which the Singapore Flight was based. There were a number of airstrips between KL and Singapore, some maintained by local rubber companies, to which one paid single landing and take-off visits.

At the end of March 1958, I departed by train for Taiping, where 7 Flight was based.

NORTH MALAYA

Taiping, which was alleged to have one of the largest rainfalls in the world (I was never able to confirm this, but certainly it was one of the wettest towns in Malaya) is situated in the State of Perak, known as the Silver State, on the

9

Western Plain which itself stretches up virtually the whole of the Malayan Peninsular. This plain consisted of a mixture of swamp, small *kampongs* (villages), fishing villages, and plantations. To the immediate north and south of Taiping is the main western range of forrested hills. To the east of this set of hills is a central valley dotted with *kampongs*, and at that time surface tin-mines. The way into this central plain is via a valley through which the railway line runs. It was also the 'rat run' for pilots returning to Taiping from anywhere east or southeast. This was particularly so when cloud was about: one did not as far as possible fly in cloud.

Taiping was the onetime capital of Perak State, and boasted a racetrack, which by the time I arrived had fallen into disuse. Just where the valley opened out into the central plain is the town of Kuala Kangsar, the home of the Sultan. It was also the battalion base of the Royal Australian Regiment. It too had a strip.

To the north of Taiping are the states of Kedar, Perlis and Pinang. The RAAF base was at Butterworth, which had at the time the third longest runway in the world. Stationed there were Canberra and Sabre squadrons. It was situated opposite Pinang which also had a civil airfield. The most northern civil airfield on the west side of Malaya was Alor Star, close to the Malay-Thai border. It was also the home of one of the Malay Regiment battalions.

The operational area for which 7 Flight was responsible covered Perak State, and the area of most interest was along the border, and in particular the forest-covered range of hills in central Malaya up to and including the border. The Australians had a company base at a place called Grik. This was located quite close to the border immediately south of the border where the Thai part 'bit into' Malaya known as the Betong Salient. It had a landing strip. There were refuelling facilities at all these northern strips. The one at Grik was frequently used by the flight.

The other similar camp was at Kroh, located very close to the border on the western side of the Betong Salient. A Malay Regiment unit was based there. It,too, I was to discover, was a frequent stop-off point during day-long operational flights.

SCENE SETTING

My first week was spent on the ground. My immediate task was to sort out my maps. This involved the use of scissors and glue. The maps were the familiar one-inch-to-one mile maps produced by the MOD. Essentially, one stuck four of these maps together, and then folded them into a form of concertina. This enabled one to readily fold the map to the required area. In order that one was not caught out, the sets of maps overlapped. It was a lesson one relearned every now and then when one flew off the map in one's hand and found (or rather did not find) a problem in locating exactly where one was. At this time the maps covering the central range in north Malaya did not have contour lines. Instead there were form lines. The reason for this was that accurate survey had not yet been done. This made accurate map reading both from the air and for those on the ground an interesting exercise in guess-work. In fact, by the time I came to the end of my tour, all the maps had contours. But until these arrived, we had these form-line maps which had also odd-shaped white patches with the word CLOUD written in them.

I was also briefed on the task of the Flight. 7 Flight supported the Commonwealth Brigade, the Headquarters which was at Taiping, as was the 1st New Zealand Battalion. Besides the Australians at Kuala Kangsar, there was a British Battalion stationed at Ipoh.There were a number of minor units also in Taiping as well as the Military Hospital.

The Gurkhas had been in Malaya right from the start of the emergency, and there was a Gurkha battalion also at Ipoh. The Gurkha Brigade Training Depot was at Sungei Patani in Kedar. All recruits came there before posting to their battalions. It was about thirty minutes' flying time from Taiping.

The flight had its base, consisting of a cookhouse, *bashas,* flight-office and operations room all within the confines of the main administrative camp. Its flight workshop was on the civil airfield at which were housed the six Auster 9 aircraft. There was a small tower in which the duty RA signaller sat with the HF set. There was of course during working hours a civil control organisation with which pilots logged in and out on VHF.

THE RÔLE OF 7 RECCE FLIGHT

It was quite simply to support the brigade operations. At the time, *Operation Bamboo* was the name given to the jungle operations in North Malaya. It was a convenient name, and was still in use three years later when I left.

The first task was the ferrying of single or pairs of passengers from one place to another. The only practical way, for instance, for officers to get to briefings at Grik was by air. Incidentally the Grik-Kroh road was 'black'. That is to say, military movement only took place with an armed escort. It was the only 'black' road left when the Emergency formally ended in 1960. It remained 'black' thereafter, and was still 'black' when I departed in 1961.

GROUND OPERATIONS

Essentially, in the Commonwealth area of responsibility, each battalion had its piece of jungle, and maintained a permanent presence in it. The Briggs plan was well established, and all *kampongs* and towns were surrounded by wire. Locals were searched on going out to work, and food was not allowed to be taken out. My impression was that in practice Malays were not searched, neither were Europeans. The Chinese tended to be stopped. The aim was to deny food to the Communist Terrorists (CTs). This was effective, and those relativly few active CTs in the jungle tried to grow their own food, or they lived off the *sakai*. These people, who still lived much as they had done for years in their own settlements in deep jungle, grew hill *paddie* in large *ladangs*. There were a number of CTs operating in South Thailand in the Thai state of Pattani. The political situation was interesting in this respect, as the majority of the locals were Muslims. Malaya was a mainly Muslim country: thus, there was an area of potential clash between the two national governments.

Malayan and British army units were not permitted to operate north of the border. However, the Malayan Police Field Force was, under certain conditions. We pilots were allowed to fly over the border, and in fact did so on a regular basis both immediately north of Alor Star, and in the Betong Salient in particular. But more of this later.

22 SAS were also deployed from time to time in the Commonwealth Brigade area. They operated under the control of 17 Division, and

15

all their operational messages were routed via their HQ near KL.

In my first week with the flight, I flew not at all. I listened in the crew-room to my fellow-, and very much more experienced- pilots, with frustrated envy. At the end of this week on the Saturday morning, Clive Russell drove down to KL with me as a passenger. I rejoined my family to find that Rupert had arrived. At the end of the next week I took the train to Taiping with the family and Rupert. He travelled in the guards-van.

Very kindly, we had been fixed up with a Larut Tin Company house. This was a traditional wooden Malay house on stilts. However, the ground floor, surrounded by wire-netting to keep out the *mossies,* provided a rather nice sitting-room. The kitchen was at the back, as were the *armah's* quarters. We took on a Chinese woman and her daughter who stayed with us for three years. She was a great cook, having spent the previous three years with the Brigade Catering Officer!

LARUT TIN HOUSE

SERIOUS FLYING BEGINS

Two of us had arrived in 7 Flight at the same time. John Naylor, who passed out with me from Sandhurst in 1951, had been a course ahead of me at Wallop. However, he had managed to fix himself and his family to go by troopship. Having flown the Flight Commander on a training flight, and done some practice message and supply dropping on the airfield, John Naylor and I were then sent off together to fly round North Malaya. We visited virtually all the airfields and strips that we were going to use on operations. At each halt, having refuelled, we

17

swapped seats. At the end of that week, I was invited to go on the Aircrew Jungle Survival course. I flew an Auster on a one-way journey to the main workshops at KL Main where it was due a major service I was then flown by another pilot to Singapore.

NOT SO SERIOUS JUNGLE SURVIVAL

The Jungle Survival Course run by the RAF was mandatory for all aircrew and RASC air despatchers. The course - a motley collection of RAF pilots,army air-despatchers and two army pilots, assembled on the Sunday evening in a pretty basic *basha* and waited. At an indeterminate time (it was dark) an RAF senior NCO barged open the door, hurled in three live chickens with a cry of, "Here's your first meal." He then left. The chickens remained uneaten, and alive.

The Course itself was interesting, consisting of a series of lectures on survival techniques, followed by practicals on cooking to survive. We were then to go out for three days and two nights equipped with what we might reasonably expect to have on us if we had come down in the jungle and lived. However, the Americans came to our aid. A party from the States had come over to test their new, yet to be issued, survival rations. These were in tins, and highly concentrated. They seemed to think that we British were the best people to be tested upon. We were split into groups, each group with different amounts of concentrates and water. I was in the much-envied group with the most generous amount of nosh and, praise be, unlimited water. I enjoyed the three days. It was in fact a glorified scouting expedition. At night, we all set to making out beds of saplings,wood and *ponchoes*. I had the impression that the RAF pilots were not enjoying themselves.

The penultimate day was spent on an escape and evasion exercise. Having been dropped off quite a way from the camp, we were invited to get back undetected. If/when caught one was locked up and then put through a severe questioning by the staff.Virtually all were caught. It was difficult for tall Europeans dressed in jungle green to walk around in Singapore and not be noticed by the local police who were in on the game, or the Singapore Regiment who were also looking for us. At the end of the course, I took the train back to Taiping (no friendly Austers available I fear).

OPERATIONAL FLYING REALLY STARTS

The next day, having done an hour's worth of circuits and bumps, I went off on my first proper operational flight, which was a Visual Recce (VR) This was of two ten thousand metre squares (I see from my log VD90 and 91). These were in the main range east of Ipoh. I completed three sorties of 2.05,1.30 and 1.30 hours, refuelling at Ipoh twice.

I cannot say that I achieved very much. I knew that CT camps had been spotted from the air. The operations board in the crew room had masses of pins in, all representing the result of VR. It was in fact an interesting historical document in its own right.

The coloured pins consisted of (1) large red, a CT camp confirmed (by ground troops) originally spotted by the flight, (2) large black - suspect CT camp,(3) green pin-*Sakai Ladang* (these were graded from class1 (occupied with crops growing) through to 7 (overgrown *ladang* not in current use).

It was a peculiar fact that if CTs used an existing *ladang* to grow their own hill paddy, unlike the Sakai who scatter sowed, they planted in straight lines. Later in my tour

20

another pilot spotted a plantation with a nicely fenced-off area in the corner of a *ladang* with paddy planted in straight lines as if in an allotment. Sure enough, a subsequent ground operation found the CT camp nearby.

However, I spent my first sorties beginning to think out, as all pilots had done before me, just what was the best way to recce a 10,000 square of jungle. Received wisdom was that the CTs were most likely to choose a site off a main ridge on one of the subsidiary ridges. One looked for signs that the ground beneath the trees was bare where normally it would be covered.The *bashas* (huts made of wood and branches) themselves would not be green, but brown as the folliage used for the roof would discolour in time. Later in my tour I was to see four such camps, of which three were in South Thailand.

During the third month of the tour I was checked out by the CFI and authorised to carry passengers or rather as the chit signed by the squadron commanding officer, at the time a Lieutenant Colonel B Story, RA, stating that "(I was) permitted to carry an essential passenger in Auster Aircraft". I was now a fully-operational member of the flight. For some reason the Flight

21

Commander then conceived the notion that I was unique, and as a result I found myself doing a great deal of Artillery Spotting (AOP) work. In fact, of the pilots in the flight, apart from Clive Russell, John Naylor and myself, there were no gunners. There were two RASC (as it then was) and two infantrymen, one a sergeant pilot. Sergeant Law was subsequently commissioned into the Army Air Corps.

During the months of May, June and July, 1958, I carried out twenty three separate AOP sorties in support of 1 NZ Battalion and 2/6 Gurkha Rifles.This was not the close support normally used in the conventional operations for which one had trained.

Basically the supported battalion would have deployed, leaving parts of their area of responsibility free of troops. The artillery fires would be directed into these unoccupied areas with the intention that, if there were CTs in there, they would be encouraged to move out, possibly in some haste. I see from my log book that on 2nd June I carried out a shoot in the 1NZ area. About a month later, it was reported that a CT camp had been hit and in July a CT from that camp surrendered. I have to say that at the time of the shoot I did not see any camp, but did direct fire at likely camp sites. At any event, the flight was given some credit for the surrender of the CT. Most went to 1NZ, who brought him in.

Another entry in my log for 2nd July (on 1st and 2nd July I carried out nine AOP sorties, refuelling at Ipoh and a small unmanned strip at Sungei Siput) all in support of 1NZ. This battalion ambushed 3CTs who, on the day of the shoot, were caught moving out of the area being shot. So the concept of this tactic did work.

In June I also began to carry out a number of Contact Recces (CRs). The CR was possibly one of the most valuable things that pilots did to help their supported batallions. At the time, the maps were not entirely accurate. The form-lines were a matter of judgement I suspect. All this had changed by the time my tour came to an end, as proper survey of Malaya had been completed. However, patrols needed to know where they were, and the only people who could tell them were the AAC pilots.

To carry out a CR, one needed to know the approximate location of the patrol, and the frequency on which it operated. The patrol needed to know the time at which the aircraft would be overhead. If all went to plan, and it usually did, the pilot would arrive over the general area. He would then start looking for an orange balloon in the jungle canopy. These balloon kits were carried by all patrols. To fly them the patrol filled the balloon with gas. This was generated by putting crystals into water. The reaction produced the gas, and the balloon was allowed to rise as the line was let out. It was a most effective means by which a lost patrol could be found.

The problem as far as the pilot was concerned was, having spotted the balloon, to work out where the patrol was. Remember that the map was not entirely accurate, and form-lines were not the basis on which to tell a patrol where it was. It could take up to twenty minutes or even longer to produce a guaranteed grid ref. There were a number of things that could help. From the air, rivers were easily seen, and they were very likely to be accurate on the map. The other assistance were the high peaks of which there were many.Using these, and by flying directly over the balloon towards the peak, one would take the back bearing. Repeating the process with another peak, one then had a point on the map where the bearing-lines crossed - thus a pretty good idea where the patrol was. One had to be certain about the peaks, however.This service was used a lot generally when a new deployment was taking place, or as sometimes happened when a patrol began to doubt where it was. Jungle navigation with the maps available at the time was not easy, and when operating at the limit of the area of responsibility, patrols had to know exactly where they were. Having worked out the grid reference and checked it, the grid was then passed to the patrol by the HF radio. On landing, it was also given to the battalion ops room.

As well as the unaccommpanied VR sortie, we also carried passengers on what were called "pax VRs". These were in general Commanding Officers, Company Commanders or Patrol Commanders having a look at the area into which they were about to operate.This was a much-appreciated form of support.

FLYING HOURS AND COMPULSORY
REST PERIODS

At this point it might be worthwhile talking about the hours that all pilots were flying. Recently I have visited RAF Shawbury where AAC pilots are now trained, and have had the opportunity to talk not only to the trainees but to squadron pilots visiting the station. The hours that they are permitted seem very little compared with what we were doing in Malaya.

Generally, pilots were not supposed to fly more than fifty hours in any one month.Every third month in theory pilots went on a fortnight's leave. These leaves were usually taken at one of the rest-houses dotted about Malaya. The nearest to Taiping was at Georgetown, Pinang.This was the one to which we always went. It was an extremely nice hotel adjacent to the beach.

The hours that I flew in the first five months with 7 Flight were :-

April 21.05hrs (including Jungle Survival Course)

May 38.55hrs   June 44.10hrs

July 50.20 hrs plus 1.10hrs night flying

Aug 60.05hrs plus 0.55 hrs night flying

In September, the family spent a week in the Pinang Rest Hotel. The division of tasks by the end of August that I had logged was :-
VR 70.50 hrs, AOP 38.45 hrs, CR 16.35 hrs.
I had also dropped some 1,490 lbs of supplies to patrols in the jungle in twenty-six different sorties.

SUPPLY-DROPPING IN MALAYA

At Wallop, the system for supply-dropping was to fly in over the DZ at just above stalling speed with half flap. The load, if it was being dropped by parachute, would be on the passenger seat, or if there was a passenger, on his lap. The parachute would be tied to the load with the line attached to the strut or the step immediately below the door, which of course had been removed.

In Malaya, this concept was discarded. We flew in at high speed with no flap. The point was that in the central range the winds and down-drafts were unpredictable. It was better to take no chances. In general, we all flew with the doors off, unless one was ferrying passengers.

Most supplies - and these ranged from radios to rations - were dropped by parachute.

Most of the DZs in the jungle were cut by the patrols themselves, and were therefore as small as possible. It was not funny cutting down trees, and the fewer the better.

There were two types of parachute. The most popular from the pilots' point of view were off-green, and fairly small. Their speed once the chute was deployed was slightly faster than that of the other type. This second type was pink. It was a larger chute, thus when deployed had a slower descent speed. This meant that the chance of it being affected by the wind and being hung up in the trees was more likely. However, whichever type of chute was used it was essential to be accurate.

The drop was effected about a hundred feet above the jungle canopy, and this meant that the chute would actually open as the load reached the canopy, hopefully in the middle of the cleared area.

On one occasion, when supply-dropping alone, my load, which consisted of two 10-man ration packs, had not been correctly tied together. When I pushed it out, it fell with one pack in front of the strut and one behind. The chute remained packed. I spent about ten minutes (it seemed longer at the time), having gone up to a safe height, leaning over and pulling eventually successfully the load back in, sorting it out, returning to the DZ. After apologies to the patrol who had been wondering what on earth was going on, the drop was completed.

Clive Russell became the Squadron Second-in- command, and John Chandler, a Royal Inniskillin, arrived to take over the Flight. After a year, he left to go instructing at Sandhurst, having been awarded a well-earned AFC. By now, I was regarded as reasonably experienced.

Flying in Malaya on operations was tremendous fun. We all had a sense of achievement. Flying single-engine aircraft, mostly over primary jungle, meant that at the back of one's mind was the possibility of engine failure. This had been happening every now and then. The alleged cause was thought to be fuel aeration. The Auster 9 had the Bombadier 205 or 208 fuel injection engine. It was very efficient, and certainly more powerful than the Gypsy Major Mk 7 with which the Auster 7 was equipped. The Mk 9 was much preferable in Malaya, and those who flew the 9 had great respect for, but did not envy, those who flew in

Malaya before the arrival of the 9.

In January 1960, the Seremban Flight lost a pilot. Virtually every pilot in the squadron took part in the search. In fact he was found some weeks later. It became clear that he had suffered a loss of power soon after take-off. The wings were painted with a dark camouflage colour. As the two tanks were in the wings, not only did they absorb heat but so did the avgas in the tanks. What could happen was that in the heat, the fuel on its way to the engine boiled - hence the loss of power.Two steps were taken. Bright red dayglow was stuck on the ends of the wings and tail-planes. And the area of the wings which held the two tanks was painted white.This later stopped partial engine failures.

In December 1958, there was still a considerable amount of AOP work. I spotted for the 25-pounders of 100 RAA battery, and a medium troop of 2 Field who had just taken over from 48 field. The effect of the mediums in the jungle was considerable There was no delay in seeing the fall of shot. With the 25-pounder there was usually a delay whilst the smoke rose to the forest canopy. Every now and then there would be a high tree burst which made things easier. On a particular shoot with the medium troop I was engaging a *ladang* which was situated on a forward slope - that is to say forward in relation to the gun position. I was flying between the gun position and the target when to my horror, I heard the word "SHOT". With AOP shoots the rule was that all engagements were on a "fire by order basis". The next few seconds went very slowly, as I was between the targets and the guns. The Gun Position Officer was removed from my Christmas Card list.The shooting was extremely accurate, however.

During December, I carried out nine AOP sorties lasting altogether fourteen hours twenty minutes flying time. It was also in December that the flight was asked to do some target marking training with RAAF Butterworth. The most accurate method of getting bombs on the target in Malaya was for the Austers to be used to indicate the target with a magnesium flare. These were fixed beneath the aircraft on a special fitting which was only put on when the flares were required. The other time that they were needed was when night-flying. When released, the parachute was immediately deployed and the flare activated. Clearly therefore, the closer to the jungle canopy the better as one did not want the flare to be floating down as the bombers were making their final run in.

The flare could be dropped on the target or intentionally off the target (say 100 metres north). The operation required the Auster to fly in at 90 degrees from the bomber's approach. The flare would be released 60 seconds before the bombs were to be released.The Auster pilot would be in communication with the bomb leader and would be told, "Bomb release in 5 minutes." From then he timed his run-in on a predetermined point on the ground, at a predetermined speed - 70 knots. He would indicate to the bomb leader, "Two minutes to marking - one minute to marking -target Marked." He would then clear off. But - there was always a 'but' - he had first to confirm that the flare had indeed been released, and that it was on target. If off the target, he had immediately to give its position in relation to the target. It sounds fraught, but in practice I never heard of things going wrong.

There was a famous occasion when a camp had been spotted in the south, and it was decided to bomb it.The ground patrols were sent in with body bags, but due to safety would have quite a march in once the deed had been done. Unfortunately the RAF decided to try out a method of directing their bombers using radar.

The theory here was that as the grid of the target was known and the radar could be suveyed in the directions to the bombers it would render target- marking unnecessary.

There was considerable teeth-sucking in 656 Squadron, but the RAF was adamant - they were going to trust their radar. The reason that I include this story is that the bombs fell nowhere near the camp.This was no surprise The grid reference produced by the pilot was from a map which was not accurate, as the maps produced the following year were. In any event, I gathered that a pretty blunt message was sent which in effect recommended that target-marking using the Austers was less likely to produce errors.

We continued to exercise with Australians who were most hospitable. There was also another attraction. They had masses of Libby's fruit juice - aircrew rations - and were happy to supply their friendly target-marking *poms*. I took off from Butterworth with the Auster groaning with the weight of boxes and boxes of fruit juice. It was as well that I could take off using the Butterworth main runway and land using the

Taiping Civil runway. The juice lasted us for months.

One of the advantages of being in 656 Squadron as far as the pilots were concerned was the distance one was away from the squadron headquarters. The flights were in the pleasant position of being "under command" of an HQ which one saw very rarely. In the case of 7 Flight which was collocated with HQ 28 Commonwealth Brigade, it was in support of the brigade, but not under command. The Flight was very much its own master.

The Flight Commander would decide on the next day's operations. The aircraft and pilot would be allocated to the particular tasks. Units would put in their bids and it was rare that all bids could not be carried out. A signal giving the daily flight programme would be signalled by the brigade to all who needed to know. This included the RAF Air Traffic Control Operations Room. But once a pilot started out on his day's flying, if an immediate request came up, for instance, if one was carrying out a VR mission and landed at, say, Grik to refuel, he could change his programme for a supply-drop, or a CR. So, all pilots had the power to self-authorise. This flexibility was essential if the flight was to do the job of supporting the troops in the jungle. It was not given to the RAF pilots on helicopter patrol insertion missions, sometimes to the irritation of the ground troops.

A plus for pilots was of course that, having flown on a day's operation, once back at Taiping, normal social life continued.

It was a strange sort of life that the pilots led. On the one hand, during the day or night when flying on operations, we were all carrying out vitally important tasks in support of the units operating in the jungle. On the other hand, once the flying was completed, normal social life carried on. By 1958, most of the restrictions on travelling by road were no more. In that sense, the light aircraft pilots were in a different position from those whom they supported in the jungle. I think that, as a result, we were all determined that missions would be carried out, whatever the conditions.

SOCIAL AND SPORTING LIFE

The Taiping Club was the centre of social life in Taiping. One had to be a member, and as with all such clubs the usual application procedures were followed. The main event of the season was the pre-Christmas party. These were pretty riotous.

On the three years that I was there, one of the contributions of the Flight was to drop Father Christmas at the Childrens' Party which the garrison wives ran. For the weeks leading up to the day, the flight would receive parcels well-packed up and labelled. In fact, each year there were two such parties, one for the NZ families and the other for the HQ and other unit families. The presents were put in appropriate sacks.

At the predetermined time, the Auster would appear, circle the children with a red-coated Father Christmas in the passenger-seat, waving furiously. The drop would then take place, some four hundred yards away. The DZ was conveniently situated behind a clump of trees. The dummy Father Christmas, fixed firmly to a parachute, would be hurled out, the 'chute would open, and Father Christmas woud be seen floating down. He would land out of sight of the children, and, lo, a minute later would appear in a Landrover, with sacks of presents. I got to do the drop at my last Christmas in Taiping.

The drop on the second Christmas, that is 1960, was nearly a PR disaster. The Auster appeared on time. Unfortunately, when the dummy was thrown out, as the 'chute opened Father Christmas and his head parted company.The 'chute, now opened with the head, landed behind the trees, as did the body, which arrived rather faster. This was, so I was told, accompanied by the massed screams of the children. However, the WO acting as Father Christmas was up to the mark. The Landrover appeared with Father Christmas standing in the back with a large bandage round his neck. Thus Father Christmas was once more master of the situation.

As far as sport was concerned, the presence of the 1st Battalion of the New Zealand Regiment meant that rugby was the major game. The fact that the Australians were not too far away at Kuala Kangsar meant that there was always a good needle- match every now and then. The NZ inter company matches were of a high standard. I had joined the Ipoh club, as it ran a civilian rugby team. This consisted of planters and ex-patriate policemen with a few locals. Their number increased while I was there.

The major rugby competition in Malaya was and, I believe still is, the HMS Malaya Cup played for by the States. In the 1959/60 season the Perak State side was run by a Cornish tin-miner. He had moved to Malaya immediately after the war. He had the good Cornish name of Polglass. He also ran the Ipoh club side.Games were played on Wednesdays and Saturdays in the late afternoon.

Having played a couple of games against the Kedar police and an Ipoh garrison side, I was selected for the State Trial. This was 1NZ versus a State select team.This was the first time that I came up against the Kiwis actually on the field. As hooker I was well in the thick of it. One of the Kiwis, a large Maori front row forward known as 'Shovel-Face', came up to me during the tea after the game and told me that I was in the team.That season Perak played all its potential opponents in a friendly match. If the Malaya Cup tie was away, the friendly was played at home and vice versa. However, our first match was against Negri Semilan one of the weaker rugby states in the south.

This was won quite easily as was the next game against Kedar. For some reason I was not selected for the Selangar game to be played in KL.Possibly just as well as Selangar had an extremely good hooker by the name of Jope. He was alleged to have been near Scottish honours at the time he was sent out to Malaya. I ran the line and observed with interest as Perak lost and the Perak hooker lost most of his own put-in and all of his opponent's ball as well. I was back in the team.When it came to the cup matches, the State team, twelve Kiwis, two Brits of whom I was one and an Indian, by race, but by nationality Malayan.The skipper was a Maori called Huia Woods.He was the tracker platoon commander. Subsequently he joined the Parachute Regiment. I was sad to see his obituary in the *Telegraph* a short time ago. It failed to mention this aspect of his life. There were also two Maori All Blacks in the side.In the event we swept all before us until the Selangar match, which was played on the Ipoh *Padang.*

The Kiwi scrum-half and I had decided how we were to at least get our own ball. The team itself was confident about all aspects of the game except for the tight scrums where the KL experience still remained. We had decided that the ball would be put in quickly with no warning. I would strike as soon as I saw the ball. It worked. There was clearly a relief when we got the first scrum. As the ball came back, a Kiwi voice from the second row called, "Well done, George!"

The final played in the Merdeka Stadium was against the Singapore Civilians and ended in a nine - all draw. No extra time was played as the Yang di Pertwan Agong could not stay past the programmed time.

Malaya Cup Final 1959
Author being presented by Huia Woods –
"Shovel-Face" Christie (nearest camera)

Author Line-Out Jumping at Ipoh

RICHEY JUMPS FOR THE BALL IN A LINE-OUT

PERAK'S George Richey, with outstretched arms, jumps for the ball in a line-out during the H.M.S. Malaya Cup rugger match in Ipoh on Saturday when Perak trounced Kedah by 35 points (four goals and five tries) to 11 (goal and two tries).—Straits Times picture.

Perak strong as ever again

(No lifting in those days! – Author's note)

I had also seen the Brigade Commander, Brigadier Mogg, who later became Deputy SACEUR, and he agreed that a Commonwealth Brigade team would tour Malaya. In effect, it consisted of most of the State players plus a few Aussies and Brits. On the Sunday the brigade played a KL garrison team and won. We then proceeded by train to Singapore where we played RAF Seletar, Nee Soon Garrison and a Singapore Army side. With a 100 percent record we arrived back at Taiping where the tour ended with a game against a Perak Select which went our way.

The following season, 1959/60, no friendly matches were played. Selection was more difficult as the 1st NZ were being replaced by 2NZ in the first half of the season. In the event about half the team were Kiwis, but the captain was an Ian Forbes. He had played centre in the London Counties team that had beaten the South African Touring side a couple of years before. Again Perak reached the final, but lost out to Singapore Combined Services.

However, this year the Commonwealth Brigade had a more interesting Tour. 2NZ had won the play-off between the Malaya Command and the Singapore Army Cups. It was the winner's turn to go to Hong Kong for the Far East Cup. From memory, that winner was a regiment with "Lancs" in its title.The Brigadier thought it a good idea if a Commonwealth Brigade team went to HK.This coincided with the last trip as a trooper of the *Nevassa*. So with the Kiwis and their reserves went about eight Brits and Aussies and their families. We all paid our way at the special concessionary rate available if there was room.

We also paid for our hotel accommodation. There were, it seemed at the time, to be three rates, the American,the British and the local. 2NZ won their game. We then played a HK A XV with the eight Brits/Aussies,the 2NZ reserves with other places being filled by 2NZ players. This game was also won.

However, as the *Nevassa* spent about ten days in HK there was a gap up to the game against the full HK side. This gave a chance for all to have a good look at HK and the New Territories. The singing of the Maori soldiers was remembered by my two children, by now five and three, for quite some time.

It also coincided with the wedding in HK of one, Charles Muntz. He was a fellow officer in 49 Field Regiment in Colchester from which I had gone to Middle Wallop. The Regiment was now in HK.He was one of the most destructive officers in the gunners and his stag night held in the Hong Kong Club was such that he and most of those present were banned for a time. I was told this at the wedding reception by the President of the club who mused that he wished that he had been at the party.

Charles was due to play in the match, as was a Sapper, also a second row forward against whom I had played in the Gunner-Sapper match in 1954/5 season. We made plans, which although legal then, would certainly not be allowed today.The match was great, and we won. The next day, *Nevassa* sailed with us on board. We were, however, able to get the two main HK papers. We eagerly scanned the report. One report stated that this was a great match on which to end the season, with quarter not being given by either team. The other report was somewhat different, stating that this was the dirtiest game that the writer had ever seen. One can't please everyone.

7 FLIGHT'S SPORT

Apart from the local Soccer League, I believed that the flight should concentrate on one particular sport in which the flight could compete on equal terms with the larger major units. This was tug- o' -war. I considered that an 88 stone team whether picked from a unit of six hundred or, as in our case forty, still only weighs 88 stone. A team was selected, and training commenced about three months before the start of the athletics season. Fortunately the admin. sergeant, a certain Sgt Fenlon, was an experienced tug- o'- war man. I had captained the 49 Regiment 100 stone team which had won the Colchester Garrison and 3rd Division competitions in 1957. Training sessions were held daily. The flight ran a fund which was financed by selling the avgas tin containers. We kept a proper fund with income and expenditure, with receipts correctly recorded. Subsequently, we found that this was not on. However, as we were using the same contractors who were buying army surplus anyway we felt that morally we were OK. After each session, therefore the team had a fresh pint of milk. By the time the Taiping Garrison sports were held

45

the team was able to "press" against a 3-tonner for five minutes before the actual training session. We were also able to pull the 3-tonner backwards with it in forward gear.

Come the day, the team won the garrison 88- stone competition with ease. Our most surprised opponents were 1NZ. They had problems on the day as it seems that they hadn't taken the weght limit too seriously. This was OK for the 100-stone limit, but eight Maoris weighed rather more than 88-stone. We dispatched a weakened 1NZ team in the garrison final without much bother.

However, they vowed that things would be different in the Brigade Competition in two weeks' time. But three months hard training paid off:and all opponents were taken in two straight pulls. The Malaya Command Competition in KL was a different story. We made it to the final, where we came up against the Gurkhas whose coach produced an interesting technique. He had a stick with a coloured flag at each end. When the pull started, he flicked his wrist, and the team moved relentlessly back step by step on the flag movements. The comparative success of the flight 88- stone team meant that next year we entered a 100- stone team as well. We swept all before us. This time we beat the 2NZ teams in both weights. In the final of the Brigade Competition we took the British Battalion 100-stone team in seven and ten seconds respectively. Then came KL. Again our 88 stone team lost to the Gurkhas in the semi-final. They went on to win. In the 100-stone we reached the final with straight pulls, where we then came up against another minor unit. It too had an experienced coach, and quite clearly had done some training. The first pull was the hardest we had ever had. I was told afterwards that the tape was so near to our line that the judge had actually prepared his arm to raise it when the tape crossed the line. I was at number six, and was actually coaching from there by indicating to our ninth man, normally the coach. Suddenly the rope gave, and that was it. The team's training came to the fore, and the first pull went our way. It seemed to last for hours. We were told afterwards it was three minutes. The second pull was over in a minute. I think that it gave the lads a great sense of achievement, and it was the only Commonwealth Brigade success of the day, as 2NZ came second to the Cheshire Regiment in the Athletics.

COMMONWEALTH BRIGADE FINALS 1960
Light Weight Team
(taking the 2nd New Zealand Battalion)

Heavy Weight Team
(taking the 1st Battalion, The Forrester)

THE SECOND HALF OF THE TOUR

Rather than a repeat of my general flying it might be more interesting to describe the flight's rôle in a number of specific operations. In May 1959, John Chandler had spotted a probable CT camp in the Betong salient. For a number of reasons, it was virtually certain that what he had seen was a camp of some size, and that it was occupied.

It was agreed with the Thai authorities that a Malayan Police Field Force with Thais included would be mounted. Air Recce flights were laid on for the Force and Troop commanders to show them the route in, the main north/south ridge along which the approach march would take and the actual ridge running off the main ridge (it ran West/East) on which the camp was situated.

The march in started from Grik and it took three days for the force to reach the border. CR missions were flown each afternoon to confirm to the ground commander exactly where he was. In the meantime, Anzac Force consisting of a company each from the New Zealand and Australian battalions moved in to occupy the border area, along the southern edge of the

Betong Salient in which was located the camp.

Once over the border the PFF moved very carefully. CRs were carried out each evening.Four days later the final CR was given, putting the force as close as 200 yards from the camp site.The ground commander was given the bearing from his balloon to the actual site.

There were at this time three Austers in the area. John Chandler and John Riggall, who subsequently commanded a Beaver flight in the Borneo campaign were going to buzz the camp once the ground force was in contact. I was there armed with a camera to record the events.

In fact, the ground commander did not have to call the aircraft in - the firing could be heard in the air. We were told afterwards that the morale effect on the attacking force was significant, as the Austers roared over the battle. The fire fight lasted for two hours.

In the meantime, the force occupying the ridge on the border had been resupplied by the flight. I personally carried out three SDs, dropping 250 lbs of rations. Other pilots were similarly involved. A report then came in that a CT had been ambushed and shot by the Australians. By a coincidence, the grid reference given was exactly on the border. Some weeks later it was suggested but never confirmed that a patrol sitting on the border had got pissed off and moved north. The CT was caught well inside Thailand. The body was carried back to the border, and the incident then reported. A LZ then had to be made for a helicopter to fly in to remove the body. It was the state of the body which apparently suggested that death took place before the day that the incident was reported. All this was kept pretty quiet, and this is the first time that I have mentioned it since leaving the Flight. I remember no names.

In the debriefings afterwards it was found that the camp was very well equipped. It was said it had medical drugs there not available in the local hospital. The Flight was presented with the flag, red with a star on it. A picture of John Chandler and John Naylor examining the said trophy with a *pangy stick* (see next page) also presented, appeared in *Soldier Magazine*. The *pangies* were used as unpleasant additions to the pits which surrounded the camp.

John Chandler, Sgt Law, John Naylor examining the CT Flag and *pangy stick*

FLIGHT COMMANDER

John Chandler left in March 1960, and I took over the Flight. My February log is counter-signed by John, with me doing the business as Flight Commander in March. Lieutenant Colonel John Creswell was the Squadron CO. Coincidentally, it was in March that I departed for one of the periodic rests at the Pinang Rest Hotel.

In June the Flight was tasked to keep a ground force, which was to be deployed in the central range near the Thai border, supplied. It had been mooted for a while that in some circumstances resupply by RAF could give the game away. Dropping Zones (DZs) which had to be prepared for the RAF were fairly large for obvious reasons. For a start, the drop had to be carried out at a fair height, and the loads once on the way down would be subject to the wind.

We in the Austers dropped at virtually treetop height. The ground troops only needed to chop down two or three trees for this to be enough for us to do the business. I was asked if the Flight could do the job. There was no way that I was going to say no. In fact it took a massive effort by the Flight. All six aircraft and pilots were involved.

My personal effort which, I emphasize, was matched by the other pilots, was to carry out nineteen air drop sorties in four days to 2/6 Gurkhas, 8PFF (Police Field Force), 1/3 East Anglians, with one sortie to drop 65,000 leaflets. This involved thirteen flying hours. The total effort by the flight was therefore in the order of seventy eight flying hours, and some one hundred and seventy sorties. These were mounted from Grik with the local Australian company organising the ration packs.

As a one-off, it was an interesting exercise. I don't believe a similar effort was made, but it did show what could be done in an emergency. The flight had of course to curtail most of its other operational activities.

PILOTS

Sgt Law, Captains Williams, Naylor, "Rupert", Richey, Smith O'Callaghan

NIGHT-FLYING

All flights carried out periodic night-flying as part of their pilot training. As far as 7 Flight was concerned, this followed a routine pattern: a cross- country flight north to RAAF Butterworth, and return. The landing lamps were put out, using the main runway, and all went to plan. Both John Chandler and I tried out a form of tactical landing system.

Basically it involved using Landrover headlights, with two safety lights fore and aft of the landing area. The Landrovers were set about seventy yards apart facing a point some fifty yards down the runway. There was a permanent safety lamp fifty yards down the approach flight path and another four hundred yards past the landing point.

The drill was that the ground crew would brace themselves when the pilot was on the downwind leg. As he turned in on the penultimate leg, the vehicle headlights would be switched on, and the pilot would land in the area of light.

This was an interesting twist to the normal night-flying, and never caused any problems. However, it did give me an idea: I

55

knew that some operational night-flying had been done, but no-one seemed to know very much about it, except that one flight had done quite a bit of flare-dropping at night.

If it was clear - and most nights were clear most of the time - then navigation was easy. The jungle stood out, and so did the rivers.The main hills could be identified. However, an accurate grid reference might not be so hard to get. I thought that a system of triangulation might be an answer. After getting agreement from Brigade, I visited 1/3 East Anglians. They were operating in a jungle area south of Taiping, only about fifteen minutes flying time away. We agreed they would deploy three directors from the mortar platoon along the road east of the area of operations. The road ran in a north/south direction. We devised a system of signals, using the landing lights of the Auster. Three flashes was the stand-by signal, and a five-second continuous light was the one on which to take the bearing.

In May 1960, I flew six night VR sorties. The first worked a charm. We spotted a fire. Sgt Law hanging out of the aircraft (the doors were off) gave me the warning signal, followed by, "Directly overhead." By the time we got back to base, the bearings and the grid of the suspect fire had been signalled through.

The result was that the sytem had proved itself. The follow-up was less dramatic. A young officer had to do some fast talking, to explain why his patrol had a fire going which not only gave his position away to the flight, but quite possibly to any CTs in the vicinity.

A few days later we located another fire, which was well away from the known positions of any East Anglian patrol. The result of that follow-up remained shrouded in mystery.

Where I really wanted to go was over the Betong Salient area. We knew there were CTs there. The existence of the camp attacked in John Chandler's time showed that.There were a number of problems. The first was the time and distance factor. The area of search was about forty minutes' flying time away from the home base, Taiping. There was no question of using triangulation. Then there was the fact that one would be flying at night over the central jungle range and all that that implied if there was an engine failure.

I had a word with the Australians at Grik. We decided to test the feasibility of landing and taking off from the Grik strip.This strip was not flat. It had a significant slope. We all preferred landing north to south as we then landed slightly uphill. However, there was a hill to the immediate north right under the approach path.They agreed to put out the usual six lights along the left side of the runway, with two on the right hand side. A safety light was also put out on the top of the northern hill.On an agreed day, I flew to Grik and carried out a couple of landings and one take-off. All was well.

I planned therefore that the concept of operations would be a daylight landing at Grik, when refuelling would be done. Take-off would be about five minutes before dark. (In Malaya, there was no dusk as we know it. One minute it was light, the next minute it was dark.) After the VR I would fly over Grik, flash the downward ident light and proceed to Taiping. The Australians would give me fifteen minutes before taking in the lights.

For my first sortie, I took the faithful Sam Law, who never complained, but I sometimes wonder if he thought that I was completely mad. In July 1960, I did four sorties over the salient. I notice that my last two were done solo, for what reason I cannot imagine. The lightning was somewhat off-putting. There seemed to be a hell of a lot. The navigation proved easier than one might have thought. We did find and plot the odd fire, for which there appeared no logical reason. However, as they were all in Thailand there was not too much that we could do about it. A friendly Malayan Intelligence Officer (MIO) who had contacts with his opposite number over the border did say, however, that these reports were useful in that they might well confirm other intelligence of routes and frequency of use. So I didn't feel that it was a waste of time.

My last night VR was on 29 March 1961 when I took Malcolm Fleming, my proposed successor, as my passenger. We actually landed at Kroh in daylight, refuelled and proceeded to the VR area. I don't know how much night-flying he had done, but certainly he hadn't done the sort of thing that he was about to witness.There was the usual lightning, and I had got used to it by this this time. So I was able to make the odd comment which was, as far as I remember, greeted in dead silence.

After the completion of the VR, I proceeded to Grik. The lights were deployed. I flashed the downward identification light and flew south. Within probably five minutes, we ran into light rain. This is where I made a mistake. What I should have done is to have turned 180 degrees and landed at Grik to await clear weather. I didn't. We continued south. Within a short time, the light rain had turned into heavy rain. We were now in a classic Malayan local storm. Forward visibility was nil.

To the right was the range of hills which ran all the way down past Taiping. There were two ways through. The first - the Ejock gap - was north of Taiping, and led out into the western plain. The other was to the South of Taiping, and of no use to me. I called up RAAF Butterworth who kindly informed me that there was a storm to the northeast of Taiping. I said that I was in the middle of it.

It was, I thought, too late to turn back to Grik as, if the storm was moving north - and that is what it seemed to be doing -I wouldn't be able to land there anyway.I had no intention if I could help it of climbing, as to be in the middle of a storm in an Auster was not good news. This had happened to me once in daylight, and the clouds were going up faster than I was.

The solution was to continue southwards down the central valley and on dead reckoning turnwest southwest when I calculated that we were level with the Ejock gap. Malcolm watched the giro compass as I was having quite a time controlling the aircraft which was bouncing about as we went deeper into the storm.We both kept our eyes skinned and I again contacted Butterworth. They gave me a fix and once more informed me that there was a storm in the area.

Suddenly, I saw lights below, and I saw that we were heading into the western plain. Equally suddenly, we were clear of the rain. The rest, as they say, is history, and we landed about seven minutes later at Taiping. It was a bad error of judgement, and one that I should not have made. I suspect that I was a bit over-confident.I became a less bold pilot for the rest of the tour.

THE EAST COAST

In July I was approached by the Military Intelligence Officer (MIO). He was keen that we should carry out a sustained VR operation over the border into Pattani on the East Coast. It was suspected at the time that there was a CT force in the area which appeared to have been left alone for quite some time.

The plan was for the Flight to set up a base on the airfield at Kota Bahru (KB) right up on the North East of Malaya. John Naylor, who knew all about allowances, was the administrative king. Basically the ground crew set themselves up on the airfield. Two pilots at a time flew over from Taiping. This took one hour forty minutes' flying time, and they would remain there for three days. The relief pilots would bring in one or two ground-crew, whilst others of equal skills were flown back by the pilots returning to Taiping. We each spent three days at a time on the East coast. Immediately south of KB was the so-called Beach of Passionate Love. It failed to live up to its name.

The Operation became official and became *"Operation Actor"*, and started on 2nd July 1960. Including getting to KB, I logged ten hours thirty minutes flying time. This was matched by the pilots. The MIO was in KB throughout the operation. After a gap of three days, I went back to KB for another ten hours forty minutes.

Operations in Op Bamboo still went on, and I see that in the days back at Taiping I logged fours hours twenty five minutes. This included a 100-lb supply drop to 2NZ, taking off from Grik for the actual drop.

I'm not sure as to the results from our concentrated VR over Pattani. We certainly found what could have been CT camps. A number of groups and single *bashas* were seen and logged, in pretty inaccessible places. I felt that some were too obvious. However, the MIO, a Major Meneiff, was satisfied. He maintained that much of what we reported was in line with other sources. He did make the point which may have been valid that as virtually no air recce had been done for a long time -certainly 7 Flight had done none since I had joined in 1958 - the idea of concealment from the air had been forgotten. Anyway, it certainly put our hours up for July. I flew 55.05 hrs that month, and most of the other pilots had flown the same.

I took some photos with a box camera of one of the sites that I had spotted and still have. They are colour, but not all that clear.

THE JUNGLE FORTS

There were a number of jungle forts which had been constructed during the early fifties. They were in the deep jungle, and when I was out there manned by the PFF. The SAS also made use of them. Their main function was, I think, to provide regular comunication with the aboriginals as well as discouraging the CTs from dominating them.They were resupplied by air. The two in our area, Tapong and Kemar both had air strips. The RAF single and twin Pioneers landed on them fairly regularly. One day, whilst doing a series of supply-drops from Grik, a twin Pioneer landed, refuelled and took off.Half an hour later, I flew over Tapong to see said pioneer with its nose in the ground at one end of the runway. As I circled round, the pilot came up on VHF to ask if I could contact RAF KL.

He then read out his Incident Report.I forget how many items there were in it, but all the paragraphs were lettered.I then flew to a great height and was able to pass the whole report to RAAF Butterwoth who passed it on. However having spent nearly twenty minutes over Tapong I began to wonder if an Auster could land and, rather more to the point, take off.

Of the two forts, it was Kemar that looked the easier of the two. Its strip ended looking over a steep valley side.Its problem was that there came a point on the approach when the option of going round again ceased. This was fairly early in the approach as there was a pretty steep hill facing one. There was therefore one way in and one way out.

2 Flight based at Ipoh had in fact landed at

Kemar and taken off. I was slightly pissed off, as the fort was in our area of operations and not theirs. However, now I knew that it could be done, the 7 Flight pilots were tasked to have a go.We went one better, and in my log for 11th March 1961 is the entry - "First Auster into and out of Kemar with a passenger". In fact, I took two passengers in: Captain Roberts and Sgt McDonald, a new pilot to 7 Flight. McDonald came out as a single passenger with another pilot.

However, four days earlier I had landed solo at Kemar, taking off from Grik where I had deposited a Colonel Aitkin. He was due to be flown back to Taiping some hours later. I see that I took off from Grik, and landed at and took off from Kemar. From there I flew to Tapong. I well remember that I did a number of approach runs, and going round again to see if the exercise was really on, I decided that it was, and landed on Tapong. The take-off was only slightly fraught. I took the Auster as far down the strip as possible, and then executed the short take-off procedure.There was, as far as I could see, plenty of room between me at the jungle canopy as I climbed away.

It so happened that the day after the

Kemar take-off with a passenger, Superintendent Yusof Khan, the commander of the PFF, was in Tapong . I therefore landed and had a word with him. It was he who had commanded the PFF during the Betong Salient Operation, and as it happened, was to command the last operation with which I was to be involved in, two months later in April 1961.

Having landed, I talked him into being the first passenger to be flown out of Tapong. To his credit, he agreed and the take-off proceeded. The trees were a bit close, and I found out later that the fitting for the flares was still on. This of course increased the drag. We landed and completed the Tapong log, as well as my own.

Some years later, when Yusof attended the Imperial Defence College, he came to stay with me and mentioned the Tapong incident. He recalled that he had told an RAF pilot, who was seconded to the Malaysian Airforce, that he had been flown out of Tapong in an Auster. The officer refused to believe him, and only when a photocopy of the Tapong log was sent to him was he persuaded.

THE FINAL OPERATION

In October 1960, having finished a sortie out of Alor Star, I had to divert round a local storm. As a result, I flew down the Betong Salient slightly east of Kroh. Looking out of the port side I saw a *basha* hidden in the jungle. It so happened that the light was just right. The *basha* itself was on the side of a hill. As soon as I got down, I reported to Brigade 10, who in turn telephoned the MIO. It turned out that the existence of the CT camp was known about, but not its precise location. Apparently, CR was not to be flown in the area in case of frightening the CTs off. However, all was well, when it was explained that this was a complete, but fortunate, accident. It was not until April 1961 that an operation with the Thais and the PFF was mounted. I was keen to take part, and was given a dispensation to stay in Malaya an extra month. I should have departed with my family on 10th March. It was interesting that the three years tour rule was strictly kept. When seeing off the family at KL, we recognised families that had been on the Hermes three years to the day in 1958. I had flown Rupert to Pinang and the Ben Line took him to Hamburg, where Jamie Turner, one of the pilots in 7 Flight when I arrived now stationed in Germany would care for him until we arrived in Minden in May.

The operation followed much the same lines as that which the Flight had supported in the Salient previously. 8 PFF went into the jungle on the 1st April. CRs and SDs started on the 5th April. The operation was to end in tragedy. An MIO had asked and been given permission to go in with the ground force. With hindsight, he should never have been allowed to go. He was large and not jungle fit.

On 9th April I did a CR in the evening and night-flew back to Taiping. The next day I did another CR, and by now the force was close to the CT camp. I then flew a three-hour sortie with an Inspector Issa, as we waited for the hoped for contact. Sadly, the next report I had was personal from Yusof Khan. The MIO had died. Subsequently it turned out to be heat exhaustion. We returned to Kroh to pick up some axes, and dropped them in the trees. The PFF had put a balloon up. The axes were received, and a Landing Zone (LZ) started to be prepared. I now had to return to Taiping as my tour had come to an end. I had time to brief the Flight before flying to KL with an aircraft due its major service.

SUMMING UP

This account would not be too different from one written by any of the pilots who served in 656 Squadron during what was known as the Malayan Emergency. I think that it was the longest serving British Unit in the Campaign. During my tour, the Squadron celebrated its 150,000 operational flying hours in Malaya.. Lieutenant Colonel BB Story, RA was commanding at that time.

All pilots had the time of their lives out there. Not only was the flying meaningful, as we knew that what we were doing was much appreciated by our supported units. I well remember the CO of 1NZ saying quite openly that they would not be able to operate without the support of the Austers.

The social life was great, as were the allowances at the time.We had a degree of freedom in our flying that has long since gone. Self- authorisation was a must at that time and enabled pilots a degree of personal responsibility not given to many young (in the main) captains.

I really started this because of a suggestion made by one of the Shrewsbury RAA. His view is that it is a pity that the memories of the old and bold are being largely lost as the generations that took part in some of these largely forgotten campaigns die off. I have had the advantage of my flying log book in which not only are the hours flown shown, but also the type of mission carried out. As with most pilots most pages have notes either in pencil or ink as to what went on at the time. I am surprised, but on reflection not so surprised, how clear my memory is of what happened, and how I thought at the time. Indeed I have better recall of Malaya than of much more recent times. Maybe this is something to do with age. I must say that family photos taken at the time did help.

RETURN TO MALAYA

In 1966 I was posted from Borneo, where I was a Staff Officer, to 95 Commando Light Regiment stationed in Nee Soon with the Commando Brigade. In 1967 the Brigade did an exercise in North Malaya. It was interesting to be flown as a passenger in a Sioux helicopter over the area immediately south and west of the Betong Salient. What struck me was the vast mount of primary jungle that had been cut down. Certainly in 1958-61 there were Chinese loggers at work, but the scale of the clearance was a shock.

The other more pleasurable aspect was to play and referee rubgy on the Singapore Padang .But best of all was to take the regimental 7-a-side team to Ipoh when we represented the Singapore Combined Services "A" team to play in the Malaysian Inter- State seven-a side tournament on the Ipoh Padang. I saw many old friends from the Perak rubgy days. The event was made more pleasurable as we won, beating RAAF Butterworth in the Final, having disposed of Selangor in the semi-final.

In 1975 and '76 I again returned to Malaysia as a Lieutenant Colonel instructor at the Joint Warfare Establishment. Each year we ran a week's course at the Malaysian Staff College. Its buildings were built on what had been the air-strip at Noble Field, the HQ of the Squadron. Neither the Directing Staff nor the students even knew this, and the name was no more. However, each time, having given my part of the lectures, I was able to fly to Pinang where my old friend Yusof Khan was the head policeman. We had a right royal time with a few of the old intelligence officers in Georgetown. I suppose that age tends to make one look at the past with rose- tinted glasses. Whatever it was, it was great fun. I, with I suspect others who served in Malaya in the fifties and early sixties, left a little of my heart behind. It was a tour mixing fun with a sense of achievement, and I am glad to have done it.

LT Col G.H.M. Richey RA

ABOUT THE AUTHOR

George Richey was educated at Haileybury and Imperial Service College, leaving in March 1949. He served the, then, compulsory four months, in the ranks as a Private in the Queen's Own Royal West Kent Regiment before entering the Royal Military Academy Sandhurst in September 1949. He was commissioned into the Royal Artillery. His first two tours were in Plymouth and Colchester, from where he was posted to Middle Wallop as a trainee light aircraft pilot. On completion of the flying course he was posted to Malaya (as it then was) in 1958. Subsequently, after a tour in Germany he went to Staff College. After a staff appointment, the last four months of which were in Borneo, he was posted to a Commando Light Regiment Royal Artillery in Singapore.

He then served in Germany on two staff appointments before being promoted to Lieutenant Colonel as an instructor at the Joint Warfare Establishment. He took early retirement in 1977, and moved to Shrewsbury. He was elected as a Conservative County Councillor in 1985, and as a Borough Councillor in 1991. He was elected the Mayor of Shrewsbury and Atcham for the year 2002/3. He was married in 1954, but was widowed in 1971. He re-married, and he and his wife, Mary Anne, live in West Felton. He has six children, four by his second wife, who resigned from the Army before the birth of their son. At the time of publication, he is still an active local councillor. He is currently President of the Shrewsbury RAA, and also of the Shrewsbury Rugby Football Club.

APPENDIX

HOURS FLOWN FROM "SPROG" TO "HAS BEEN".

Middle Wallop 1957 Chipmunk June 20.35 July 27.15 August 8.00
Auster 6 and/or 7 August 7.45 September 22.25
October 34.25 November 24.5
Auster 9 December 23.50
1958 January 25.35
Total Hours at Middle Wallop: Chipmunk: 55.50 Austers: 138.50

Malaya Auster mark 9

	1958	1959	1960	1961
March	26.00	50.10	56.20	56.20
April	21.05	60.40	59.30	27.50
May	40.00	14.10	43.35	---
June	44.10	68.00	68.50	---
July	51.30	51.10	56.05	---
August	61.00	26.50	50.15	---
September	38.00	52.10	42.15	---
October	49.40	32.50	22.35	---
November	59.40	58.25	61.05	---
December	54.20	49.15	47.25	---

	1959	1960	1961
January	39.50	53.20	18.10
February	50.40	22.10	35.05

Total hours in Malaya

1958	1959	1960	1961
445.25	554.10	484.05	137.25 (four months)

=Total Hours flown in Malaya 1,721.05 in 38 months.
Average hours per month, marginally over 45 hours.

SORTIES BY TYPE OF TASK FLOWN IN MALAYA
(A sortie begins with take-off and ends at landing)

Training & familiarisation flights	168
Visual recce by day incl pax VR	360
Visual recce by night	35
AOP artillery missions	46
Supply dropping missions	240
Contact recces	64
Communication flights	275
(ferrying passengers)	

ROYAL AIR FORCE

LIGHT AIRCRAFT SCHOOL

......ELEM..... Flight

YOU MADE IT!

Date 15·JUNE·1957   Hrs 7   Mins 10

_____ Student

_____ Instructor

揭露驚人消息

一百一十八名馬共人員
在吡叻州先後集体出來

聯合邦代理總理兼國防部長那督雅都那昔，於一九五八年七月九日，在怡保舉行各報代表招待會中，揭露一項驚人的消息，指出自從本邦於一九五七年八月三十一日實現獨立之後，除了已經先後公開發表在全馬各地（包括吡叻州在內）出來自新的一百八十六名馬共人員的姓名與詳情之外，在同一時期中，又另有

一百一十八名馬共人員在吡叻一州之內
先後分成數批集体出來踏上新生之路

這一百一十八名馬共人員之中，包括：

一名	州委
四名	區委會書記
七名	區委
十三名	支委（包括同級的小隊長在內）

這些人的名單請看後頁。

除此之外，保安隊伍又擊斃了負責領導南吡叻整個地區馬共組織的 **州委江儒** 和他的警衛員南滕。

上述這些消息，

是緊急狀態十年以來最轟動驚人的消息。

在山芭裡的馬共人員聽到了之後有什麼感想呢？

記着 這不過是在吡叻一州之內的成績而已！
一百一十八個聰明的人出來得到新生活，
兩個不聰明的人在山芭裡無謂流血送死。